A CHILD'S
NIGHT DREAM

A CHILD'S
NIGHT DREAM

OLIVER STONE

ST. MARTIN'S PRESS ⚞ NEW YORK

Book design by Gretchen Achilles

Library of Congress Cataloging-in-Publication Data

Stone, Oliver.
    A child's night dream / Oliver Stone.—1st ed.
        p.   cm.
    ISBN 0-312-16798-9
    I. Title.
    PS3569.T64157C48   1997
    813'.54—dc21   97-15347
                                                         CIP

FIRST EDITION: OCTOBER 1997

10   9   8   7   6   5   4   3   2   1

CONTENTS

PROLOGUE

THE ORIGINAL MANUSCRIPT of this work was undertaken when I was nineteen years old in Guadalajara, Mexico, in 1966, and was finished in New York City in 1967. It ran more than a thousand handwritten and partially typed pages, and was rejected by a handful of New York publishers. The act of writing it caused me to drop out of Yale University a second and final time, and precipitated not only serious clashes with my father but an increasing isolation from American society in general.

In an act of despair, I threw several sections of the manuscript into the East River one cold night, and, as if surgically removing the memory of the book from my mind, volunteered for the Vietnam of 1967. Intent on forgetting altogether the narcissistic experience of confessional literature, and seeking the anonymity of a soldier's life, I turned down officer's candidate training and insisted on rifleman status in a front-line combat unit as soon as possible—in case the war might end before I could participate.

My desires, for a change, were granted and after training at Fort Jackson, South Carolina, I was shipped to Vietnam in September 1967, precisely on my twenty-first birthday. Ironically on that night into day, we crossed the International Dateline, omitting my birthday, which thus became the first casualty of that war.

In Vietnam, I tested all my true values and managed, barely, to survive fifteen harrowing, yet oddly illuminating and sometimes incredibly beautiful, months in a country still strange to the Western soul. When I returned to America in late 1968, I had moved from the world of novels to the new medium of film, which I think suited the sensitivities of someone who had spent fifteen months in the jungle, learning to survive off the six senses free of the inhibitions of thought and choice. After some erratic stops and starts, I entered the New York University Film School climate of 1969–71, grateful to have anything in my life, much less my life, and for many years I never looked back.

Some parts of the original draft were lost or misplaced by my father as he moved residences, but sometime in the middle Seventies, I gathered together all the existing pages I could find into a shoebox, which I stored in various closets through the ensuing years. In the middle Nineties, an editor by the name of Robert Weil from the St. Martin's publishing house in New York, having heard of the book in an interview I had done as a filmmaker discussing my past, wrote and asked in the kindest way to read it. In time, coming to trust this gentle but authoritative figure, I turned the yellowing contents of the shoebox over to him.

I have no idea how he plowed through it all and made the copious notes he did, as the manuscript was mostly out of sequence, a jumble of type fonts, and raw handwriting on various paperstocks, with crucial pages missing. Yet he persisted, generously excavating from the ruins some essence of its original beauty—a beauty of language and feeling that I had intended but forgotten, but which he insisted was worth fighting for.

Given that this man had helped Henry Roth complete his novel after half a century, I had to assume he'd stay the course with me. And as a result, Robert Weil is far more than the editor of this book. He has in essence made possible its rebirth, and to Robert Weil, I am deeply and forever grateful.

Reluctant to actually sit and write and edit, I stalled the process another two years and two films. Confronting me were some seven hundred pages of highly dense, experimental language; on numerous occasions, I had to crack open a dictionary to find out what some of the words actually meant, as the style in parts was unashamedly invocatory and wedded to the epic novel of old, but with a determinedly "modernist" punctuation and spelling. The time periods of the novel were conceived in a freewheeling stream of consciousness, born of my seduction by James Joyce, shooting back and forth from one childhood I had in the America of the 1940s and 1950s to another that I experienced in the France of that same era.

In that vein, the central character is cross-named William (after my American father's preference) and Oliver (after my French mother's preference). Both names are used in this book, William being the more practical and anonymous American identity chosen for me by a father who, deeply scarred by the Depression, insisted that a man should not distinguish himself by any exterior mannerisms or names but only by his work and his mind; and that any instance of declaring oneself, of saying what one really meant, was a form of gigantic hubris that would be gigantically punished. Whereas Oliver, or "Oliverre" as Mother used to call me in her thick French accent, was the name that, though grandiose and embarrassing by the rules of the men's institutions I attended, was secretly preferred, the name I always thought of myself as.

Thus I stumbled between the two identities in the first years of my life, a child born of two strong parents, breaking brooms and fucking and fighting to the bitter end over private detectives, illicit rendezvous, custody cases, and all the other medieval divorce proceedings of the 1960s New York legal code. Although I grew up a child of privilege, without brothers or sisters to share what was mine, and enjoyed many good and happy times, there was, after my parents' sudden separation in 1962, the darkening sense that there was no security in the world. Throughout my childhood Mom was always disappearing in a cloud of perfume and jewelry, neither of us quite sure when she'd return, and Dad was generally enigmatic at best, and, in keeping with the habit of the age, unwilling to express his emotions or physical feelings to his son, and rarely to his wife. The world, it seemed to me from an early age, was always moving precariously at my feet, as if I were five years old again and struggling on a fast-moving escalator at Bloomingdale's.

I raise this because the nature of Time itself in this novel is elusive and uncertain, and I have come gradually to the feeling that in some way I have lived several lives at once, cursed and blessed in that regard. Having become Buddhist later in life, I accept the doctrine that all time is illusory, that all things are circular, and that all things happening in parallel universes do not occur literally in chronological fashion. You can be old when you're young and, obviously, cheerfully young when you're old; our perception of time and life is truly in the mind. What happened to me in 1965, or '67, or '73, or making illusions such as films in the Eighties and Nineties about my experiences in Vietnam, only reinforces my sense of a mélange of key events that mark our lives, events that we seem to gather into our consciousness before we die.

And I believe it is in the moments or days or years before your death when you truly live outside chronological time. It is then when you remember the "poem" of your life—its essence, rhythm, meaning, whatever—sometimes lonely, sometimes beautiful, always unique. The bad parts of life, I find, blend into the good parts, because we can never appreciate the good parts had we not experienced the contrast between good and bad—all of it illusion in the end, or *samsara* as the Buddhists say, the great circling wheel of life with its six realms in which we abide until enlightenment comes.

Even back in 1966, unconscious of Buddhism and its meanings, I called this work *A Child's Night Dream* because I was possessed of the feeling that I was living in a dream. My mind as a young man was too often *not* in the "present moment" of Buddhist teaching, but very much fleeing from the fears I had of this life, and hiding in the recesses of memory and fantasy, inventing for myself better or worse worlds. But looking back at my life now, I realize that it *was* the Dream that propelled me forward into all my memorable actions—the Dream allowed me to believe I could do certain things in my life, as impossible as they seemed, like go to war, go to sea, make love to exotic women, have children I could create and love as ongoing reincarnations, and make movie illusions that others would see. All this comes from Dream alone, for without it, there is, for me anyway, no going forward or backward or even sideways to Something; without Dream, it is just Vacuum—the living of quotidian life, the maintenance of body, food, sleep, but mostly maintenance, the more and more so, as many of us realize, the older we get.

When I first went out to Vietnam in 1965, it was as a teacher at a Catholic private school in the Chinese quarter of Saigon. I had taken a year's leave of absence from Yale. This was during the Kiplingesque early days of the war when Vietnam still resembled an exotic French colony. The first American troops were untested and blindly optimistic, and it seemed everyone, except me, was getting rich at the nexus of war and oriental corruption. I ranged freely during this period through Asia—into Laos, Cambodia, and Thailand, which, as they contribute to key memories, are described almost interchangeably in the novel.

When I returned to America in 1966, it was as a "wiper" on a Merchant Marine vessel. Landing in Oregon, I drifted down to Mexico, where the passion to write suddenly erupted one afternoon in a cheap hotel room in Guadalajara. I stayed for several weeks, going out once or twice a day to breathe the air before retreating back to my monk's cell.

After returning to New York, I circled warily back to Yale, but found the pursuit of the novel so consumed me that I simply ceased attending classes. As a result I flunked each one of my courses, and enchanted with Asia and the Conradian imagination, I withdrew from college in late 1966 and cast my fate to the winds of introspection.

As described earlier, after the book's initial stillbirth, I willed myself back to Vietnam in the infantry, where I was finally able to participate as closely as I could ever want in the only war of my generation. It was from these experiences that later in life I forged the films *Platoon, Born on the Fourth of July*, and *Heaven and Earth*, yet everything described in the novel was written *prior* to my actual combat experience and is imagined by the author based on his peripheral knowledge of the war in Saigon and his travels to the interior.

In the same vein, it was impossible, as described within, to be a soldier and travel to Laos and Cambodia where there were no "rest and recreation" facilities for our troops. It was also impossible, if you were a soldier, to return to America in the Merchant Marine, which is a private organization. The military would've flown us back Pan American either in the paid passenger section or as a body bag in the cargo hold. It must be clear by now that I was not—and am not now—that literal a person in relationship to time or place, but there was a reason, I believe, for this illogicity—the forging of the Dream, and it haunts and wracks the manuscript to this date.

In a larger sense the Dream has a fantasy element, wherein the young man within, wrestling with what he will and won't do with his life, recounts a set of future possibilities as if in fact he'd already acted them out. I am convinced that the reason he pursued these fantasies for such a large portion of his every day was so that he could free himself to withdraw, to retreat to the comfort of nihilism and the concept of suicide, in order not to have to suffer through the "tedium of this life's sweat."

It all seems to me now a strange life, but no more or less so than other lives. In the movie I made based on him, I still vividly recall Jim Morrison turning to a friend, casually stoned as he often managed to be, saying, ". . . this is the strangest life I've ever known."

Yes, what other life do we know but our own? By that standard, every life is equally strange unto itself. Which thus becomes the question: What *is* this life for? Where and how do we, as individual egos, intersect with the life force? Am I authentic? What is real to me? Is there future or past or parallel life? Are our imaginations real, as Hamlet asked? "The security of forms" that I sensed so fearfully when I was younger now appears to me an early precursor to the concept, and the fear, of leading *other* lives—of partaking in reincarnations that occur constantly throughout our passage, which we deny and deny and deny to the point where the Dream dies.

Yet I truly believe the Dream is enduring and resonant and fragile. I only wish I could have known it sooner and trusted it more. Be that as it may, I have attempted, with thirty years' perspective and instinct, to cut through this huge rainforest of memory to the core of my young mind. I have tried in spots to enhance some of the surreal transitions of Dream, and, in other places, have rewritten in the style of the author without, I hope, adulterating his thought process of the time. Insofar as I never really finished the novel or presented it in any coherent order, I have taken the liberty of putting most of it in chronological form, beginning in New York City, 1965, and ending in Mexico in 1967.

It is finally an ambivalent feeling to look back upon yourself in this way. Part of me begs forgiveness for my nakedness; the other voice is harsher, perhaps satanic, and whispers to me as it did that winter night long ago in the middle of the Pacific, *"Jump . . . Jump!"* It tells me I should put myself back in a closet, even burn the book once and for all, and thus never allow it to see the light of day.

I have chosen, evidently, to reveal myself as I was then. And in this search to know who I was and have become and will be, I implore you to look to the creative nature of the search itself, indulge it if needed as you would the child in you, and allow that the process of every evolving soul often begins with the ugliest of forms. And all forms, as the young man inside found out, change.

I am not ashamed. And similarly I hope you will allow yourself, as with a powerful drug, to go with the tumble of time and images that rise and recede in the Dream, and remember, in the deep memory we have, what it means to be nineteen again. O that glorious cursed time!

—AUTHOR

(1997)

My subject is war, but the poetry is not with pity, nor with dust or earth, nor with water, the poetry is in my soul, in my city of sin, in my seat of sorrow. Symbols by the seven I swear I know not. I know what I see, is my subject, is my pity, is my poetry. . . .

Thus I was conceived by my Father, born of my Mother, suffered under both, was crucified dead and buried. The eighteenth year I rose again from the dead, and ascended unto heaven and sitteth on the right hand of God the Father Fiction, from whence I shall come to judge . . . Mother, Father, and Myself, amen.

PART ONE

AMERICA

1. NEW YORK

SHYLY INTO THIS Tuesday night party in May of '65. The year
the world hinged. All of seventeen. Here on West 57th Street.
Do come. With your erection. It may wish to emote. In tune
with Truth. What am I looking for? And tomorrow, at Yale,
where I'm supposed to be tonight, the last examination. In
Ancient Greek. Which I'm failing, and if I fail tomorrow, I
somehow sense. Some great Big Break in my life.

In this giant artist's studio on this hot drinking night full of
fame. And the matching music, frugging bosoms. Painters and
moviestars. And plebians in the street passing and pointing and
looking up with disappointment at the giant picture windows.
Silhouettes of souls who never worked a day in their lives. Why
is it so? That we work and they play. And yet we marvel. At
the wetness of Fame. These people wrapped about the bark of
a tree. Famous and never to be famous. This columnist of the
gray hair. That moviestar. A tropical growth of eyelash guarding
her eyecave. Embarrassed to be here. With the black hairdress-
ers who introduce themselves as Socrates and Caesar. Designers
with long curly hair, earrings and boyish sweet-sixteen faces
ready to undergo the popper and the knife. Glittering metal
dresses. And bosoms caked with white makeup.

3

Such colors! What a party! For the truth is, it is. And that one, the tall strange-looking one with the long red hair? Who paints magnificent photographs. With neon tubes. And in that corner. With his wife. The novelist. Born in Bulgaria. Boozing down gin into his pot. Really want to talk to him. But I won't. . . .

Waiter delving in drinks. Various people, with stony faces, casting about the room to let you know you are held in cherished contempt. Who are you?

"What is he?"

"Actually he's a woman now—I know—he looks just *awful*, but don't tell anyone I told you, or he—I mean *she*—just would *kill* me!" Bzzz, bzzzz.

"How *marvelous* an idea, come talk to me about it." Heh heh, bzzz, bzzzzz,

"I'm bored, baby. Let's split. Cha-cha."

Seals, undismayed, sunning in summer. Seal summer. Their insunsilent light beetling over the merry sea. Mother's portrait painter, Otavio, in his whiny Chilean voice complaining, "Now there're *so many* famous people, don't you think it's much more fashionable to be *anonymous?*"

Titters and bored laughter.

O who was that who simply left? I think that was whom I was looking for. Was I? Will I remember this party in future years? When I'm a doctor and bring hope to the sick, when I'm a lawyer and bring clarity to complexity, when I'm a financier and bring bigness to smallness, will I . . . will I? Are you alive, Oliver? In this room full of fame. I touch the top. With my fingertips. And with my toes, do I really feel anything?

Though not one neurosurgeon. Or handyman. Servant of mankind. Too dull. I wish I could meet a banker or a strongman. Models three thousand feet high. Long aloof noses. Airy tread. They slip through the crowd like panthers in the night and from the treetops contemplate the bald heads of wealthy males. Might marry. Then, their fickle souls willing, they dance. Sovereign and suave and sinuous, tepidly without charity. So nice. But beware the morning. When you awake and, seeing your bedpartner, squawk and squirm away. Because she or he hasn't read a book in ages. Though she or he does watch television.

It scares me sometimes, it scares me very much. That I am not a faker. Looking with lust. As they retire to the toilet. Pretending to be witty. To be gay. Pretending that I am what I am not and wanting to be what I am. But confused. By it altogether in sum. I am paranoid because it is as if the imminence of my greatness were an open secret. Seriously now. There's this immense gap, as deep and dark as the interstellar night through which the cold wind blows. It lies in the feeling that everything of the present is overshadowed by the past. I stub my toe, I curse, I think on the battle of Cannae, and I ridicule my hurt. I hear of courage and I think of Caesar marching into Gaul. I dislike somebody and I tell him so, not so much because my emotions outlaw him but because just a quarter of a century ago, some forty million people were brutally killed. What point could there be in my pain, you see, what significance?

What a party! Oliver in the corner full of facts, his mindlips churning with pros and cons and contretemps. People pointing, frowning. A few weeks ago an essay was returned to me, it was a humilifying experience but no more different from a thousand others. This testicle of an English teacher telling me I had a preponderant dislike of the way things were done, that I made things up, and he was smirking through the cancer at what he thought was the approving reception of his words; he was entirely bald and he was laughing, his hairless arms crossed on his white knuckles in delicate equipoise and private insanity, smelling of soft buttersweat and repressed fantasies. Laughing and laughing, he laughed without reason; and the whole class began to laugh, until they were all laughing and laughing, because they were laughing at me. Haw Haw Haw! Haw Haw Haw! All the ribs quivering and going Haw Haw Haw!

Haw Haw Haw!

Everybody. People. Party. God. And above all, women. Laughing!

> *O but I know I'll be rich someday. Faraway.*
> *For the time being*
> *Just stay*
> *A—*
> *Live.*

And marvel at the wetness of fame. This girl in golden horsehair. On every billboard on every highway in America. Sipping coca-cola. Looking for virgins. American dream. People pass and wish. Now she's coming to me. Is she? With cloven-hoofed André, who walks like a female but has breasts like a male, Pan God sent for a handjob. *"Ah, Olivyeah! Ça va? Tu connais Samantha? Sammie?"* Nervous as I speak I know not what. *Oui*, sava baby. Your polite little breasts. Lay my *triste* head. And your trunk. Around which, raving footloose maniac as I am, I would like to wrap myself in storm, snow, or sleet.

Greek. Eeek! Must possess that tongue because if I don't they shall not promote me. And promotion is what . . .

Samantha putting the cigarette to her lips. Krak! a cigarette bolt, kernel of the Swiss night. Now enwombing it with a gentle ovoidal greeting, smoke eggchanting, tumefying, the cancer devour, dentists in dreams see sets of teeth clacking through the night and I see cells of iridescent convicts in my hell, private hell. Whip! Krak! Owled deep in her throat of birth, she says in a voice deeper than mine, remotely rumbling German-Swedish in its design:

"I know your mother," she says. As if that defined me. Her gold hair flowing in the wind.

"Yes," I skip by it, pained by the thought of her vast usurpation, everybody I know knowing my mother. "Are you enjoying the party?" I ask, not knowing why because I'm not.

"Are you?" she asks back, the prophetess.

"Oh yes." Not really. No. Who knows? Pause. "You know you're very pretty." God what stupidity comes from this whiny voice of mine!

"Am I?" She acknowledges me, growing a little bit bored, I can see. "I don't think so."

"You are!" I blurt again. Oh God!

Then without any warning, she wonders, "Why don't you look in people's eyes when you speak?"

O? What does that mean? Pretend not to listen. Can't possibly look her in the eye. Would die. And her thigh. My. How do I measure love? What is the smell, what is the sound? *Clickety clack.* Her earthy good-looking feet in high-heeled shoes clicking down Fifth Avenue and her shaved Dior armpits sweating silver dollars in the springsun. And under her dress. A surprise. Don't look! But in the interval. To be misunderstood. All prophets are. Unrecognized. How old I feel. For my age. Busy probing to the bottom of life's meaning. Its flesh, its bones. Reading Lawrence's *Seven Pillars of Wisdom.* His fever. Wrestling with the devils. Emerging to lead the Arab hordes to independence. Me too. Want to be a common man—Nostromo. Bonded with the earth. Must forgo college.

7

So, what do I say now? O this nervous nothingness. Have another drink. Say it's hot here. I do like the sun though. Especially in Lisbon, and you? Over there in the corner. Changing the subject, do you see her? The star of La Comédie Française back in the 1920s, yes. Friend of my mom's. Ho ho, has she had her day in the sun! Looks like a lizard. Or a harlequin. Withered harlequin.

The golden girl looking at me, her eyes like Greek Goddesses of judgment. This malice comes, you know, from nervousness and nothingness. I too am a part of all I have met. Heh heh. She mumbles something to cloven-hoofed André, distracted now by two boys giggling suggestions in his ear, is that a popper I saw flash me by?

And by the way, I add, trying to regain her attention, you know in the corner over there, the former reigning beauty of Paris, *La Comtesse Je Ne Sais Pas Quoi?* Yes, that one. Former protégé of Picasso. Still has it, don't you think? Oh that name! Anyone could take a dump here on the floor and call it a ''picasso'' and they'd all worship at the fecal altar.

My schoolboy cynicism hangs there, like bad morning mouth, Samantha sniffing it. All these words. Opinions. Yours, mine. Who cares? Why speak? Making now for the backstairs of my mind, like Edward Hyde, mounting them at a fugacious speed. Reaching my solitary quarters. Little cackles of malignancy. I am crept in favor with myself. Like a spider who speaks. And crawls. Suppose I actually looked like Edward Hyde? Wouldn't be my fault. Walking down the street and somebody's heart stopped while staring at me. No. Though I must admit. Some strangeness pricking in my head. As if a krait snake had escaped my intestine and was mad and loose among the sundrenched rocks of my brain.

Samantha's body leaning more and more to André, excluding me. My eyes wandering off to hide somewhere beneath the growing mountains of sweat which come on so so fast in moments like these. Amazing how quickly my cells burn their molten wax onto the surface of my pores and into the waters of the world. Why do I even bother wearing clothes? Nothing for me to hide. Everybody knows everything. It's too late now. The alienation started the day they stole me. From the womb. In Paris. I remember. The long swim. Acidic passageways. It was dark. My sperm tail wiggling. I was a nervous baby. And thus never was the center of things. A Galahad in a sea of troubles, as strong as I am witless, and Samantha, yes, Sammie, please, what: be nice to me.

Lock me in your thighs. Bury me. Me o my. In the earth. With the worms. Hide the world. By hiding me. Sweet deception. As the waters gurgle by. And from the liquid cave I poke my head and see. What Eve first knew in Paradise. Which is the roar of the Planets. And the sweet retort of the Kataract.

And then she, who calls herself a fabulous beast, she who sets afloat a thousand pavilions, of blue and white, and red and gold, which sail softly, like a coif in a snow-laden squall, over the whitewinter Alps and settle themselves like parasols on the Champs-Elysées in the spring. Ah! she reaches over softly sweetly and, with a thousandshipped face, in dismissal lays her parfine hand on my squalid pathetic claw, not without sympathy.

"You're hot," she notes with disgusted empathy. Anxious to leave. I'm slipping fast . . . grab it *now*! "Nice to meet you."

"No, please! Don't go!" I don't say. As she goes away. Forever. Nor look at your thighs, no nor tread on graves of grass, nor enjoy yourself unwholesomely, nor fuck other women, nor do this nor that, believe me, he smiled weakly, like a gentleman, in a gesture of congenital forfeiture. As her fingerflowers move away, on their hundred and twelve odors, and Samantha smiles at another in the Spanish sun.

No doubt I am worth one brief comment. Thinking me sad and scholarly. And possibly boring. Looking at my clubfoot. A pity. And pity by pity reach into the stars. And with my great big meaty hairy paw. Smash much glass! O why! Have I not done what they tell me to do in the books? And that is to care, to be a man, to flatter the rest of humanity! My person. Murderer. Dreamer. Intellectual. Like a little gibbon trapped in a tree. Monkeyskull. And yet I've failed Physics, Economics, and now most likely classical Greek. Strange sad sample of thought. That I've come under the influence of the Polishman. A world never clearly defined, neither humorous nor tragic, yet expressive of my deepest, most unconscious desire, is there really such a thing as *un paradis artificiel,* an oasis of frangible understanding? Or are these the ravings of an ancient sailor living oh so sensibly in London clubs dreaming of old storms in the Southasian seas?

Is there an exotic world? Is there adventure? Is there Romance?

Conrad's world draws me. ''Beware all ye who enter here, Abandon Hope!'' And one day live in China. Manage a factory full of women. Little caps on their heads. I wouldn't be embarrassed. Volleyball games on Saturday afternoon. I'll blow the whistle. Keep score. Referee disputes . . . yes.

What a party! And in the morning, I will awake and, in amaze, masturbate. These feline faces, bones of china, tiger women laughing, reality reeling behind the laughing crying face of Fun Fun Fun!

And lastly Mother who, sweeping aside fun for fucking, makes her entrance. The cynosure of discriminating eyes. Classical features. In her gown. Growing out of the ground. Knows everybody. Even me. Invited me. She has aged a bit yes, with time, but grows more attractive, more complex, more radiant. Her limiting factor in the past had always been her Virtue. Now, without a husband, she blooms. Like a huge orchid which brushes aside all other flowers in the field, and opens its emperirich mouth to swallow all the million billion trillion bees spiders and birds, she blooms. Puff!

As her son, thinker, thinks in the corner, perplexed, grown too old with thinking, and too little fun. And murder.

"Antony," her lover coming through these crowds to greet me bigly. Used to play water polo back in the Colonies. Till he got serious and came to the City. To meet the women who could afford him his cups of wine.

"Allo Ollie, 'ow ya bin," in his Australian bushman.

I murmured, "Fine. And you?"

"O can't cry, I'm 'igh."

"How so?" I inquired.

" 'Ere," 'e said, and proffered a freshbaked cookie. I declined, secretly frightened of him. Married three times, two children, tried to kill himself more than once. Like my father, frightened of that which I could not comprehend.

My father and I had had lunch that afternoon at the Palm, his favorite redmeat haunt, cartoons on the wall, the smell of beef and smoke. We talked. Of many things. Such as his insurance policy. My chances. His chances. Slipping on snowy streets. Skiing without his glasses. Being clawed to death by a falcon on his way to work. "What would you do if I died, Huckleberry?" Death. His ultimate frustration. Every morning at three dread stalks his atmosphere. When I sleep I sleep. Not he. Frightened of philosophy. He coughs, he groans, he totters on the brink; and when he breathes, he rauks on his rhythm, and his rhythm damns his dream. An arthritic doglike friendly scotchsmell that clings to his body and clothes. In my sleep I smell him through the wall. The static breathless irrevocable commotions of Death: promotes, haunts, and wracks his scotchmind! Moors and ghosts and an insane soul to bagpipes whistling over the mists. It is not strange that the purpose and passion of his noctambulation is urination. He must urinate for fear that if he didn't render the yellowed pomp from his system, he would be cold and corpsed by morning. Because he knows in his gut that Death steals by night, twixt two and five; and so each night, he fights, fights viciously, to remain alive.

In the eleventh year of life, I fought madly with my father and under the influence of my rage cried, "I hate you, I've hated you from the day I was born!"

I remember particularly his face then, shivering with mute, incomprehensible hurt, numbed, turning and gasping for breath, he was so surprised, so anguished. His face revealed all this to me in a moment, and I immediately regretted what I had said. "Forgive me please, forgive me Daddy!" . . . and I remember feeling a very strong urge to be cradled in his arms, to be perhaps blessed. He was not an affectionate man, not given to displays of emotion, but he was a powerful, barrel-chested man, very much similar in my imagination to a Jewish patriarch who commands the unfailing obedience of his Son and who in turn raises his Son to be a Father unto his own Son. But!—and thus perhaps the reason why—his soul knew not really the word of God, he accepted not the resurrection of Jesus, nor comprehended the grandeur of the spirit world, all of which by instinct I knew and yes! wanted wished him, my preacher my Father, to teach and pass on to me, as in my knowledge, God-fearing Abraham had done with Isaac and when called upon yes! to sacrifice his Only Son to the Lord God, he *did obey*! But he had no such Father my Father, and thus by indirection I had no Father because I could not obey him.

And thus it went, on and on, Father insecreting three vodka martinis to his brain, more than usual, and me one, more and more ruthless. "Dad, don't you understand, don't you understand? I have desires, wishes, that are different from yours!"

"We're all different, kiddo," he replied, reflecting his own fears of the Depression and not getting a job back in '31. Until Dad, not having read fiction except Mark Twain millions of years ago, not believing in such journeys as Lord Jim's and Tom Jones', said, "You can't be an individual in this world, Huckleberry, and expect to get away with it. Only a few do." Then added, "You're a bright boy—if you drop out of Yale, you'd be making a big mistake! You want to be a rebel, but the rebels don't win in the end." Or something like that, it's hard to remember how a long-dead father talks.

And then I, exasperated and familiar with the several examples of Goethe, Mill, Wordsworth, and Plato, who all experienced despair at a young age, and wanting furthermore the rough life, wanting to flex my mare's muscles and be a hero, and a killer besides—*if* necessary—exclaimed something to the effect of "I'm not bright! You mean jaded, the very finish of wit. I am as an ape to Ruskin, and we as a century are as apes to the nineteenth century!"

Father, his red face swaying from side to side under the demented martini moon, then made some condescending remark about the need for common sense in a confused century. Ignoring the interruption, I continued, "Why, what's happened in the interval? Two World Wars? But why, how does that explain the loss of intellect since the Victorian days, what does war do to the soul? You see, Dad, I must leave this country which I hate but I also love because it is big and beautiful and undeveloped and pure despite talk of its perdition, and yet it is intensely uneducated. That is why, don't you understand, I am leaving. To learn why we are what we are."

And finished, something to that effect, enrapt with the truth of my statement. I don't exactly know what my father then said. All I heard were the words, "You're nuts!" That in effect was what he meant. That neither he nor my mother had ever really *believed* in me, unable to realize I was a person separate from himself, something other than his flesh and blood, someone with a soul of his own. *I don't believe you.* It rings to this day in my ears, challenging me to take the untenable position. I was fatally furious, the dialogue proceeding apace to an unnatural conclusion that ended with me rising from the table in the hidebound restaurant full of laughing dying red faces, the vein in my forehead visibly swollen, I shouted at the befuddled figure almost thrice my age, "*Don't you understand,* shithead! I'd like to kill you, you're such a, sucha, sucha . . ."

And swept out, knowing I had said something not only illogical but also too ugly for repetition. Father in the redmeat restaurant, in spite of his state, shocked. At his plumrose plethora.

> *Who*
> *One innocent day,*
> *Feather-fledged,*
> *Stole a summer's stroll on the street*
> *When the big wind came up*
> *And whoo . . . whooo*
> *Went and blew his son away*

Poetry. Fire. Flew. I go. Smash the barriers, fight off the bloody scholars; they read and they read, they read until their eyes go blue. And yet they never understand. Sad scholars who see not the sunset at sea, the fastfading margin of experience, the nature that is one with Ulysses, who dared strive with the gods. Scurry forth to sea. At once, at once. Sad scholars. Sit by your magic lanterns in gabled rooms. Refine your rhetoric. Become as perfect as possible in every thinking way. Ye have toiled hard. Ye merit the laurels. Sad scholars.

Sad little Olivers. In the vice. Who am I, in my little college room, going home and saying, "Father, you're wrong, Eliot's poem is structured on the belief that . . ." as each eight-thirty morning, two million workers pour into Wall Street to give their souls. In hordes that pass me by. Fear stepping down to my simple level. The plexus of irongray life. Even Father, who makes five times more than the average man, says he's poor. The women who want this and that, bric and brac. What right me, what right life? Squeeze me, you fleshridden pythons of eternity. Coils of slime, as the day is long, despair distinguishes itself in extinction. Of this special species. Stone people. Novelists write about us. I belong in a book. Not in a life. Where it is looney. Where do I belong? Where if they wanted me, would they send me; would theology explain why and say, dear butterfly, your *locus naturalis* is? South of simplicity and east of evil? I read of this theology. It makes me feel good. Theologians are warm and good people, they reach out from the page and say you are sick rotten ugly and addled, and forget it Oliver, unless you turn your fear to faith. Faith in Jeesus. And love in God. And kiss the lipless Holy Ghost. How does it go—"neither death nor life nor angels nor principalities nor powers nor things present nor things to come, nor height nor depth nor anything else in all creation, shall separate us from the love of the Lord?" Or my father's favorite quote on the Temple walls, "Love justice, do mercy and walk humbly with thy God." 'Tis beautiful 'tis that. Tit for tat. I'll give you my Beauty. You give me your Truth. But don't bamboozle me.

Taking leave of the vulgar novelist, Mother at last making her way to me in the corner. Hi Mom. Was that you there on the day I was born? In '46? Could you, so bright, so beautiful, really have been in that hospital? Occupied totally. In bringing me to the light? Kissing me and saying, "Oliverre!" in an attention-getting French olive accent, "Why are you staying in ze corner, zere are so many girls wanting to meet you?"

You me. He she it. These girls. Meet me. Why?

"Zese are girls you should know, not the whores your fadder sees."

Warm waxen well-known breath. Her telephone was Templeton Eight: tee:eee:ate. Her son, by now maudlin and drunk and embarrassed, looking at Mommy, my mommy, beginning to birth the pain in his throat, it aches so. Your age. Your age. Admit! Admit! How old you are, how old? I don't know! cried the voice born of Kafka. Always lying Mother—her age, her operations, the divorce, reasons to dump me in these camps they call summer. "Just a *white* lie," you always said, but how could I trust you ever?

"Don't *start*, willya. Leave Dad's girls out of this!" My sarcastic manner, angry at her, who are you to judge? Tell me all the time whom I should see. And whom should fuck.

"Living zere off 'im, taking 'is money, tramps! It's not a place for a boy to grow up. Fucking every thing he saw, he was a pig your fadder . . . his whores . . ." Steam pouring from her nose with the unsaid words but so terribly hurt had she once been, Mother, she broke a broom over his head three months pregnant into the New World. In decadent later years, regaling her friends at endless dinners, "O zen she call me a beetch,

16

this leetle floooozie Lou like, and she hit me with her zandbag you know, but she don't know me! I take her dress like this! and I tear it all ze way down ze front! She look so surprise! She scream at me, 'You beetch!' and then oop! I hit her with my wight hand! Zen she fall down, Lou is white, he never believe this!''

Her friends all laughing as I listen. Mother, revved on wine and weed, launches on into another tale of a late evening in the snow, wearing her long leopardskin coat. When she took a lengthy leak in the shadows off Fifth Avenue, so long it sounded like a horse stalling, and her tuxedoed manscort, giggling, grew impatient, ''Come on, Jacqueline!'' And Jacqueline saying, ''Yes, yes, I am coming, don't leave me!'' in the shadows in her leopardskin down the taxpayer's drain pissing. Until a traveler came out of the white waste and asked, ''What's that there, in the shadows?'' Mom trying to be inconspicuous, crouched in her great fur. And the manscort, laughing, said, ''O that? That's my sheepdog.'' And the table tumbled into tears of moon gas, and I thought to myself, the fabric of fantasy is rent when fiction to fact is lent.

''I never see you,'' she to me says now, ''you never come by,'' as the waiter gorges us with new drinks and Otavio asks her if she's coming later? Of course I am! Because *later* is the place where Mommy always goes. And she's right. We never do. See each other like mother and son could, should. As close as we could ever get, in the summers in France, naked in the shower, Mommy would ask me sometimes, ''Oliverre, bring me ze soap, darling.'' ''Yes, Mommy,'' in my nerve-wracking charcoal gray suit and neatly combed black hair, the pith of tiny gentlehood, I would pass the soap, gazing upon her *corpus nudus*, the sensation as exciting as an airplane first dipping into a lacuna, swooping off with my genitals. Oh I had seen my mother naked many times in the gargoyled bathrooms of old Paris—always late morning, she never woke before eleven, and then in irritated humor, abhorring all questions till noon, a silk shade above her brows as she sipped from a tall orange juice glass with wine and cigarette mouth, wincing as the light tumbled over the rooftops into her regal bedroom.

At her *toilette*, where in ancient France the courtiers watched the Sun King pee in his chamber pot, little "Oliverre" would stand in obeisance at bathroom's edge stealing glimpses from the many angles of the many mirrors, anxious most of all to know where she would leave me that night. Waves of her deep black cunt hairs appearing and disappearing through the steaming shower glass. A silly pink flower cap on her head. Suddenly she looks bald and ugly. But no matter how disgusting I've seen her, sick or on a toilet seat, I'm still deeply drawn to her femininity, to her all-knowing, forgiving body with its earthy black bush. We talk through the water in French. "Where you going tonight, Mom?" Tension overflowing. She mutters something I cannot understand.

"Oliverre, bring me ze soap." Yes, of course.

"But am I coming with you tonight? . . . Please!" Such a gentleman I was then. You and I, Mother, when the evening is spread against the sky, shall stroll down the "Champs Eliza," as the English say in their frightful French accents, arm in arm, mother son, and I shall treat you to tea and *éclair,* an orb of white bread baking hot and sweet, unkissed, unbit. Psss! The shower has been wrenched on in this eloquent bathroom. But still no answer. She adjusts the rubber wedge on her head. In she goes. "Mommy?"

Speak to me. Her rubber flesh, seen at intervals through the French glass.

"No, darling, I can't . . . not tonight. I 'ave to go to the Rémoulades, it's too adult for you. But tomorrow night, we go to the movies. *O zut!* No, I can't. I forget about . . . but we'll be together all afternoon, hokay?"

"I really want to talk to you," she says now, trying. "I never see you, you never come by," she repeats herself, the noise of the party robbing her of much memory. Her face more masklike now at forty. "Really . . ." her attention now taken by someone else. Calling out to him, *"Oui, chéri, tout de suite!"* I'll be there, as I split my infinitives with my son, because I belong to the world. And I am everybody's friend and know any name worth dropping. After all, I am Madame du Vin, the biggest whore of all!

O Mom, once indeed you were my mother, one of the sweetest kindest gentlest of mothers. I loved you without bounds, and now, and now to force my face to look upon you, to hear these words, to batten on this moor, my God! can I not say I have been most foully deceived? "But what!" she protests, "I have been the best mother! I have always loved you. . . ." the denial and the denial and the denial, creeps out this petty pace, O Mother! For all the liquor I've acquitted myself with here, do you know how long it's been since I've touched a girl? How long? A year, Mother, a year. Yes, and in its stead, the cruel sickness of masturbation. In the tub. In the early morning hours, and worst of all, in toilets furtive, O Mother, I am ashamed to say this to you, forgive me but I shall lose my sanity if I stay at Yale! You guarantee me future wealth and position if I graduate, and I guarantee you the vanity of insanity! O Mother! Is it so difficult to sleep with a girl? Is it so difficult to be an animal?

Mother looks at me, understanding, pitying me and, contrary to what I expected, says, "but you're not the only one who hasn't had zex, darling. Antony and I haven't made love in two months, he drink too much and he . . ."

Two months. A year, Mother, a year!

Well, she says, that helpless fear in her eyes, what can she do for a grown son, what would you do if you weren't in school?

O a steamer to Australia. I'll farm! A wild people, divided into three parts, fierce in their beer, where the women are tall and marsupial and at night leap over the moon.

Mom puts her arm about my shoulder and kisses me, uttering a soft motherwolf growl. Saying, "Come, I want you to meet Monique."

Yes, Monique meet. It is meet, I meet Monique. And we talk. I laugh loudly and say nothing, till she vanishes. And why not, what have I to offer? Money, job, *savoir-faire,* responsibility, puppy love? Don't even make my bed in the morning. And dislike asking the vendor for his newspaper, scared that I might insult him. I set myself apart from my fellows, who share my sufferings, but in fact I am no different, only more vain. In its waking hours, a jaded intelligence, the idle puppets of a scholastic imagination, but when have you last kept company with Homer, Shakespeare, Dante, Milton? You have forgotten your forefathers, you have forgotten to see clearly, poetically. My ethic is hangdog humbug yes, I am angry, I am vulgar, I am proud. And I have sinned. And to think. Of my beginnings and its puritan ethic originated as a child of chance. As purely simple as that. So pure it renders living almost abstruse. The puritan shines its lighted beacon through all fogs, walls, and clouds, it creeps, intrudes, and climbs, and makes us as young and innocent as any child who has just set his shaky foot in the world. It damns us when we don't, and it pursues us when we do.

Mathematical, law-abiding, and severe. It gloats. And, o Jerusalem, how it begs me to deny its existence. Absalom.

Walking out onto 57th Street, svelte bloodvein of the city. The party fading into the museum of memory. Models with hair and tits like Indonesian shadow puppets in the windowlight. Anyone calling out to me? Second thoughts? Come back Oliver? No, the wormwood is. Mom is right. The pursy sheets are already composted. Sweeping up over the New York skyline in purple haze, the fingers of the dawn weep before me. Profane, profane! My profile in the Seine. I am awake brimming with alcohol flat on the brain, staring flatfaced into the pond of myself. Seeing back God. The King with the White Beard on the playing card. "Thump Thump!" I Am He Who I Am. Lanklean curls. No more! No more! I weep. Cry in the night, howling *"iboo ibooo, Oliver Oliver,"* as I rest in her breath in her breast my head on her bosom and weep. Weep. Weep.

I ONCE MADE love to an angel.

She descended in the midst of the Peter Pan night, and alighted on my jeesus-cold floor. She told me in the sweetest of voices that she'd had a long and tiring trip, but that she was happy at last to be at my side. She approached the bed where I lay. My hands were poxed with chickencold, and I watched her in stony disbelief. Her fortune of goldenbrown hair, high-peaked, cascaded down her shoulders. Loops of locks fell about her perfect chiseled face, dimples dancing on her cheeks. And in her eyes there flickered like cinema frames of modesty, lust, and drollery.

I said to her something like, "jeeze, an angel."

What else can you say? She placed her hand on my face, on

my eyes, this angel did. Her eyes were other eyes. She had *seen*. She lifted the bedsheets. Her long hair was parted down the middle. Her lips were moving up my firmflat stomach, her honeyed tongue flicking with lizardlips at my navel. An angel interested in this kind of earthly stuff is rare. She paused and whispered in French, *"Tu n'étais jamais adoré par une femme comme je t'adore. . . . C'est peut-être trop tard, mais je veux une fois dans ta vie que tu connais l'amour d'une femme, d'une vrais femme. Oliver, je t'adore."* Which can mean, "You have never been loved by a woman the way I love you. . . . It may be too late but I want, perhaps once in your life, to show you what it is to be loved by a woman, a real woman . . . I adore you, Oliver."

As my sculpted cock slipped gently into her sweetened rim, swallowed. My fingers in her hair, her angel eyes looking through me.

Above the fucking sounds, she murmured, *"Je t'adore . . ."*

. . . I once made love with an angel, but I don't remember where or exactly when or how to find her again.

2. YALE COLLEGE

A MOONFACED WEREWOLF clock beating on the plaster wall. A blackboard and a four-eyed wonder proctoring this thing called Greek. Clock ticking and tocking. Ten skulls, cluttered with craniums, writing, erasing, thinking, mouthing silent vestiges of memorized milestones. Have no pity on this one wedge at the back, dotted with holes, emptied of brain fluid, ravened by whiskified afterthoughts of other smells, boys and girls laughing, playing with frisbees on the quadrangle, pollens dancing in the spring air. I'm swimming in the flesh of large murky brown catfish in Mississippi swampgrass. The blond willows look like Ursula Andress. The unsought, unbought, unstudied beauty of life, bring it back, please!

But I can't, because *this is it*, time has unpoetically slowed and crawls—something here I believe about Xenophon's sacrifice to the gods, must be liver of some sort, Greeks always sacrifice livers, in the aorist gnomic active, perhaps passive, or perfect middle, or indicative, or operative, or infinitive, or perhaps simply the dative of reference, yes I think so, must run through that once more, but I can't because there's a restive baby octopus on the tip of my penis with a massacracious tentacle stretched back to my prostate, massaging it, and because that fat creeping slug of time on the wall keeps grinning and grinning. And so does Ursula. Must find some love, and there is a long list of things which I have to do, like get the rental car up from New York, see the janitor, catch that fellow who has my liquor glasses, and in short wholly evacuate: this American landscape. And all the same, as things stand at this spot in time and space, I haven't a worm's chance of passing. Nor will the great wagging dwarf on the wall cooperate.

And so, with one convulsory nervous shudder, telling of my misery, and the terrifying contemplation of life's oracular mysteries, on the parched blue schoolbook lying before me, I now bring this once comely forehead and its sad thinking sensation to silence.

3. AMERICA FAREWELL

A COLD WINTER'S day in early 1966. The solar plexus of ululating ague. Purple clouds peeping out of scorified scud. A slate gray sky where sparrows take the tumble, and all which rises must fall again. New years into the new decade. The Sixties.

On the road to the airport, I wish it'd snow. In winter we never notice. That there are no smells whatever but that of the cold. Dragging its tail across the silent world, hushed after the Great Birth. The Grand Central Parkway is paved. By the way. You might wish to know. That the road to the airport is functioning properly. Yes, and I'm going to board an airplane. Which flies. Taxpayer's money, they're taking me seriously. I wouldn't. Tomorrow San Francisco. Then Hawaii. And then?

My parents and I had dinner last night at "21." The school-itch of woolen trousers nipping at my legs, these rich people, married, drinking from glasses with liquid within, talking with the relaxed ease of a limp, assembled at this fabulous eating house of the dead and the living, the ugly and the handsome, upon whose allheads falls the snow. The metaphorical miracle. Yes.

My anal sphincter tightened and through the flaw in my

duodenum, a flotilla of warm breath blew. Mother weeping without noise. Who ever gave her son this idea of joining the Army? Looking at her ex-husband with ever-lingering doubt, hoping she was wrong wrong wrong. That instinct could be wrong, that somehow her son would be the same again. When she next saw him. Whenever *that* would be.

But secretly thinking: somehow some friend of her husband would pull a string or two. And her boy will not have to go. Perhaps just before flight time. Which only makes me angrier with her. Don't lose your temper, O. You're a military man now, above this sort of "civilian shit." Oh this soldier's life. Can be lonely and hard. Little nutcracker Southern drill sergeants with mean asshole mouths barking out the endless months in the pine forests of the Carolinas, hating fucked up Northerners and Puerto Rican street assholes. Left me alone though. Said I was "edeekated." That I am. Scholar. Poet. Adventurer. William "Bill" Stone. Lending to this world an androgynous image. KP. The night I broke five hundred eggs, one after the other and the ghosts of the yolk dried like blood on my fingers. Never had I ever murdered like this before, a *frenzy* of slaughter! And standing in the rain in my poncho looking at the puddles, sad leaden emotions. And thinking no more of nothing. Not even getting laid. And by whom.

O but it's over now, Mom. Put it behind you. It's better that way. So when I die, wherever I die, bury me afar off. In foreign graves running with grenades. And call it New York. Because words signify nothing, full of sound and fury. Memory a rope. Up which I climb. Looking down. For fear. Of falling or forgetting. Awakening in your breast the dizzy. Mother speaking and speaking, weeping and weeping, on and on. The omophagous omphalos of infinite ousia. Eating outward from my stomach: phlegm and rattling spittle and all. Fearifying me.

Branding the burning air of Satan on my breath forever ever. For having done her wrong. Doing by proxy to me, for the queen bee in drag, fag moll, her sting, her carnivorous tail, proteanized penis. Satan!

And I'm so fucking mad, besides, because there are times—oh there are times as bare as a bodkin—when I know I simply want to take this woman in my hands and simply shred every last fucking breath out of her system. Stabbing her to death. Eek! Ook! *"Tu m'as tué!"* Yes! Je Tay Tooay Brutus.

On my other flank, Father. Fat cat, growling lowly as the formless darkness sweeps in. His steak was juicy and good. Enjoy it while you can because in Peking they have your name on a file. Wall Street. Liquidate. The son too. Fabulous formless darkness.

Father uneating, staring stared unstarting. *"Anything* I say, Oliver, you make fun of. I give you everything you want and for it I get nothing but an ungrateful kick in the face."

Now I know for sure. My father is a coward. O too bad too bad. What else do you have to say, old boy, what else do you say? Sheaves of cigar smoke and cluttered brains clicking and clacking. Ho ho. The difficulty lies. I am wholly sympathetic. An immoral degenerate war. Toilet: capitalists only. And remember, if you're late, tell your friendly pilot to fly faster. Ho ho.

Oh and I can also tell you Mother was one for bed sports she was. Father never was. Something brutish and short in him. Deep revolving dredging delving Mother. Cut his throat in leaves of plaster, as he dangles, dangles from the walls of her tangle.

Must get away. Must. Intimations of suffocations. And in China I hear told of Chinese women who squat by sides of roads and ask you questions and cuddle you kindly and take their drawers off and spit into the stars and swim into hell and crack earthy jokes. O yes. In dreams. Poems poetry. Across athwart, these girls, in dreams, they come for me.

The taxi pulling up to a curb. Sonic thunder on the horizon. Announcing departures. My anal sphincter tightening more and more. Emerging into the crowds. Unspeaking. Must hurry. We're late. Checking the duffel bag as it pounds off my shoulder and clobbers me on the head.

Father and son peeing together in the men's room. Mother sobbing silently outside. Funny are the ways of the world. Yes, your only child he is leaving you now in the Indian Summer of your life, when loneliness resembles *la mort*. And though he won't tell you, he's crying, why inside he's crying. Whether to be merciful or cruel, this is the question. A faint quiver in either direction, taken like the size of a step, and the thing inflicted either way. O what to do! because to do is the same thing no matter what you do.

"Goodbye Mother, goodbye."

Redundant tears. Unstoppable. Broken bung. Forgive. Forget. Forgot. And on, and on, and on. Cry cry this naked land for the everlasting contradictions of its kaleidoscopic conflict, Thou art my Goddess.

Bidding farewell to Father. A hurried embarrassed goodtidingspeed and He be with You. My son. The soldier. Shook foil of hands. The smell of good whiskey on his breath. Goodbye. O halcyon days farewell, sweet scholarly fall air that sleeps in my lungs, and Saturday football games and the orange leaves crackling down on my head. Girls smelling of oak and maple country houses, from Radcliffe and Sarah Lawrence and Smith, in heavy overcoats with loping handbags and rich sympathetic faces called Susan and Sarah and Catherine, named Turner and

Barnes and Cabot, from St. Louis and Haverford and Wilmington, talking of James and Kerry and Douglas, invoking the muse of wealth and good times; to these I bid goodbye. Wresting sorrow from joy.

Cold day. Tarmac apron. Looking back through the porthole of the civilian plane into the airport building. My parents. Suddenly like an old French couple made in Cézanne. Gliding down the Marne on a fishing bark. Eating peaches. Mother in her leopardskin coat, absentmindedly waving *adieu* with the paw of her miniature, sad-eyed dachshund. Of a sudden piercing my puerile breast, recalling the freezing cold memory of my French grandfather, who only fifteen years ago, on a knoll at Château-Thierry, confronted by the green fields furrowed white with thousands of American crosses, spoke of the great World War One battle, shivering mists of steam parted by the sunshine. I am thrilled my stern French grandfather has actually come over to the American graves and has spoken in praise of American boys, my boys, now dead, so many so young; he looked just as he did the afternoon he put me on the train alone from Paris to Lyon and I looked back into the dark, grimy glassroofed station clanking with distant metal sounds, it was la Gare de Lyon it was, and watched him waving as I left. Bye bye. My inner voice murmuring in echo. The shimmering ironic fragility of beauty; dwelling on these thoughts alone. Snoozing sodality. Ah blush, beauty, thy face is blooming blue! And tomorrow there is China. Toughened combat infantryman. Droll scholar. Dying poet.

Father unlooking. Averting his eyes and holding Mother's arm in a gesture aimed at preventing the superfluous display of soul water. O goodbye you all. Rush the hurry of life. And at last. Fed with fattening food. Die. Done. Death!

And tomorrow China.

The rattle of the engine. A folding o'er of newspaper. A strange-faced stewardess trotting her mare's muscles down the aisle. A sign flashing its heart out. No smoking. No unfastened seat belt. Or was it fasten your seat belt? No matter. My belly is belted, honey. It aches. With holymorse. The blessing of God upon us all. Descending in pails of mercy. As I told my mom, don't worry. He only takes the good ones. Breast of my breast. This adamsapple is locking, and, as it so often happens in moments like these, a cold feline shiver luxuriates itself down the length of my body. Tearing the clothes from my back and leaving me frightfully naked. Please don't peek. Loneliness *de la mort*. More more than ever before. Out across the Great White United States by air. To Kansas and Utah and California. The march of this Union. Conceived in the pulsidge of an ancestral brewery. To the frontiers of Asia. The fabulous formless darkness. Throw my pellets into the storm and run. How they hate us! Fu Manchu. And comic terminologies like Mao Tse-tung and Chou Pow-pow and their samefaced smirking successors to be. The West is decaying, the energy tires itself, the arts fornicate, the outposts are abandoned; and in the vacuum arises the Orient, immortal, ommortal, flowering Father of millions, phoenix! Eek! Stinking hordes of Chinese verse blotched on my sinified mind and, Heaven jump into a Burning Lake, the tin kettle *nyow nyow* of oriental music. Books to burn, much to destroy, and much of the new to learn. I am an old man, I read much of the night, I was born a long time ago, and my habits I find difficult to change. Beethoven and Brahms. With their psalms, in my arms. And Paris. Where Monet and Renoir painted passion pink. Leave me that, mine Chopin, mine Aristotle, mine dreams, mine cinema, mine *kultur*, yes, you can have the rest. Vulpine creature of the slitted yellow eyes, glowering and gravid with deep-rooted nodal hate, who never flew Pan American Paris New York and looked on as long-legged plumed females paraded through the emotions of American hearts. How he does hate us so! Too bad.

San Francisco will be cold. Been there before. Pioneer people who know me not. Squirrels in the park won't eat my peanuts. And old showers will spill out their creaky guts in greed. If nothing else, there is one law to life boy: *move!* Good hunting all. And don't stop to think. Never regret. Never memorize. Just *do* it.

"Sir, *please* put your cigarette away and fasten your seat belt."

"Oh yes, excuse me." Out she goes. Started this habit in the Army actually. A friendly black fellow showed me how. Kools go down smooth and buzz the head with cotton-picking dreams. The engine revving and rumbling. Like coal on the cellar floor. A baby shrieking above the din. But? But if I wanted to get off now? They'd have to let me, they would, wouldn't they? Stewardess? Miss? Parents' faces being wrenched away. Goodbye. Good riddance. Not so! I'll miss you Mother. Because something tells me I'll never see you again. Now what do you mean by that? Momentarily describing my Edward Hyde face on the arc of my porthole. There, that's better. Old soldier. About to cross the Pacific, spotted from an airplane, a globe floating in the water of space, behind behung, cornfields of my soul. The bulging blue Pacific. Crawling with marinia and waves, white as the wrath of God, cascading currents of corpus, stretching all the way to the rocky coasts of China. Here we come!

Like thread lightly snapping, the angry bird lifted off.

There it goes, Mother said. With Father watching it go, quitting sound, into the horizon aimed, at distant suns catapulted. His odyssey begun.

And remember what he said, darling, before he left? God only takes ze good ones. What doz he mean? Nozing is going to 'appen to 'im. Iz it?

No Mother, God is never wrong.

PART TWO

LAND ACROSS
THE SEA

4 . DEAR MOM

APRIL 1966

SAIGON IS LIKE the flowering of an oriental despot. The road into the city is choking with bicycles and red dust and barbed wire, endless trucks of all shapes and sizes and jeeps everywhere scurrying with an invasion force intensity. Bouncing over the potholes in an old military bus, I watch American officers, their peaked hats cocked rakishly on their short hairs, charge about snappishly on the broken sidewalks like insurance executives with black satchel cases in khaki uniforms looking powerful and important. Working-class Americans in sweat-stained under-shirts hammer beams and haul crates and drive bulldozers, everywhere reconstructing the earth into an armed camp. Only a few miles outside the city, olive green tents dot a landscape, rising and falling on endless plains and slopes as vast as Valley Forge. An army is come!

I am so excited by the corrupt smell of fruit in the air. Skin-cracked ladies, neither old nor young, crouch oriental-style on their haunches and heels, looking like buzzards in the heat, hawking gewgaws all day long—sunglasses, American suntan lotion, old comic books, plastic combs, knives, toothpaste, dirty pictures. Cars and self-important trucks scream by them honking, but they don't blink or move. Vietnamese soldiers in red berets, holding each other's soft hands, walk in pairs alongside big beefy American boys who stare and snicker. Dozens of policemen in starched white fairyland uniforms and elegant white gloves poke their faces in silver whistles pushing traffic. Harsh-sounding loudspeakers garble Vietnamese propaganda, "Enlist in the armed services of your country. You will receive money and land! Join the struggle for your freedom! It is starting. Join your fellow countrymen!" Join something, join anything! The sound in the sky above suddenly exploding with the monstrous kick of an unseen jet fighter screaming past the sound barrier; distant bombs and artillery thud downriver day and night. Monstrous limbs of wounded planes and ugly signs—KEEP AWAY, DO NOT SMOKE, DANGER!—are strewn everywhere amid the barbed wire that grows like weed all through this crumbling city, streets pockmarked and rutted, now closed off with sandbags to house American billets and PXs.

Never in all my fantasies of American troops landing in Normandy, Roman forces in Gaul, Napoleon in Egypt, or British armies in India, had I conceived of the complexities in the export of a nation. Our bars, our whiskey, our peanut butter, our jeeps, our money, our prices, our Ohio State and Michigan-trained government officials, our teachers, our foreign aid experts, our secretaries, our food, our catered meals for our officers, our security, our superiority, our sex, our rape, our creation, America! everywhere replacing the old French colonial ways of the soft giggling Vietnamese who think it so funny for the time being.

The port straddling the city is crammed on both sides of the Mekong River with ships, crates, warehouses, and stockyards of incoming goods, brought together from the world over by our Government and its Money for one purpose alone—to get all we can over here as fast as we can—men, frozen food, televisions, generators, cash, coffins, beer, movie reels, snacks by the millions, cars for the generals, instant Las Vegas U.S.A.! functional, tasteless, arriving all day all night at Danang, Saigon, Qui Nhon, Cam Ranh Bay, cannon to the left, cannon to the right, action all the time! America is on the move again!

Anyone has to be stirred by it, Mother, this raw power and energy, everyone is happy and getting rich, anyone would burn to take part, to perform something of importance, to be part of this vast passion—yes, to fly out and kill in the name of country!

> Love,
> Oliver

P.S. When Father attributed to me certain morbid proclivities, I knew him, vaguely, to be in the right; again yesterday this enervating disease demonstrated itself. At the U.S. Embassy here in Saigon, I saw an attractive young American secretary walking by, whose features were thoroughly marred by fissures inflicted, probably, in the bombing of the Embassy last year. Long and deep, the sticky red files of her wound lay fallow on both her cheeks; ugly red welts inhabited her shoulders and arms. A primitive perversion though it may be, I very much wanted to own those scars. They were marks of vanity, of experience, of pain suffered. It seems hopelessly sordid of me; am I still so childish in my fantasies as to wish for a rib of scars raking my person? Is it a disease, a predisposition to death, the sign of a decayed mind?

I killed a man the other day.

I suppose it was a great event in my life, something that since childhood, when with devotion I watched the violence on the television screen, I have always more or less lived with. Perhaps I expected too much because, of and by itself, it was rather commonplace, like bumping into someone at a subway turnstile on Lexington and Fifty-ninth.

I shot him out of a tree at thirty yards. I picked him out and fired seven rounds in mad succession, until I was assured that he would utterly cease to breathe, to move, to exist; whereupon, as if in pointed irony, I heard the cracking sound of breaking wood. He was tumbling from his nest like an unseen falling coconut and came to a quiet halt on the firm intersection of two thick branches; a tangle of shrubbery hid all the emotional parts of his body. For a second, it felt deliciously good. I could almost have eaten "it," whatever this satisfied feeling was. Something had fallen exactly into place, like a bone comfortably cracking in the body. Good shot, Oliver, good shot! It seemed so suddenly strange that without even touching him, I had brought him down like a buck. A light, delightful tickle pervaded my wrists, especially my right wrist, you know, the one I broke as a child.

Yes, above all, it was the wrists which responded, as if they themselves had hurled the bullet-knife. A grim satisfaction possessed me. He was mine. I killed him. Me. Nobody else.

We were in a jungle outside Pleiku this week, 25th Infantry country, maybe you heard about it in the papers, it's history now. Many were killed. We cornered and slaughtered five hundred Viet Cong in a pincer movement that lasted three days, so they told us. Where I am right now, Death seems as thin as air. In Paris this will only be another piece of news embroidered within the thick columns of your morning newspaper. News is not made in proportion to the number of dead, we can be thankful for that—three dead in a riot in Paris is politically more important than a thousand dead in Vietnam because, I guess, politics is an interruption of the life narrative; war is not, war is a part and portion of the continuing story, just as the work of Einstein and Shakespeare was a continuing daily struggle. But it is really more than that, it is military history. Imagine a mass grave of five hundred corpses, heaps of flesh, it is quite a sight, one I am both fortunate and unfortunate in seeing. Like the decadent parties you took me to in New York, it is something I will never forget—that first whiff of serious longing, the desire for sex; perhaps Mailer and Freud are right. The two strongest principles in the universe are Sex and Death. In any case, it is a divide I have crossed never to be the same again.

Standing there looking at the bodies, most of them in an open field paralleling a small wood, I shivered in the wind. It was cold and gray and overcast with a slate-colored sun, a day strikingly depressing, apart from other days and sad in itself. There were so many bodies it seemed like the end of an era. A dark pall, signaling the monsoon, was to be seen in the distance.

The corpses were beginning to stink. Busy, crunching maggots were infesting the wounds, worms wiggled in the eyesockets of hot gas-bloated carcasses, strange sordid pathetic fallacy. Already, immensely large, grotesque flies were settling themselves down like vultures in the gullies of flesh, attracted by the ingredients of decay.

I thought abstractly of life and death, of the freak accidents which distinguish the two, of myself as an individual, as one body of boy, yearning, basically noble, virtuous, and yet insignificant. And to think how much I used to worry about myself, you remember how fussy I was, everything had to be done right or not at all; and remember the way I used to pester you every single night about why do all the other boys have hair around their "thing" and I don't, am I different? And you forever assuring me that I would have pubic hairs one day, though, frankly, I never believed you. And how badly I wanted to go to Yale. I thought if I didn't get in, life would be over and I would be damned; the ridiculously fragile things upon which we construct the fabric of our lives when, here, far away are men who have died abruptly and violently, without a trace of recognition, men who never dreamed of Yale or lunch at the Plaza, or a mother in a leopardskin coat with a brown flapping dachshund; but not once did I think of any possible injustice perpetrated in all this death. I refuse to believe it was unjust. Five hundred deaths are no greater than one death, because a man can only die once. The massive magnitude of the dead does not overwhelm my faith in a divinity that shapes our ends, because I persist in believing that each one of these men who died *had* to die. I do not seek to explain why, only they in their individual souls could have done that, perhaps sensed that they were destined to die here. I can only seek to explain my own spirit.

The night of the killing I happened across Ridgeway, the platoon sergeant, talking effusively about the day's events. I told him I had killed an NVA that afternoon. He grinned and asked me how it felt. I said casually, not wanting to boast, like some of the other guys who talk too much, "Aw, nothing special. But it felt good . . . yeah, really good." He kept on grinning. And suddenly I felt I had to get away from Ridgeway. There was something nauseating in talking of a dead man as quarry or game. Because I was the only one who counted in the interplay, not the man I killed. Instead of sublimating my feelings, I was congratulating myself in Ridgeway's presence. He was pleased and said he was looking forward to more action soon " 'cause the gooks are startin' to come across the border," by which he meant Cambodian border, which we keep crossing and recrossing because we don't really know where we are most of the time. Someone even said we were in Laos one time.

But I wasn't in the mood for combat talk. I had just killed a man. He hadn't. I had gloated over my kill. I smelled. I turned black inside—that look Dad always hated when he scolded me for "sulking," and I told him I was going "to catch some z's" which is Army talk for sleeping. But he caught the tone of my voice and looked at me like "lifers" look at "draftees"—like I couldn't really be trusted. I walked away.

But many years from now when I'm in New York toiling in an office, there will always be back here in Asia a tiny un-marked grave bearing the body of the man I killed. He saw me but for a danger-filled instant, before the lights went out and darkness shut his lids. Who is there to mourn for him? I don't feel guilty as much as amazed. I think that if I had talked to him first, had heard and seen his expression, fingered a scruple of his humanity, I never could have killed him without remorse. Words would have damned me; and yet looking down at the hand now writing these words, I cannot really believe that I pulled the trigger. It is remote, part of a misty past through which I wandered aimlessly, harmlessly, anonymously. Perhaps for this I will be forgiven.

No, I am only amazed because no matter how many years I put between me and it, whether I am thirty and married, forty and divorced, fifty and rich, sixty and wise, I will—from so many years ago—never never forget this grave in Asialand.

It's a stigma far greater than any emotional wound. It is fact! And each time I kill, a part of me dies. I lose my feeling. I lose my flesh. Guilt is self-amputation. It is more sacrificial than self-consciousness. O that I could reach up, in spite of numb guilt, and achieve the realm of action, of freedom.

Would Death then be what I want?

O for some noble thought with which to resurrect the poor poor little man I killed!

[No Signature]

P.S. Neither of these letters was sent.

5. SAIGON TEA

A BAR. SMEARED in the myrrh and cinnamon of smoke and shuttered afternoon light. Seminaked females snaking back and forth, hither and thither, with delinquent eyes and chilblains of the soul. Mistempered claviers. Scattered remnants of sore dry throats and tired limping drunken American erections dropping off to an underwear's quietus.

In a corner, secret corner. A jaded young fellow, worn with gasps and creaking springs, positions perpendicular and floors speckled with the dirt leavings of rats, lethargic and lazy, self-serving and sallow. An ugly sort of thing. What's he doing over there, anyway?

He's getting quietly sucked, he is yes, it's a special aristofat pleasure reserved by Mrs. Sex. Her Highness sucks. She senses suck, he senses suck, suck sucking away, it is written in the eye, it is served in the stomach, anthems are played, for whenever he sees a woman with blub-thick lips and her long black hair highpeaked, parted down the middle, he always has an irresistible urge to slide his manweapon into the lady's soft moist mouth of the Nile. Because sucking is an allotrope and several months ago I got laid amid fretted sheets one steamy hot night on the banks of the Mekong and nothing has been the

43

same since, aye, by the cunt who bore me, breast of my breast, what would my mother say now if she saw in such topography her son, stoned on weed and whiskey boilers, slipping his snake sweetly into her supper? Wow! This girl, this one hundred and approximately eighth girl that I've had in all these Saigon and Cu Chi and Qui Nhon bars, she just breathes suck.

"Suck suck!"

And there is in this the wry suggestion, I might add, of toilet manners, as suggested, *quidnunc,* by the lead editorial in *The Wall Street Journal* of twelve May, nineteen hundred and fifty-nine. At which *articulo mortis,* a womb escaped its wail and teased toasted into my gastric cancix lining where, wow, there it goes rolling through my belly's wall, tottering totally and trembling more than a tittle. Preaching thoughts of gloom engineered by motor parts and beers and chasers and greasy bolts and nuts rinsed in oilsperm.

O these words! Come fast when I'm drunk. In the day. By and by.

"Suck. Suck. Squish!"

I shall sleep late tomorrow, for, without doubt, I have emotions, even though you may see nothing but inarticulate vapors pouring in plenitude from my mouth, but do not err in your assumptions, being as they are . . . how do you say that? That memories collide with the indomitable wall of the present. Who was it who said he could never sympathize with good-looking men; they could take care of themselves. Obviously that fellow had warts on his nose. Because I for one can't. We can't. Incredibly shy people. Others call me on the phone and, referring entirely to themselves, they say, "We'll be seeing you later." Who's this "We" I think. The collective outside me? No dearie, this is not about "we," this is just between *you* and *me—yoomee,* yunerstand?

44

"Suck. Suck. Squish!"

"Hey, you, what matter with you! No come? Five minute five hunnert. Ten minute eight hunnert. You pay!"

Personally I object. Not to fucking. But to her. Rather greedy the way well-fed Orientals tend to be. Would carve my balls off with a sharp spoon if it gave her any pleasure. As a matter of fact, my father always supported the thesis that a woman should disappear like a piece of roast beef as you eat it. Not a bad idea. No aftereffects.

"Suck suck. Squish!"

Like a rubber boot traipsing in several layers of mud, sacs of swollen pollen, gurgling cold leeches like cold vichysoisse, sucking and burrowing in her mouth, leeches laying their cold black backs across my penis, shivering juices slopping through her deserted honeycomb, her mouth arched forward like a dragon's cernuous snakehead, gulping in gobfuls at my peter, o hideous hump, go on! Milk me more!

"Come on you, you come *now*!"

My cock disappearing in her orifice. Egolice. Any moment now. Beginning to hold back. It's like a machine. Feed it, it craps. Fuck it, it comes. Tethered together in space, love, like barbells, orange-colored barbells; my resistance bulletproof, my soul lickerlined. I never sucked anyone off myself, though at Mother's parties, I'm always offered the opportunity. Okay, I did it once . . . twice, just to see. But I always preferred the front entrance, more generous a hole. And too many cocks tend to wither at their extremity. I suppose that's age, but then again it has much to do with diet.

"Suck. Suck. Squish!"

Which raises the rub which of the composers best accompanies orgasm. I should think, personally, the organist Bach, high shrill Brandenburg Concertos wailing in the rear as the male jerks convulsively and rips his penis on the iron threads of her steaming cunt. Hideous how!

"Suck suck! Squish."

William O. In a privileged retreat where the monks come and go in whispers, quiet, eat in silence, like ezra in his pound, wrapped in a floppy hat and scarf and looking into the french *métro* a rainy day in 1920, and seeing leaves, the boughs of the trees, and sounds that sough, o poetry, when, like a very bad dream, coming with swift tread through the smoke-enshrouded darkness, one yellow waiter, a deadly dull man, he appears and proffers a glass of cold "Saigon Tea" which he says is whiskey, to which the belle-dame raises her dragon head and, rubbing her customer's drunken meat with a free hand, drinks swiftly in refreshing gurgles, as he watches. So this is America, the little yellow waiter must be thinking. *Toi oi! Chee bee.* This is what we fight? Rubbing his head with contempt.

Handing the empty glass back to the waiter, she lowers her dampened mouth back onto her customer's cock and swallows it whole, while the indifferent waiter to the client below rudely says, "Hey! you pay six hundred *P!*" ("P" is for piastres and *"pay, pay, pay"*) and put forth his rude little hand. As the belle-dame sans merci continues to complain, confusing me totally with her menu prices.

"Twenty more dollar joe you pay I suck you, no pay no suckee you joe, you pay hokay?" Something like that, to which I reply.

"Shut the fuck up you fuckshut up you, fuck you!" Or something in reverse like that. The customer named Stone now seen unleashing his fury. Suddenly pushing the belle-dame off, she thuds heavily onto the floor, rather rude of him yes, but who does not like coitus interruptus, and turning to deal with the impolite waiter, a penis already pulsing heatedly, his poetry purloined, the *métro* roaring off down the wrong tunnel, and behind it the legacy of wind that picks his floppy hat from his head and violently dashes it onto the tracks where it is promptly crushed by an oncoming engine, and only violence to the rescue, he belts the little waiter across the throat in an act truly of aggression. The waiter is seen toppling backward into an unoccupied table in the darkness. Screech and crunch! Tables overturning. Glasses breaking. Liquid dripping. *Chee bee! Toi oi!* Check that out, brother.

The customer now sticking his hand in the cunt's face. Chow baby. And giving it one horrifying wrench. For the road. Screams. Grunts. The knight extraordinary, now grimacing with bated teeth. Kill one, kill them all! M Pees whistling in the distance. Changing his mind and relinquishing the scene before I truly destroy this entire bar and everybody in it. Stumbling toward the rear exit. I shall remember this place. I shall remember never to return. For fear. From within. A fat sphinx-smiling Oriental holding her head in scalding pain, parrot screeches coming at me. Flinging the ugliest epithets you ever heard from woman to man. Not a Valentine card exactly. Threatening to kill me. To disembowel me. To vivisect me. I am hurt.

Stone out the door. Smell of cat's urine on the wall. Breathing deep in his Circean head. Stunted sperm, hot smell of sex. A bad night. A bad year. Another year yes. Gone with the Asian wind. And out, out into the air. No longer do I feel, I only imagine that I feel. And hence feel. To feel.

Sordid base and rank, ashamed in shame, he slinks around the corner, never looking back. And darts into another bar lined with women selling Saigon Tea.

6 . THE MERRY MONTH OF MAY

THE CAMAU. MAY of '66. The merry month. A thick hot breeze thrashing in the leaves. The rainstorm has come and gone.

Like a windy day on the coast of Florida, down in the Keys, when the palms heave to and fro. Something like a sirocco.

In the center of the small village, in dust I stood. Looking on. In this hush huggermugger task. That is but whispered.

I remember the gaping raw sting of the wound on my abdomen. Rubbing up on my loose-fitting buffdundrab uniform. The name "Stone" printed on my hairy chest. Son of Atrides, and Stonides, of *Iliad* fame. Oh what a name. So short, so strong, so unto itself. The Indians once told me stones are the most revered and ancient of recording devices, having seen and witnessed all since the beginning of time. And that perhaps I am here on this earth to write of these mute histories—just another stone, an "oliver" stone.

They took the girl with the red welt on her left ankle, her wrists bound like a squealing piglet, into the center of the town, beneath the mottled sun.

But she didn't squeal nor scream, pigeonlivered, but stood thick squat unpretty girl of twenty. With beautiful sheening

49

black hair, laden with lice living and dead, raddling down the small of her workhorse back.

On this day, the last of her life, because she was brave enough to throw a grenade into a parked jeep. And killed three officers. And got away into the fields. On her way back to the cave, when she was found and flushed and almost killed. Crouching in a rice paddy. I always thought that was a lie. That she'd been betrayed by one of the informers we paid in the village.

Her ankles were contused and torn, her wrists were shredded, but she was all tiger in her extremity. Big lips, brown saucerlike eyes, a flattened pugnacious nose, I would look for her in Paris one day, but now the sun was lowing in the sky. I studied her haughty hate from inside my ancient stone face. Her blear sun-filled eyes gazed out onto the paddies comprehending all.

It must be sad to die with the sun in your eyes. On a day I did not realize then. Would change the way I lived my life. This woman. The first woman whom I would ever know.

For only a second, do we die. Then it's death. A state of status quo. Which gives no pain. It's the transference of the spark. That drills to the nerve. And in this case. Kills.

I think I'd rather do it with the sun in my eyes. O I don't know. It's so irritating to have to die. Scratch my abdomen. Feel the grooves and ridges of your fluted hurt. Pass pity.

A crowd of peasants pushes forward to see. Uniformed guards circling to keep them out. *Pro forma.* As the diminutive, barking captain forces her onto her knees. How ugly a woman is when she crawls, when she is pushed, her head stretched and level with his holster. In which was a pistol.

We are going to make an example of this girl. Who won't cooperate with the authorities. The law and the order. Working for the Viet Cong. And, as has been borne out by unmistakable sources, by which we mean to remind you villagers that informants are everywhere, she is the assassin who yesterday killed three of the Central Government's military personnel.

Oddly fitting, isn't it, that Communists are yellow. They go well together. The color and the idea.

We have been lenient with her. Asking her to reveal the exact location of the Communist arms cache in the mountains. She has refused to cooperate. Let this then be an example.

Pro forma.

His tintinnabulous voice ranting and raving in fierce-mouthed monosyllables. A man of grandiloquent authority. Who would pull the trigger. Madman. One to fear. For these are a hairless savage people. Different from mine. He works his work. I mine.

So that when this is over, and I am yetalive, we shall sit in the shade of a local tavern and talk. Much beer. Dirty English. Dark brooding pigmentary skin, stronglystout, from the north of Vietnam, split in 1954. I would like, especially when this is over. To stare into his cold stonehard heart.

In the West, you know, we are led to believe that a woman is inviolable. I don't think I'd even touch one unless she asked me to. Mustn't hurt their feelings. They're sensitive creatures, girls.

"Find 'em, fuck 'em, forget 'em," Father used to joke. More than once, not quite a joke.

It's funny to be standing here listening, not understanding a word. Sense of the unreal. Inreal.

The captain's voice rang off suddenly. The girl in defiant fear lay on her soiled knees in the afternoon dust. As if you didn't know. Should be sunset soon. Or as they say in the westerns, dusk. Father said it all right, "It's no bowl of cherries,

Huckleberry. Nobody gets out alive.'' If the old man could see me now. Wow! Could see me now. Like a song.

Crouching there like a poodle who has peed on the sofa. My pet poodle Bongo dying of cancer, guiltily looking right at me for having shitblood all over my bedroom carpet. How could I beat him! But I did.

Not quite like that. More fierce, she. A hater of men. Such as us. ''Gimme 'nother twenty dollar, joe!'' No, not this one. Her hatred pure.

Captain's cobra eyes closing. Lean, pointed look. Putting one single bullet into the revolver for the coup de merciless grace. Merciless misericorde. I knew he was wrong. I would have galvanized her. A hundred and ten volts to the nipple. Big black darkened teat. ''They talk fast,'' someone who knew these things once told me drunk in a bar. Torture is best talked of when drunk at night in bars in places like Laos. But it made no difference anyway. She had to die. *Pro forma.*

Finally she saw me. Our eyes met. Our minds followed. I was white. White for well-off. Suddenly I felt it. She puckered her distant face and spat.

The only woman who ever spat at me. Strange that I didn't know her. Never saw her before in my life. Well, fuck her hate. Fuck her pride. Fuck these Commies! . . . Yet I bet you'd have liked me under different circumstances. I bet. I would've liked you. Fierce. Death, the great equalizer. You and me, different classes, different histories, untied, united. In your hate. If I'd known then. What I know now. Never would I have let you die. But how could I have stopped it? Stones cannot act, only record what is washed in the rain.

From above her head, in a disaffected voice, he inquired again. Where is the arms cache? Where o where?

She just glared at the ground. Speckles of dust. Playing about her rough naked feet, digging in the dust.

She could have spoken. Her comrades had all cleared out by now. With the arms. It made no difference. The difference being her life. But then she saw me. A rich white American. A class problem. Watching her die. In proud revulsion toward my presence. Isn't it something? A woman dying for you. A form of love.

Pro forma.

The pressed jugged crowd sucked in its breath when the dog-faced captain locked the revolver and spun the axis. Taking the single plumbiferous shaft into its chamber deep deep away into the deadly dark that peered down the muzzle at her head.

And pulled the trigger.

Click! Squish!

The heat spinning in my head, as I wavered with nausea, in this old western starring . . . The crowd, entertained, gasped sibilantly when there was no explosion, no spuming of her brain from her body. No frozen moment when death is caught in the net of a grimace. The status quo. Is *pro forma.* And it's all a question of who gets caught in the wrong headbeam when. Inreal.

Again, she shook her head. She will always shake her head no matter how many times you replay the frames; she always will. It's her nature she can't escape.

Click! Squish!

The cylinder revolved another notch. Her midriff heaved in clotted resolution. Never never.

My wound tickled me. Tickled like spider legs. God do I want a girl this moment. Though I did not know it then. Icecold cubes in my stomach. My balls frozen in liquid nitrogen. Cracking, they broke off.

Click! Squish!

Like that day outside Bloomingdale's, I passed the wrinkled hag who had the heart attack and lay on the subway grille. Most embarrassing. No one stopping, though they all knew from the corners of their eyes. Her mouth *ad hoc* open to marble. Her eyes scanning the blue azurity of a stare. Intersecting with a book under my arm, newly bought, the picture of its posed author on the rear cover—in sweater smiling, nature's boy, champion of the literary set, former caveman, intelligent, immitigable. Another crowded lunch hour on Lexington Avenue. Someone's bound to stop, to call a doctor? Hordes of Viet Cong riding out of the mountains in jodhpurs to save Guinevere. Enshrouding mountains. I walked on, disappearing, like everyone else, into the security of my form.

Click! Squish!

O come on! For Christ's sake, you could be alive tonight, eating and drinking. We could talk. We could fuck. Just because I drive two automobiles and watch television: you don't have to die. What I do, I did because . . .

Click! Squish!

And she flinched. She knew the next one was hers. In fear. In pain. In desire. In pity. In loneliness. And resolution. Her body shuddered. In that great yawning purview of the final loneliness. O the hell! Die!

The madman grunted something doglike from his gutter and then lifted his hind leg, as if to piss as he pulled the trigger.

O when a person is shattered! *S-H-A-T-T-E-R-E-D*. Like glass, yes.

Bones crack and snap at once, taking the mesomorph with it. Going soft and flaccid. Peering into the insides of a freshly toasted pulp of toast ripped steaming open.

Every eye turning on this death agony. The shattered face distorted in one final grimace. Gorging her cud. In blood. Like a cow the girl's face wheedled itself down to the earth where it stuck in the dust. Her feet rattled violently in a bouncing spasm like an old Mickey Mouse cartoon. Lice-laden black hair, siccative and dangling. The French say *Méduse,* not Medusa. Her feet now embedded in the earth, thick bare and fat. Toes pointing outward. Like piano keys. Her rump, rounding, resting on her erect knees, peered out at the world in one giant fart of *rigor mortis.*

Not a pretty sight, gentlemen. Nothing human, nothing romantic in it. The end of sex.

The crowd lingered. The captain, temporarily pacified, cocked his gun. Like Wyatt Earp. Blow the smoke away. A good man sighing relief. And commandeered the guard, breaking their breaths, to bury this body. In a dog's grave. Unmarked and running with sores. A costive person. The final insult. Added of course to a rather great deal of injury. Quite a fellow. Not many American men could claim his experience. Yet he's poor. We're rich. And no one knows what a hero he is.

In any case, she's dead.

Stonedead.

. . . so silent. Insunsilent.

And I am alive. Breathing sucking air, o *God! it feels so good! to be alive!* In that dirty receptacle of dirty facts which accumulate in the past and make life so middling. Like the way I look. Each day every day, same-faced forever!

Shuffling away on legs gazing at the ground. Only long enough to reach the ground, Abe Lincoln said. Where is Abe now when you need him? May rain again soon. I couldn't really feel could I? For her I mean. That is until later. Much much later. Can only express my sympathies. To the Camau woman. You get used to it. Maybe there's grace in the rain. Wash out this ensanguined earth. Stones should know.

The monsoon comes swiftly now. Head of a mongoose: tail of a mole. Odors in the rain. Things always happen to me in the rain. Can't write about this, can I? What do I say? War is hell. People won't understand. Yes, we know, war is hell, why must you tell us?

Because.

7 . KILLING FRANCE

PITTER PATTER, PITTER patter. The rain. Its tears dripping into the oracle of air. Playing with his nerve cord. *Pitter patter. Pitter patter.* At his feet, the earth opened and gaped like a wound, raw silk on the meat of seas. And the rain waiting for me.

My feet in alien corn. Women with kerchiefs, in the fields, bending. To their God.

God?

The eight-year-old boy, sitting at the card table, remembers now. At his grandparents' in the countryside outside Paris 1954. The long green lawn leading down to the stone bridge over-looking the valley. He never knew what grew out there. Po-tatoes. Bands of stocky peasant youths who roamed the countryside roasting harmless snakes over dirty little fires. And if he crossed the bridge into the forest, of tall trees and dead ends, wise serpents in the leafage and wild birds in the trees, thinking of the Gauls. Before Christ. Never go into a forest after three in the afternoon. The darkness tumbles down very fast.

Remember the way Jean-Claude, the bravest of the boys,

would cringe from venturing past the bridge after dark? Do you remember?

Pitter patter. Pitter patter.

Oliver was a nervous boy, much scared of mutilation, this of all deaths to him the most horrifying, and at times he would be carried away, in nervous frenzy, to peaks of instant madness.

Jean-Claude was Oliver's cousin—five years older, thinner, taller, a nervous wiry energy, his hair cut *en brosse,* French crewcut style; they slept together in the attic, trading ghost stories, and on the days the rain let up, they went out to hunt for buckets of giant multicolored snails, running the captured ones in endless chariot races around intricate coliseums of rocks and plants, allowing the winners their freedom, and eating the losers in soft butter and garlic.

Once they were chased by the never-young village toughs through the black forest, and Oliver caught his shorts in the rusted barbed wire that dotted the landscape from the gory gas battles of the First War, *La Grande Guerre* the French called it, and he fell, ripping his leg open—a painful gash of seven stitches that would never vanish with time.

The boy cried in agony for his cousin, "Jean-Claude! Jean-Claude, *aides moi!*" He was scared, bleeding, more worried about the oncoming youths who would beat him, yelling in contempt, *"l'Amérlo! Casse la gueule de l'Amérlo!"* They hated Americans even then, not because we had won the Second War for which they knew they owed us their freedom from the Germans, but because we were rich and too perfect, and jealousy pervades all conditions everywhere at all times.

Jean-Claude skillfully picked his *petit cousin* out of the wire. The French boy had no real mother of his own and so found his affection and trust in Oliver's. From America Mom would bring him *le bluejean.* In turn Jean-Claude would protect her son from the village toughs. Later that summer, she finally called from Saint-Tropez in the South to say she would not be able to come and see them after all. She was sorry but . . .

Instead the rains came.

Pitter patter, pitter patter.

Day in. Day out. The youths were forced to stay indoors and devise games. Grisly newsreels were shown throughout France of the colonial defeat in Vietnam and soon Dien Bien Phu, where the French paratroopers were encircled and captured or killed to the last man by the treacherous and supposedly inferior yellow man, was incorporated into children's war games. And Oliver, taunting his older cousin, would make fun of French military might. And Jean-Claude would mock Oliver back saying America lost in Korea, though Claude truly loved the America of the Chicago gangsters who shot their way to success and the comic book images of tough unshaven American G.I.s who beat the shit out of the feared Krauts in the Big War before all the little wars devoured it. And they wrestled together, but Oliver always wanted to lose to the heroic Tarzan core of the older boy, and always would—strangled, knifed, duped, shot, arrested, it didn't matter, the good guy always beat the bad guy in the end, and Oliver saw himself as bad.

It was a summer somehow. Their grandmother, Mémé, sickened and took to bed. The bees were ferocious, swarming in drones about the kitchen where Mémé stored the jam preserves. One morning, before the sickness, she killed forty-four bees with her swatter and piled the corpses anklehigh in the kitchen corner.

Petit Oliverre was stung twice that summer. Once right on the edge of his little manweapon. It was at a garden party on the banks of the Marne. Full of flowers and rubbery-tasting teas from India and women in lace nodding, clucking in credent Proustian prose. The boy was half-nude, caked in raspberry jam, on his fingers, on his mouth, the neck, the inside of his thigh. The bee, it came zooming down, settled, and moving sideways, it dipped and stung its little life away. O, he cried like a baby-giant, crinkling his eyes and flattening his mouth.

Mémé wailed, *"O la Mon Dieu! O la Mon Dieu!"* The adults were laughing, it was amusing and it was a summer somehow. Obviating mirth. A restless hot pollen in the August wind. And the dull hard slitting tresses of rain, full of hollow appetite.

Now do you remember?

Another time, earlier that summer, I'd first learned to kill. My grandfather Pépé had gone away and left some live fish he'd caught that day in the Marne swimming in the kitchen sink. Jean-Claude had not yet arrived from Corsica, and Mémé was squeamish about killing animals, as was my mother, who was there briefly. What would they do without a man? *"Bien sûr, que je le ferais!"* "Of course I'll do it!" I proclaimed proudly, after a moment's hesitation, the next eight-year-old man in line. Not quite realizing how cold and ruthless an execution it would be to hold them in the slippery palm of my hand, each fish struggling and leaping for its little life as I swung their terrified brains onto the edge of the white sink, sometimes leaving small splashes of red blood, the voice in my head telling me to do it, to take these fish as sacrifice, and as much as I loved animals, they must die, and I be their executioner. If I hadn't done it, to this day I wonder what would have happened in my life. All its choices came with the concept of sacrifice, my own and the fishes included. I laid all twelve of them out on the sinkboard as Mom and Mémé paraded by, looking at me suddenly with newfound respect in their eyes. Man of the house. *"Comme il est fort! P'tit Oliverre . . . c'est un garçon féroce, n'est-ce pas?"*

Now do you remember?

The boy at the table suddenly experiences the very naked and overwhelming desire to hurt someone. His own void itches him, like the rain, like the playing rain. What is its smell? What is its sound? What is the history of this rain?

At these cards, *La Belotte,* then a popular working man's game played in smoke-filled *tabacs,* and Mémé, hot and dizzied, bringing the four o'clock tea and the freshly heated chocolate bread to the table for her boys. She looks like a big rat, her left eye perpetually ducting with a tear, always moaning about money, one thing or another—*"Mon Dieu, toujours du souci."* "My God, trouble, trouble all the time trouble." Playing, slap! at the rosewood table, losing, cards shuffling, time crawling, emotions boiling, slap! the card goes down. The sound of a finger rubbing on paper. *Pssssss? Kssss?* What is the sound?

Jean-Claude. His close-cropped skull and ears stretched outward. Taut tough lean face of no suet. And grapplinghook ears of which I have always been afraid. Teasing me as I lose. I feel the fat on my thighs. The moist marrow of my bones. It seems malignant. The rain. Pitterpatting on the granite stones of the gray sad garden at my back. Some drops you know are louder than others. Can hear them. Can hear footsteps in the rain. Can't you, Oliver?

Do you, do you?

What is this voice calling to me all the time, telling me things I don't want to know? From where does it come?

This surge growing in my shoulders. It always starts in the shoulders, at the joint with the arms, sleeping there like toxic cigarette smoke. Sepsis. Sepsistic smoke. And little fragile bend-able cards to nervine the inner furor. Like the ringing rain. Drumming in my dead ears.

Thump Thump Thump

Jean-Claude now sneering at me. Slow motion. Saying something about me being a bad loser, taunting me with his hee haws. Children always know how cruelty works. They take no prisoners. In silence, his lips churning. Out with it! French? What is the sound, what is the smell?

How do I measure love?

"Eh quoi!" He demands, *"Qu'est-ce que tu attends! Tu triches ou quoi, petit? Tu n'aimes pas perdre, tu sais, tu es mauvais joueur. . . . Allez, fait suite!"* Things spoken loosely with the madness of rain.

Oliver suddenly leaping and screaming from his seat. Think-ing now in American. Foul dirty unstoppable frontier American, in terms of Kill! and the laws that adjust themselves after the fact, you fool! you French fool! you deserve to die, and I, I am all hard inside, hard as I possibly can be, inexorable like Nature, all American, all pioneer, for once for once, faced on a course of action which admits of no . . .

. . . moving swiftly and ruthlessly behind his chair in an instant's pride, grasping him at his unprepared ease from behind his back, taking his throat, in all its soft embedding flesh, thor-oughly in the small of my hand, his cartilage piercing into my palm, and, fragile, squeezing mightily with my fingers and strong frame, killing o killing, with my hands, squeezing so very hard, squeezing myself to death with him, who's to die first, o killing! Something I learned in a comic book.

My cousin not knowing why this is happening, crying croup-ously, so surprised! choking on the natural difficulty of *"qu'est-ce que? Questceque? Keke? Keke?"* Squeezing on! You shall die because you shall die! And I. I am killing you. Screaming with my mouth contorted in fury, *"Je vais te tuer! Salaud, je vais te tuer!"* Ha ha! His ovoid orifice growing red. And redder. Reddest. The red ogre of Mad Ness. The word "squeeeeezzzze." His crewcut head, *en brosse,* ha ha! bending forward now, emitting grunts from deep within his saliva, struggling to be rid of these hands cleaving stuck to his gullet, breath denied, now realizing life denied. The power the glory! Of killing! Raw brute force. Master mocking his dog. Dog meating his master. The rain without beating down in flurries of strangling finality. *"Je vais te tuer!"* I am going to kill you. Shouting these mercilessly majestic words through the rain raining. Onto the rooftops. Jean-Claude spewing up private liquids through his mouth: onto his chest he sees in the sun when he swims. Gurgling there bubbling. An ugly French face rasping red. So ugly, haha, that you deserve to die!

And Mémé. In this drama. At last pouring from the kitchen. Into my ear. Her face of deepest shock. Shrieking above the rain, *"Oliverre! Oliverre! Arrêtes! Je te dit! Qu'est-ce que tu fait! Tu es fou! Fou! Arrête ça!"* This sixty-year-old woman lunging at me with all her creaking force. Grabbing and twisting my arms with all her peasant strength. Petrified thoughts of murder. My spell broken. Hatched. Cracked. Ooze. Lose. Leaving off. Jean-Claude slumping on the floor.

"O la la, ô la Mon Dieu! Qu'est-ce que t'as fait, qu'est-ce que t'as fait! Comme tu es mauvais!" Reviving Jean-Claude, his mottled face coming round, splotchy red and white. I am looking on. I am a criminal. I am mad. And at so young an age. Why? What have I done? How wonderful the feeling. Killing. My wrath. My hate. It sets me apart.

Jean-Claude now facing me. In the rain and the violence of scurrying clumsy forms that dance to the music of ruptured molecules—never-ending violence! Crash and thud! Kill Kill!

"Je vais te casser la gueule, ça je te le promets!" Lunging at me. *"T'es fou non!"* Mémé now trying to restrain *him*.

"Arrête, non arrête! Vous . . . êtes tous fous! Mais non, vous êtes tous fous!"

Jean-Claude punching me and throwing me into the wall and kneeing me in the stomach and kicking me with his shoes and breaking my nose. In fear. In trembling fear.

8 . MEI LIN

THE REEL RATTLED. The dark lights flickered on the eyelids. The numbers flashed upside down. Eight SEVEN six five! ******two. Plat! The film focused. We have two films, the driver said. One from France, one from America. Ten dollars? Hokay?

After all I'd never seen a pornographic film, raised never to look people in the eye. The beeping car zoomed on through the glistening rich traffic of Bangkok. On the outskirts pulled up outside a ramshackle bundle of windows and shades. Conducted through the rain into an attic room. Picture of the Pope on the wall. Cloaked with stale sin peeping out from the seats of the chairs. Sit down. Sitting down. Sleepyeyed lotuseating Thai projectionist adjusting his implement. USA. 1948. A woman like Marie Curie. Anklelong skirt. Touslehaired. A large pouting mouth, floozyfaced. If ever I saw one.

And this man, thin and diffident, urinating. The jolly green giant. Closeup of his penis quaffed. Now the names: Molly and John. Good title. Sitting there talking over foul things, cognate with the insufferable erection pitching in my pants. Already? Promise of things to be. Alone in the dark room. Do I dare? The Thai sleeping, or is he? Words flashed across the bottom of the screen. John: Maybe you can help me out. Molly: Don't you worry. I'm no virgin! Ho ho. I'm relaxed. My conductor's baton. Molly is certainly not timid. Saying: Let's try it out for size first. And, ho ho, slipping her pocket into his change. And bouncing in his brood of mirth. Up and down, up and down. A tide in the affairs. And a view from the rear. Enlarged buttocks and cunt. Grind and bump. The fleshy shaft. The ironhard. The strong of groin. In the suctiontight clasp of her vagina, prolonged grunts. Pig humor. Splat! Cut. Shy John now humping aggressive Molly. The hairy tool fixing the black muff. Thrash thrash, threatening to collapse, groans the bed, and cameramen squirting down their calves, and Molly is Molly, there's always a Molly that distinguishes the thought of this world from its attendant action. Minutes elapsing into dignity, and John's wombwishing wong, marvelously erect, crouched 'neath Molly's coup de dog grace. Back where we started,

William Stone, in amaze, questioning his own virility, wondering why Adam was a lousy lay for Eve. Because he didn't use his foot? Molly saying: Hell boy, you don't need a teacher! Ho ho. My balls are baffled: that there is no one here to hold them. But must keep my face astringent. Lest this sleepy Thai see my lechery cauterized on my flaming mug: born American, seeker of sin. Molly up and down. Juicing. Film jerking and blacking out. Ohhh! On again. Quick. For the orgasm. Opening up inside her like an umbrella. See her fuck. Lifting herself off John. Camera focusing on the last trickle of snow as it melts from his shrinking gland. And drops, dripping, ah like a remorseful tear. Molly in the husky voice of a female cowboy: Well, hon, you shot your load! Yes, and now Molly, it's my turn! Here I come. Film roaring to an eclipse. SMASH! Finished. No credits. William, not delaying, bustling out. With this tremendous erection in his pants. Once knew a man. His name was Bill Boner. Lived quietly in Connecticut. Didn't join the countryclubs. For fear.

Driver, do not smile at me like a monkey. But I need a Molly. Now! Do you understand any English? Take me. I say. To the nearest whorehouse.

Beeping car zonking through the rich wet streets of Bangkok. So good to be here. The wear and the tear. Nobody to share. Thousands of lonely American boys without a clue, eating hamburgers and fries with real ketchup in air-cooled lounges and drinking foaming milkshakes. "Just like home, man!" *Home.* Why is that word so warm a sound? To every man except me. Home. Memories buried deep with our bluejeans and sneakers and Mom, served to us now by bizarre lithe smiling Thai waitresses in white. "Looking for a boyfriend for a few days honey? Well, I'm ready in seven to buy you what your gook boyfriend buys you in *five years*! Yeah, that's right, two three grand right here in my pocket, honey, American green! Couldn't spend it in no jungle. Whaddaya say?"

"R & R" they call it in the Army, "rest and recreation" lest we crack from too much murder out there in the jungle. In manuals that tell you how to behave in foreign lands, always be courteous and polite, even when robbed, remember you are a guest and use a condom at all times. The Army psychiatrists, a class like Army doctors and Army priests who never look you in the eye when they send you back to your death, even say a little sex can ease the pressure of the nerve linings in your trigger finger.

"But don't you believe it honey when I fuck your brains out for the next six and a half days, now let's get goin', time is money and first I gotta buy you anything your little candyheart desires, jewelry baby? A tattoo on your ass? And you know, maybe even get married?" Who knows, promise her anything, future mixed race, all racing down to the very last fuck the last day in the modest hotel room with no money left, just in time to get back to my jungle home, where I grunt and shit, before the dream runs out.

But for now I feel rich, clean and wholly artificial walking these clean streets. Skyscrapers spike the sky. Movie marquees and long Asian lines to see Julie Andrews with her large white horsemom teeth singing from the mountaintops of another artificial *paradis*. O that I could live there, in the icy lakes with no snakes. From the cab I see it has just rained. A certain glistening entombed in the cobbles of the yellow-reflecting streets. Going forth to fuck. How glorious. Into the depths, surrender my body to art. My portraiture postmarked on the rotted ceiling of my emotion. And my name on every stamp between here and eternity. How really bourgeois you are William, whoring about, happied and incontinent on this continent consistent with sin. Last year of ass I had was in Cambodia. Brown and rubbery woman, a dungbeetle whorehouse, squishing sounds from my penis in her pussy. O I wish, my wishes, somebody, anybody, would marry me. Then I would be a somebody. And anybody looks pretty enough once you go deep enough.

Hurry up, driver, drive. For I feel strong and practiced and clean. Times like the Meadow Club in Southampton. When I walked hither and thither smirking in the wealth of finery, the cloud of bubbled ease, the sweet unreasonableness of memory. Specially scented coca-colas each August. Watching out on the tennis tournaments aplay. Little markers and gauntfaced referees pegged about the mintgreen courts. Little signs stuck in the grass. Names of players. Laver-Sachamangari. One from Australasia, the other a Pakistani, black as a pearl, taut as a starved tiger. *Whishwhoosh, ping, snap, blam, boom,* the thunks and twunks of green balls hitting the heart of the curving racket: a volley of exhausting suspenseful length. The *oohs* and *aahs* of the damned in paradise, and a little titter of colliding flesh under the hot Island sun. Canopies that are red, girls that are long-legged, men in white, balls polite in play. And I would come away. When it was over. Feeling sticky, hot and enthusiastic like the head of a poodle flapping and wagging in the open window of a fastspeeding automobile. And when I would step out on the court the next day. For all it was worth, there was I! Weaving and warming and swarming. Singing shots down the baseline. A subtle fractional volley. A withering serve. An acute crosscourt. Game! Stone, 6–1. Magnificent times in the West. That faded out the next day. And more the day after. And so on.

Yes, I'm ready. Let us proceed. And if well done, perform. Twenty dollars. This wench. Here you go. Where? Oh. Up there. Come. Let us climb these stairs. The Pope is still watching. Effaced and energetic. From behind some jalousie in the Vatican courtyard. Like a figurine made in fiction looking out into the rain in inimical eyefuls, writing belles lettres with boring, bland banality. Horrifying things are now happening all over the world. Anacondas are eating people. Right now. But *figure-toi*. That you're pretty. And what is your name, little lamb? "Mei Lin," eh? Well, that's a pretty name, it is. My. Here we are.

Close this door. A bowl of energy in my balls. I've just been to the movies. And I was moved. Now undress for this here hottened pirate a little rude under the collar. You must forgive my haste, but this haste, it is hungry, Molly. Yes. Her puba. Was sublime. And besides I haven't seen a white woman since I've seen my mother. But you'll do. You'll do well. I'm cute, you say. She says I'm cute. Blimey if I don't besmirch you! I feel like one of Captain Cook's band, foxed and corruptive, landing in the Southseas with a seabeard. I must be ugly when I'm all hot eager panting like this.

But for now, forgive me, then kiss me. And say I'm beautiful. Before I crumple and feel humble. Pitiless with perceptivity, the icecold wind.

Whoosh. It passed me by. Into the interstellar. Into . . .

What did you say? What did you do?

You did. You do. Famous deed. Doubtfully done. O doxpite. Thorough in your seduction of this carcasslass.

Woo! The alchemy of the magicmind. Teeth pushing out from my ass. Cursed piper. I ply the musical pipe. And prance along through taverns of country greenery. Tralala. And then, when the East sets in the West, I put my pipe down. And look back. And see. Nothing but useless creativity.

And yet I sing. And yet undress—off with these jester clothes, this jocular bonnet! Horses prancing yes in the park, ballet dancers tiptoeing through the dark, come, throw it open and ah! peek into my hot cold heart. And show you my shame. Our shame. Your sweetness. Mei Lin, yes, lithe lean and hungered, slim, trim, seeped in sin. As gentle pretty, no, as gentle beautiful. As a drooping willow. Despite the dox of the fact that I have never seen a willow my whole lifelong. Despite the further fact that . . . And living in sealed cities your whole life. So sad, so pathetic, so inevitable, her piggybank owl eyes. That have seen it all. And yet. And yet I marvel. That she offers what she has to me. For so small a sum as this moneything. Ah, there is blemished beauty here. Of the second heartbeat. Of the rank that is deep. A beauty fleshed in my heart. Its hushed footfalls treading through the snow, as Bach plied his organ and bore carnival joy into the gothic streets where cathedral bells ring and rang.

And now you're coming to me, you're kissing me. I see.

Though for this you are not paid. You're cradling me. You're loving me. And yet so . . . Beautiful small sad breasts, perfect in their modesty. Fleshfolden. And if a little tugged on and worn, oddly occupying. My heartfelt sympathies. Let us now proceed, for the streets they are washed, and have been cleansed. By this rain. Which fell from the dark night sky.

I went walking once on a nudist beach and saw a German girl, perhaps the most beautiful girl I ever saw. In Saint-Tropez, oh generations ago in the West. Slim sixteen, tender seventeen, sprawling blond flesh pitched in the sand. Just like that. And on her ears were long silver sardine rings. They gleamed in the Cézanne sun. And I was overcome. There is simply something about blondes. Glistening wealthy pubic hairs. Spun of gold. The spinning worm. And I'm the spider. Though then young, too young. I looked at her. She looked at me. Nude Goddess. Into your tent. To shelter from the sun. Which, I note, is hot. Your blond legs strapped about me. Like a parachute. Floating. Floating down. I looked, and again she smiled. And I felt so small. In my bathing suit, unfree. Shyly burying my erection in the Mediterranean. Trapped in the long silences of suicide, I began to move away, although I knew she was looking. I knew she knew I was shy and inexperienced, and I knew she would be nice to me. We would talk in sign language, her with hers, me with mine. Her nude shape dazzled in the sun one last time, on her back like Nature propped on her elbows, and I like a fool, forever going south. Past past. Past the sagebrush and flat breasts and the very blondness of her waiting. Past life and all. Past.

But now let us be practical, no poet I, but a fucker be, lost to eternity. My fly unzoned and fornicating felly with this Chinese wench. Off with the rest of these clothes! Men at work. Burntoffering. Both in our childish estate. Stripped of adulthood. Peeking at one another. What is that on your thigh, Mei

Lin? Bad bruise. Oh! But what does it matter, for though both beaten, our bodies are moist with the moonstar and in our abdomen's seat, there is melancholy this night.

Here. In this house. For money made. For Mei Lin. It is you whom I want. All this time. Blind blind. The first girl I have ever loved. Why? Because there is something in your face that even a serpent, in all his uncensured cruelty, could see. It takes not a twoeyed man. It takes not eyes. It takes not man. There is no advantage in your shredded little smile. Orphanic: runic. Farewell Molly. Prithee, stay awhile, Mei Lin. And keep me company. This bewildered bull of a boy.

Moving onto the bed. Mixing our bodies in the vapors of knowledge. Looking at your prehistoric nipples. Look at them Oliver and marvel. Glued to the bottom of her distended bosom. A combination lock. The lights are out. Operated by a graduated dial. Three to the left. Four to the right. Seven over again to the left; bypassing four. So smooth for this thief. Who snuck in and stole. My clean white teeth nibbling the big money. Open it for me. I seem to be stuck. With memories that have been forgot. O now these ugly things we must do. In the light of day. Become bliss at dark of night. Mei Lin. Such an Asian girl I have never seen. Such hair never was. Because you're thick yet thin and these hairs took to your trunk. Just like twine. This prize is mine. None else to despoil her, none but me, she is me and I—I see—am becoming part of you.

Licking the little hairy leaves 'neath these arms. Spider copyright. And my warm tongue sipping the unpasteurized liquids of your lips. Such light fine black hair. How fares it? Put it into this male's mouth. And taste its grassy brim. Treading on tiptoes the path of spring. Now lick it, the chops of memory, and may you never forget till the day you die the sweet taste of this in your palate of memory. Taste. Tarry. The blossom is too sweet for cutting. For. What is it that I foresee in the foggy mists of futurity? Some physical evil. Happening, it happens. To me . . . or is it to you?

And now, as it came, it is gone. The cold fear. Awaiting. Two squelching lips cupping her cunt. Two squab feet cupping my balls. Your tiny fat baby toes rubbing up against my globes. Hemispheres. Strange that . . . that you're thin, and for one so thin, such feet were fat. Intact. Squirming and poppling in my plantigrade grasp. Like this wine, your hind, it is divine, and, as in youth, when to the gods we whispered our aspirations, of whitearmed Helens and yes—Pallas, Pallas Athena in the sack!

Changing o'er. Moving with the slow sweetness of a flower's scent. A mad method to your motion. Refined sublimed, it circumscribes all of me and, may I add, every scribe from a to z. Our simultaneous, our semaphoric, our *soixante-neuf*. My peter is scared and uneducated but you shall like it, though there be many you have seen. Why? Because it's mine, little flower, it's mine. And I'm sucking forth the swishes of your delight, your wishes, into mine, me you, you me, all *myou*, who beats who. To the orgasm.

No, wait. A few beats more, as I stand above the shaded elders of the river and drink deep the effluvia that pervade the gleaming sweat of your green pubus. Greedgraced architect 'tis I. Who build these spanking spires to the smoking sky? Earthborn giant, I volumnize the earth, my greed knowing no skull, my ambition no growth. Do I not frighten you, little feather? Aye, what not and all, what are you doing? You're reaching into my hatch of time—man made humble, into my testicle sweating in scent. Your cold finger with its nail disrobing my tinkles of first sorrow, my void, my inevitability—thus traduced by the echoes of humility, this Hercules that's who. For now is the time of revelation, the time to tell all, to you lying astride

73

me here as no other will do, clutched close to me in the bands of secrets, licking my belly like the fondest dog I ever knew. That I must disappoint you. You see . . . there's just one. With one to go. For Mei Lin, the other one never quite came down. The specialists, they all looked at it, they all tended their hopes, but you see, it never quite came down all the way, the addled one, and when I was eight, they swooped down with a scalpel or whatever it was, and took the vestige away. And told me it made no difference anyway. And Mom told me it was hernia. Though it hurt for years and years. The phantom of original sin. And I used to think that one day in the future, when I'm thirty-five, in the locker rooms of men's clubs, in the dressing rooms of ladies' boudoirs, I would say, humbly, I lost it in the war. Swooning sighs. My other limb sprouting in size. Sorry 'bout that. Sorry, Mei Lin, to disappoint you, but you are the first, next to another, my mother, who knows this. You're Chinese aren't you—opium thighs in the night, grunting sweat in the day, though I know no Chinese, pity the chaos of my lonely body. And place your perfumed pussy on my penis.

O Mei Lin! the rosejoy of your lips, softing my sadness and incesting my hard mind with bribes of an intimacy unknown, was it not so long ago when Byron in these sheets slumbered? Three centuries Shakespeare, six centuries Dante, and in the first Himself—say tell, I wish to know, of the sacred hands that defiled your temple, and stole from your organs the sweet sweat of ejection.

No, best not, fumble to kneel, and then to pray, and boldly to washup. For soon. No. Yes. You understand? I knew you would. That I'm tired of it all. I read much of the night, I go south in the winter, and you mean more than this to me, so much more, now that I am about to lose you, never to see you again. I will sit in a New York office years from now and think with prickly fever about the times of my youth, and you Mei Lin—whatever happened to you? You will be dead, Mei Lin, that's what. Killed by some awful inevitability of the East. Bad-lucked girl. It is so good to be alive when one is young, is it not? And sing in jest, in thee I shall swim till I reach Eternity flowing at my back, and cry out, "Darling, thou eyes are like shooting stars, thou ears finely cut of an Indian green nephrite, and thy mouth, sweetorder of breath, soft rainy shore of snow shaped as the green rose, that which grows alone in the throes of the Kachanjunga, faraway many days' journey across the emerald seas. To which, where we shall go together. Then. Before we age and before we die."

Ah ae. Now is the time. Curling up in my armadillo's armor. Keep the world away. This soft gran'fatherly position. Come over me now, so soft, so tender, cuddle me kindly. Keep me. The doctors also said that some day in the future, man will have so far progressed he won't even need two. Just one. Me. The man of futurecity, o woe! and now, Mei Lin of the soft plentiful hair, wrap your reservation, rotund and roiling, around my penis and let the lightning roll. Before it's too late.

Not so much of me left, arriving at this rendezvous shortly, your lithe movements over my body, gentle heaves, looking down at me like an eave, what is in that look? Your eyes are open, you stare into me. I hope there wasn't pity there, sorrow certainly, the lack of lust, yes, in times crescent, in times future, that is the moment I will recall, and that will bring back the sweet taste of your hair, that single look from above, your secret eyes, our secret together, that I am a train, lumbering through the sparse night. Too. Too. Did you know that the Northern State Parkway in the spring is a most beautiful highway on which to travel? Did you know that the train from New York to Chicago, the *Lakeshore Limited*, heads north and swings through the plains of Albany, yes, to avoid going through the mountains? I thought I'd tell you. It's warm, the mounting mouse in my blood, ooo, faster, faster, you must go faster, Mei Lin, dammit, you must go faster, your hair like that in front of my roving eyes, am crying, a few sovereign sorrows, they beguile the tutored airs of our distilled lives, lay on tears, like the tonic toys of dalliance, piping out, it hurts, it hurts, the sting of sweetness, weakness, *in saecula saeculorum*! Oh yes! I shall have to pick you up now, and, o, roll you over on your back, o because I, more or less, more than, rather would, o . . . God! . . . is it always like this?

9. DEATH COMES IN THE AFTERNOON

THE TREES WERE green with wet that jungle day in June of '66. Turbulent afternoon shadows camping in the gullies. The twenty-five sticks of June. On this day Custer and his men were wiped from the face of the earth. Ninety years ago.

Moving fast over the surrounding ridges. Swooping and sousing, the camera whirring. Lush green, coming down the northeast ridge of the Ashau mountain range, in the wide open distance the smoking fires of Laos, where the rivers with panthers run and press with the question of who laid waste to the land. Just who? You wild wild American boys called Tex and Bones and Ripper. Know no evil, see no evil, it's my movie.

Moving in closer, the rain falling musky and thick. Wet and tired infantryman of the rear security, their numbers thinned by battle, now trudging through a sloping meadow, circular and waisthigh in vegetation. Two hundred meters in width to the camera's eye and stretching downslope half a mile, to the entry of a dense wood, which the First Platoon now enters; the Headquarters Group, Captain Crisanthefoi and Sergeant Ridgeway trailing with the Weapons Platoon. Behind them Second Platoon. And now, at the far end of the meadow, emerging from the upper wood, Third Platoon, Lieutenant Perkins in command. My platoon.

The youth William Stone, black-haired with strong forearms and a Mongolian electricity to his face. Moving the camera in, even closer please; we know what happens now, and in the face of what's to come, we ask for a hero. Possibly he could be. If he willed. But doesn't want. Because he has killed already. No brute, he too is worried and would say. Thinking of the Gauls Before Christ. Never go into a forest after three in the afternoon. The darkness tumbles down very fast.

Am I coward? Like my father? His name on his shirt, spelled "Stone." Born on a Sunday morning in '46. Now '66. Only twenty when he . . .

"Time? Tick tock. Hey—got the fuckin' time?"

Answer him. Words forming. Yet no strength with which to speak.

"Broke ma watch, man."

" 'Bout ten thirty," Raines grunted. A handsome, dark-haired Southern boy.

"Hour to chow," someone else said, spitting.

"My feet're killin' me, man," Greek chorus of infantry, idling the air with longing.

"I figger two more clicks today, it's a bitch! Fuckin' heat."

"Fuckin' country. Fuckin' mountains. Fuckin' sky, man. I hate this fuckin' place."

Stone fucking thinking, how many men have I killed now? Do you remember? *Pitter patter.* The VC you shot out of the tree. Tumbled down like a hard coconut. The one in the Ashau as he was crawling into the abandoned bunker. And the one in the spider hole, looking at you just before your grenade went off under him, and splut! he collapsed like a small building. It wasn't so hard. Mostly luck. How many others? You couldn't count them, could you, in the commotion? In your loincloth, with a flamethrower, running through the mountains screaming like an Indian. Why not? Say what is not possible in this life, say it and you are a fool like Father who says it's a tough life because he never knew how to kill what stood in his way—to overcome! And said life comes up and eats you when you're not looking, the dull the dreary and the dry, goodbye goodbye, fools who never saw life, who never danced contorted dances on nutty floors in nutty dinner jackets with nutty arms that could strangle the living shit out of you. O no! Not that!

The lick of the whip in an orange sky. *Snap! Snap! Snap!* It flared crimson orange and gold and pounced into my eardrums. Dirt like dryness in my throat. A tongue of land detonated. And in the resumed sudden silence of this field, I can almost make out a farfetched dog barking behind a stucco wall, somewhere perhaps in Mexico in the 1950s, and the eagles in the mountains are peering down at me through clawmade field glasses. I must be mad, but don't fret, they'll soon bury my sorry ass on the day the cannibals come out to play and Mommy and Daddy crying over the taxes on my G.I. insurance, but hey I'm not alone anymore. I'll go down with my unit. Raines and Rizzo, Maloney and Crazybush, who did a year at Elmira and was half crazy Indian and sent his old lady all his money for Christmas, right before she ran away with the biker next door and . . .

Bam Bam Bam! A slow but sudden boredom of riflefire from the meadow below. Crouching. Looking. The fire suddenly surging, picking up, intensifying. Then, *crackety crack wham bam,* and "INCOMING!" Hitting the earth. Machine gun delving into our midst. A bit high. Dull terrifying thuds of bullets whacking into bark. A cry. The sly silliness of first fear. Creeping along its tree. Into bullets. It's like riding the subway. Look-ing out from my earthbound position in the rain at the dark sky. Lines under my hollow eyes.

"Sit tight. Sit tight!"

Sitting tight. First practical application of the art of war. Crouching in a military costume, what fell fate could be fore-warned? Thinking no fuckin' way they gonna get me to attack that machine gun no sirree! That French Army crap, circa '17, waves of slaughtered men. Who'd go now? Sit tight! Yeah, we know. Everything except what's going on. Like at the Yalu, I'm sitting there frying c's, minding my own fuckin' business, and who comes wading across the fuckin' freezin' river in the middle of fuckin' winter, yeah, kiss my ass, a million fuckin' chinks! What'm I supposed to do? Sit tight? Hope they don't see me. And thinking, I'm getting paid for this. Twelve cents an hour.

The Second Platoon disappearing in the woodline to the right, chasing the ghost. Down a wooded slope. Very quickly, the last packmule disappearing in the wood.

Just what the NVA regulars want. What's his name, Crève-coeur, broken heart? Liver of Christ? Some name like that. Anyway the captain. He won't close up the perimeter. He'll leave the meadow open 'cause he wants to sucker 'em into a fight. The First Platoon at the front, the Third in the rear, and the Second forming the apex of a new triangle. West Point tactics. Like Custer. Won't work. The man with the weird name is gonna kill us all, ho ho, this battle was lost on the playing fields of West Point, it was won in tepee tents where tea does not titillate.

Very heavy concentrated fire from deep in the woods. I'd say 50-caliber machine gun. Right on top of Second Platoon. Ambush! Then a sputter. Sporadic fire. And over the radio, the insane static: "We are surrounded. Repeat—surrounded. Come up on our zulu tango seven, we are meeting main force, a battalion, maybe more. We are . . . !"

Now heavy fire to the front, downslope six hundred meters where the First Platoon, with the Headquarters element, lay in the woods. Across the elephant grass it was impossible to see. The rain still falling thick and heavy. On the radio an unidentified voice: "We're being overrun! Roger that. We're pulling out!" Then it squawked.

Take a peek, O. See what's really going on. I know they tend to exaggerate.

Whing! Wow! Six feet from this moviestar face. Like a flying fox. He's behind me. To the right. In the tree.

Whing!

Moving away. Someday: infrared bullets. Will announce the end of war. Stone turning. Through a film of water.

Wham! Wham! Wham!

A 50-caliber not more than sixty meters to the left rear, opening up. Crossing into the killing zone. Low this time. Bark and earth flying, with low silhouettes, through my atmosphere. Shouts. Hoarse yells from the cave. Winding in the leaves. The fox *volant* through the trees. Ghost of a panther's soul. Coldness cataracting. Jungle soul of songs. The rains. In rich drenching folds, slitting down, miring the earth, dimming.

Fuck, I muttered. Must keep calm. Must not think. All I know is Gee oo dee. Must relax. Oldest law of life. They did it on the sanguinary fields of Troy. Masturbate. Balms the walls, ungyves these knots, washes out the mouth of malcontent.

Abridges the doleful worm.

A night in the bed. She will come for me. Her blond hair floating in the breeze blowing at the window. Smiling. Her body thick, squeezable. The lunging hungerford I never had. Flexing her thighs. Saucy wench. I leer. Come here. Her legs, erecting themselves like nutcrackers and—

"Mortar incoming!"

Whoosh! Whump!

Whoosh! Whump!

Heads low, men scurrying from rockface to rockface in the rain. Cry Alleluiah, Alleluiah, Alleluiah!

Whoosh! Whump!

Whoosh! Whump!

Dull deadly thuds spluttering. Tornout grass, golfed up, poppling weakly through the rainheated air. God's next to worst work. Rockets are worse. Shredding to bits and pieces, balls and all, a giant upheaval, a Doctrine of Final Things, killing men who never believe they're going to die, who can't possibly believe that. . . . Looking up. Into the face of the man lying astride me. Why, it's Crazybush! His eyes opening, fearified. Cries of "Medic! Medic!" A severed tree trunk inches from our bodies. A few feet away, the stunned and battered coal black face of Sergeant Washington bleeding bright red from his mashed nose. Heading toward our hideaway. Didn't quite make it. His last moment between living and dying. What the fuck *happened?*

One less. Yes. And not many more to go. You get to a certain point, and you know you're going to die. It had to happen. But it fits that soldiers are the ones who get killed. They are the restless bitter ones, aren't they? They believe in nothing. Neither God nor Ursula Andress. Is it that belief which divides the world into the You and the They? O to be rich someday! And marry a high-fashion model with cheekbones in her cunt. New York. Paris. Dreams. Without dreams, Death.

One thing I've noticed for the first time is Nature, and how very full it is. I want to write about that. So that when the Angel of the Lord asks me again what are you looking for in life, Oliver, I shan't be nonplussed this time and say something silly like "Happiness"—no, I shall say—"its Fullness, that's all, its Fullness." Now that I know this, that faith is my fullness, I can lie silently in the smallest stillest spot of Nature and witness each struggling sample of life. Some discharge of energy. A leaf that falls. A caterpillar slinking along a blade of grass. A bee burying its head in the flower's hour. Or simply a sound. It never stops, not for you, and have you ever noticed that it is those who are afraid of life who shy away from its Nature, 'tis so. Once I was the transposed soul of Rimbaud, fleeing all moral courage and reading *Vogue* magazine. And suffering as I looked across the abyss at complacent Beauty. But now I am a soldier and as when I was young and scraped my knee and Mother said, "now be a little soldier and don't cry," now I know for certain that she was right and that a soldier is a soldier and a soldier can never cry.

A voice crying, "Where's Minerva?"

Another wailing voice, "Tell Bissel to get up here fast!"

Who are these people named Bissel and Minerva? My second cousin on my mother's side, François Goddet, he lost an arm somewhere around here. In a place called Jars in Laos. *Plain de Jars*, he said. Incoming mortar. It blew up. That was about fifteen years ago. Poor kid. He never believed. And now he's a one-armed car salesman in Paris. Where memories of Mother who walks down the Boulevard de Courcelles past le Parc Monceau flitter mothlike across my mind. *Clickety clack* go her black alligator heels with the shiny black alligator bag swinging, smelling of Chanel perfume, as she heads off to Van Cleef in the Place Vendôme. And then perhaps to Dior at four. And at five she will go to see Mémé in the Rue des Quatre Fils. It was in

Paris she introduced me, for the first time, to homosexuals with kind sweet svelte malemasks, now lounging in Egyptian luxury of penthouses on la Place Vendôme. They knew I liked them, their movements were lithe, their brows beautiful, and their faces mythological. A woman by nature is tender, but when you discover a man that is sweet, O 'tis a gift given of God to a race of centaurs.

But now these bare and withered men smell of butts and I am become an oldworld Westerner in the East, another drop of greatness shred. Little yellow figurines in green uniforms swimming in my eyes, scurrying about at rifleslength yelling vociferously at me, pointing at my testicle, and threatening to disembowel me. Two fifty-nine. *"Eh, mon vieux, ils t'ont pris aussi, les salauds, les petits salauds!"* Ghosts of French soldiers at Dien Bien Phu. I met one once in Laos. What will they do with me now? Send me north to savageland? Break my arms and legs and then pull me apart? Never be the same again. Never see Paris again. Wandering along the unlit streets of Montmartre looking for where Loyola lived. Paris! Mother! In treachery yearned my squeaking heart waving its frilly *mouchoir*, Mother, how could you . . . let me go? Bells tolling tolling. Threeaclock. Threeaclock. Threeaclock. This Sunday afternoon in June. The twenty-five sticks of June.

The man we called Crazybush looking sightlessly up at me. One eye gone, but the other can see. Gripping me tight. Our bodies moistened in the thick rain. And once he was an Indian. He loved me in his way. I too loved you. Moving away now. Into the rain. His ghost crying.

The 50-caliber tracking down the *piste*. Maloney rolling out into the killing zone. Semiconscious, his right hand and half his scalp missing. "Maloney! Get back! Get back!" He couldn't hear. Confusion. The thick squat bullets rising to meet him, quick like the sea. Rolling in. Got dusted, Maloney, the machine gun surging off down the *piste*, into the open meadow, where the rain was still slanting down hard.

This I feel. A curse. Mother said it more than once, "You could be killed over there, Oliver," as if I were incompetent, somehow not man enough to take care of myself; I hated her motherlove arrogance. Did I listen? Did it make sense? Mothers are cowards. Curses passed down the vaginal passageways deep to man. True as true can be. I told her that I didn't really want to go back to Yale, I was an adventurer, just like her, and went to Vietnam instead. But I wonder what she'll say when she finds out about this, my limbs stiffening, waiting in this groin wound of a rottefield in Vietnam, a lily and a daisy both, and the buttercups tumbling in the breeze, though I could never tell which flower was which, and overhead the receding rumble of another unseen warplane heading out over the South China Sea. Mother loved me deeply, I know, and had me baptized in the Cathedral of la Ferté sous Jouarre along the banks of the Marne where the Great War was fought and my grandfather Pépé was gassed by *les boches*. I meant to write about it because it seemed so very beautiful, and so mixed up it'd be a dream, a child's night dream. But I could tell the truth.

An eerie stillness dancing through the jungle. William on his stomach alone, drinking from his canteen in great surging gulps. Before the attack. Suddenly exhilarated, deciding to dig a hole. The size of the pad doesn't matter. It can be a duplex on Pacific Palisades or it can be a shithole in the jungle. Right now, it's a shithole. And I intend to make use of it. Bury myself. Atavism. Because I once was a worm myself. Until I packed my bags in the foolish fickle past. *Whing!* A sniper. Should I tell you about the bee that bit me once on my peter? *Whing!* William digging in a way you'll never be. Mud beneath the nails.

So caught up in this I can't think of anything else. My Uncle Roget lives above his stationery store in Paris, and my Uncle Leo lives in a house in White Plains with a bunch of cousins whose names I don't remember, only their lack of interest. No, there's not much money here, in digging your grave. Right now they're making, in an equivalent amount of time, twenty times what I'm making, in Paris at the cocoa market. Where I worked one long summer ago.

Through the rain, a dark moving body. Sergeant Ridgeway! What do you want, leave me alone! His impassive face with the wide cheekbones. Large leathery hands. A competent man, made for war. "Six is KIA!" Lieutenant Perkins, he meant, is dead. A vision of him dead. "They'll be coming up the middle. Try to split both platoons, get us in a crossfire."

Looking me in the eye. Soldier to soldier. Man to man. Unpaid unhappy. Can't promise you the cavalry will make it this time, but. But what? He winks. "Stay dry man. Gonna be a long afternoon. You okay?"

"Yeah, you bet, Sarge! Four months and I'm gone!" I lied, wondering why do I say all this, why do I speak at all? Deathbed repentance. Baby, you and me we know. That this is a movie.

And, turning to leave, he cracks, "Don't forget to save your water, troop." He smiles.

Riant rhymes on the road to dusky death. Mouthing a lifetime's mirth. His large frame moving away through the rain. A good man. Snipers hurling in the lead snowballs. Rocket rounds lazily pounding in on First Platoon. And mortars, massive and mad, landing sloshing deaddrowning hard in the midst of men. At this moment! In this very flashing fiery instant of thought, my painless thought, who and how are these men dying? Slowly or quickly? Painlessly or painfully? And I their student, the student of simultaneity.

Looking down the long row of faces peering out at the jungle. Times of turmoil. Thinking of each man in his home. Flowers and palm trees embroidered on his sport shirt, and white socks in ancient slippers. Potbellied rooter of the baseball game. Cutter of lawn. Reader of sports page. Cursing his wife, mother-in-law, and ugly little children he always seems to have. Nor will they sense the blinding pain when the lead fractures the brain, its memory, its life. That's sad. Denied deprived. Lying there huddled up with pieces of your body blown far apart, ugly distortion, blatant bloture, chafed lips parching, functioning ceased, earthworm fertilizing the earth; they'll throw a poncho above us, their voices humming and buzzing, and exciting our envy, they will shake their limbs and provide the mirth of movement, ho ho ho, and they will repair to the States, home of the hotdog, and they will copulate in sheets, and they will lounge in baroque movie palaces watching Julie Andrews yodeling on Swiss mountaintops, what lucky fuckers these; and then, completed of their sorry task, because they do feel sorry, the medics, they will throw me, wrapped in a winding sheet, gently into the deep red earth, where, God above, of all places I don't want to be! With the earthworms, your inadvert friends. In the earth on which you fell when you did it, when you died. O, if they could jettison me into space, slip me into blackish snake water! But not the deep dark brooding achromatic earth, not that, not that! Shivering. Brrr. It's cold. Don't think. Don't wonder why, fool, it doesn't become you to gainsay the gods, the trouble with you Stone is that you're too intense. Struggling just to exist, it must be a hard life that; the solution is to start early and bark about howling your guts out in parody until they accept you as just that and then say you are no longer a parody because all laws adjust themselves after the fact. O why is it that you can do and do and do your very best and do as you are told to do and still be dead?

"D'ya hear that?"

"Think so, what was it?"

"Dunno . . . think it was . . ."

"Listen!"

"Yeah."

"Fuckin' gongs man! fuckin' gongs, willya?"

Clash, boing! Clash, boing! Fusing with the slush of rain, from the distant wood, a cakewalk hinting of Debussy and little Alices with golliwog curls, playing pianos and eating sweets in consummation. Do I hallucinate, acidhead, out of the wood an army of teeth and silver bullets?

Clash, boing! Clash, boing!

What a rain! Stealing away our air support. I knew I'd always die in a final bursting blow of rain. We must have a rainbow. The rest is silence, see. And the Channel, I say, is too choppy this day. Thus I suggest complete withdrawal. Begin again another day. Easy now. One and one add up to two. Old Chinese proverb. Music in the jungle. An absurd association that, by its very reality, borne out by reiteration, cannot help but conquer habit. Because the moment when habit is eroded and crumbles, then it is the man either dies. Or lives. Thank you, gentlemen, that will be all for today. And they want me to go back to Yale as a student. Christ! How frightened I am. Of the whole big world. All of a sudden. Today. Should have pulled up the sheets and slept. Swallowed my toad. Because there is no guarantee, gentlemen, none at all, that any of us will see the sunset again. Sink back now into the depths and feel the ironcold reality, the pointed steel piercing the gut of fear, feel the infinite patience of watching a fungus growing on a weir, the hopelessness without end or beginning of making it. Just making it baby!

Hysteria had now gripped Stone. I could feel it in me, from very youth, when I pounded on my knees in rage at not being able to defecate; my anal sphincter having contracted in petulant reprisal, in monkey's mockery of my meaningful wish.

A trumpet now spoke. Echoed in the woods. Six notes. Toy trumpet. Through the rain in inimical eyefuls. Sound of William's teeth clacking together.

Why you bastards! I murmured. A voice in the cold rain. Whose? And it was funny because just then a large raindrop splattered with a large splunk on the rim of my helmet and exploded into my two eyeballs. And it means: start thinking. Because there is something to remember. Cymbals. Of my guilt. One Friday night at Yale, at Mory's Tavern with friends sitting there in the easy warmth talking, laughing over foul things when Alex (for Alexander), one of my old friends from primary school, suddenly said after ten years buried in the immense caverns of his mind, ''Oh Stone, you're one to talk, you killed that poor Bongo!'' He laughed wickedly, finding it funny that Bongo, the poor beast, could have died of cancer of the rectum needless to say, a slow and painful lingering death, he ho hum. So funny. What do you mean Alex, killed Bongo? After ten years, I said, why do you suddenly bring it up? The eyes of all my friends feasting on the sport. Chase me up a tree. Tear me apart. ''You know,'' said he, ''you know better than I,'' the words reverberating like a carillon in my ear. You know Oliver, you know better than I. That I had beaten him, made him my catspaw, ridiculed him to his dog's face, that I had impressed upon him so many humiliating tortures, this I knew, but how did Alex know? What secrets revealed him by He who watches, what douce spirits have hovered over me in the shadows of my life? That I, Oliver, am a killer! And Alex, something else you don't know: that once Bongo had quit this life in mortal pain, I broke down and cried, and refused to see my father, who never liked my dog because he lacked discipline, for an entire week. Poor Bongo. In his youthful grave. He'd still be alive now had it not been for me, me, me, me! Who have killed? What right have I, nay what right to demand the right of surviving? What shall prevent this? At last. What code of purity, of honor?

Did I ever tell you that I dug up Pee Wee the parakeet a month after he died? And found a wormeaten body which I distilled in my chemistry set, mixed with my urine, and gave to Karlo the butler to drink? That too, and more, much.

The silver whistle now shrieking in the rain.

"Here they come!" some disembodied voice yells.

O don't look! Don't feel the fear. The belly in the fear.

Out of the woods, the hordes now come. Yellowfaced and poor. Little people. Two hundred. Four hundred, what does it matter? More and more. Out of the Belleau Wood the day you dug up the battered shell from 1917. *"O la Mon Dieu, ô la Mon Dieu!"* your grandmother wailed, the day in the rain she poured out of the kitchen into the porches of my ear, *"O la Mon Dieu, ô la Mon Dieu!"* and the rain fell and fell, o yes, symbols. Symbols in the rain.

The hilarious rapping of the trumpet crying Charge! The cymbal and the whistle shrill. Wild contorted mouths yelling mute hate. Stone firing in short, controlled semi-automatic bursts, O Holy Christ, Sweet Mary, Martha Luke and John! Ra ta ta ra ta ta! The figurines disappearing like popup targets in the elephant grass. No jamup, no confusion. Reappearing. Heading for First Platoon. Flanking to hold us off. Can very faintly see them. The empty puissant convulsions of grenades. Tossed, imagine, into nests of men tight and gasping for air, before they drown, jampacked, subwayed.

And in the room, the women come and go, *"O la Mon Dieu, ô la Mon Dieu!"*

Closer, their short jerky movements, in heaven water, announcing themselves with painted passion. Knees to the wet earth, sloshing onward, prepared, in a bloodthirsty frenzy of death, to die. To die!

Fictional mass, farting ass. My fingers torn and bleeding. From what? Am I hurt? Pain shooting through me, numbing me. In the muddied clip of my M16, I ripped myself! Fuck! Idiot! In my pain-bleeding hand now, an iron lump of jungle fetor, studying each pebble, each lump of dirt inches from my eyeball, each drop of shit a liter of time. A new relative significance.

Looking up. Soon doom.

Yaaaaaeeeeee!

Louder. A little louder.

All about, cries and lungbursting shouts of mad lusty American men chasing after death. Shitting for the very exhilaration of their narrow devout lives. The coming forth of it all. A willingness to die. Because never again will life rise to these heights! Americans, without helmets, with stringbean faces, grasping their picks and shovels, locked in limb-to-limb death grips with their small slippery soulless foe. Grappling dwarfs in the distance. Tumbling to earth in anguished arabesques of shock, hurt, death. Americans firing low, automatically, hardly looking. Into a delirium of despair, where Death has another meaning, another time. You would not want to be there that day.

"Get down fuckhead!" Something red and black flying out of the earth! Look out! *Pow!* It smashed me on the right side of the brain, throwing me down hard on my ear in the rain. Blackness. Twenty seconds, five seconds, two seconds, who knows in the madness of time? Coming to. New World. Stunned and dizzy. Where am I, looking out of paper sockets that hold my eyeballs? Mottled mass of images. Shifting human forms. Meeting volleys with their bodies.

A man, cursing, disappearing behind a pile of smoke, reappearing for an instant, bouncing to earth and lying there limply, his body crumpled in a new shape never seen before. Forever. A mass.

Three-hundred-foot trees. Ghosts everywhere. François—my cousin, the French soldier! Was that him! A woman beneath, thrusting up her landscape, breast of my breast, a time of tribulation, falling back down, upon, on. Some lower level of holy animalism.

Another raindrop plashing on my nose. Thinking I'm hurt worse than I really am. And my mind reeling through space and stars and wind with the blow to my ears. A burly figure coming at me through the trees. Is it us? Or them? I can't tell. I doubt I want to believe. The probable truth.

This life is one long chain of paradox. Like a parachute. Opening up finally as you fall toward dusky Death. Down down, the laws that adjust themselves after the fact. The *compos mentis* of sangfroid. You see, that's it. A man can only go on living if his knowledge of God deepens. Otherwise he dies. That's what happened to Keats. He died because . . .

The man shooting at me. Missing. Close now. Shooting again and missing. Am amazed. He's coming up fast, too fast, eager for his kill.

The frame of knowledge reeling by historified, inreal. Do you too believe in adventure? Would you trade places with me right now? To be at this moment of history, *mano a mano* with my enemy? It's true I always wanted to be an adventurer. But really never was because I was puritan at heart and too smart. Manyeyed. Out of the mainstream of time. I can't die. Can I? Like the end of *Richard III*. Beetlebrowed, effeminate. Not believing it was over. On the plain at . . . what was it? Bosworth, Bosworth Field. By your eleemosynary leave.

I met one once. An adventurer. In Laos. A small, wiry, handsome French paratrooper, *un légionnaire*. With his tightly drawn, having-suffered face, like a mask seared flaming shut with kegs of iron brandy, mean as a swan—a year in a prison in North Vietnam, beaten and starved, and when finally released, he returned to France in order to volunteer for Algeria, where he killed a quite colossal number in retribution. And when that war died, he returned to Laos to advise the bony natives not why but how to jump out of these rickety airplanes. One night at a lively, packed bar on the Mekong banks of Vientiane, the wartime capital, recoiling off the streets where hideously made-up Laotian transvestites were begging me to fuck them and there were no real girls anywhere to be approached in that fairy kingdom, I drank and drank and wanted to be his friend. Wanted him to teach me, to like me—I am young yet and still pay meet adoration to my household hordes. And oh, he was charming in that snakelike French way of Baudelaire, Verlaine, and Mallarmé, who cultivated the abnormal artificial and neurotic, now called "decadent" or "symbolist"—i.e. "I see things other men don't see," exclaimed Rimbaud peering up Verlaine's asshole. Why not? Which is what my handsome and heroic paratrooper wanted to do to me! Suggesting it in surprisingly tender tones. Did I hear him right? Oh my God! What do I do now? Allowing him to show his vulnerability, so badly did he want me.

I am embarrassed and, suddenly nervous without experience, I tease away his queerness so at odds with the hardness in his handsome male face, whose proud wrath I underestimated when without warning, he grabbed me savagely with fast slicing sharking reflexes and pinned me against the bar. Death in his eyes, six inches shorter than me, but truly terrifying. A pyramid gaze, centuries old. Fuck me, kill me, there's no difference once you've crossed the line, as he had long ago. I'd betrayed him. The bond of the brotherhood which I'd mocked. No longer. I pleaded in my best conciliatory French. I meant nothing. I totally respected the French, despite the loss at Dien Bien Phu, despite the fact that every bullet you soldiers fired had to be accounted for. Despite the fact that you couldn't fire unless fired upon. Despite the further fact no one gave one shit of a *Bon Dieu!* what you were doing here in Cochinchina—the lost patrol. Oh, a lot of despite doxing thee. In doxspite. The doxspite of inwit. Inreal.

Then he smashed me, the little Frenchman did. In the eye. *Crunch!* That was real. I like fights. I like to break through the treacherous crap of facial beauty, immobile and meaningless. And stick my tongue in the bitter soul, the brackish crap of conflict. The crap that counts.

Crack! Crack! Crack!

Stone, through shredded bleeding fingers, firing clip after clip. Just fire! They tell you just pour it out there and the ghosts will go away. My 16 jamming now! Oh fuck! Is this really happening to *me?* Cheap plastic black toy assembled in some fuckin' factory in Connecticut. Fuckin' worthless now, all for money made. The burly attacker coming screaming through the trees. Fuck!

Get to work, o please! Hurry. Ripping my fingernail a second time, tearing my flesh, blood all over, extracting the jammed bullet. Shit! It burns. What does it matter! Hurry! In with the new clip! Load it! *Karromph!* goes the gas lock. Now aim! Where the fuck is he? Oh shit! Get out of here!

Moving fast. Then suddenly seeing the NVA! Crouch! He was there all the time! Doesn't he see me? He doesn't! Fuck! Get him! He doesn't have a chance!

Tchak! Tchak! Tchak! Six seven cracks from my smoking hot barrel. It actually works! Look!

Whamming, his big body waxing with the rain, madness mastering him, river of thought dispiteously drowning. Now dropping, writhing like a baited worm. Now disappearing. In the ankles of the grass. Gone

And on.

And on.

And on.

Down through Laos. Into Cambodia. In the rain. Into the whorehouse I came. Bruised human flesh, horny for love. Rain, rain! Forever, in places of sunless seas, in hostelries. I reeked of the dog odor the rain paints on the body. And the old cyclo-driver breathed into me the animation of decadent poverty. A soft sweet wheedling murmur designing the shapes of love from his wizened cricket throat. We bicycled through the wide empty boulevards and ghostly still markets of the capital Phnom Penh, past the deserted French bistros with the impeccable white-shirted waiters standing there, waiting on the wraiths of former customers, hundreds of empty tables still freshly set with starched linens and fresh flowers and gleaming silver, such patient, smiling sweet people! The rain mercilessly beating down on the canvas covering my head with its Mongolian blood and pierced ears where my burly forefathers embedded their charred stakes, for what else is the rain but memories slapping up against my head, an imagination, immense, of memories, rainy youth foregone, foregoing?

As I disembosomed my stilted soul to the old cyclo man, his knotty legs turning, knit to furies that are wed to Fate. Weaving Fate. And in the spinning wheels of his cyclo, I saw my life—important to me, meaningless to anyone but me. It would have to be someone special, I told him. Because I am weary and misused, and the woman who will do this with me must not be older than I, yes? And she will be good, won't she? Not some dog? O yes, he assures me, "number one, the best! No more American here. In old days people happy, people rich. When American here. Now go way. Now Government own everything. Communist! Paah! Me show American pretty girl. Me can do."

His sister, his mother, Brigitte Bardot! Anything the horny heart wants! Why is it I believe? That you are really Santa Claus disguised as a cyclodriver? Here in Phnom Penh in December. Without snow, without gay gifts for me 'neath the trees. But now I wouldn't want you to think that if I took you to Capri, you'd take advantage of an old woman, tee hee, but do ignore my uncertainty, would you, I'm silly tonight, even hairy-chested American men sometimes grow silly on too much whiskey and marijuana, you know why, so take me. I say. To this cathouse that is Cambodian.

"Hokay!" said he enthused and, singing the sweets of life from his insect throat, cycled me in his spider's web over to the slums, into the whooshouse, which was in the end no thousand different from another, the girls no prettier, the smell no more edifying, the walls cracked and boarded, the mattresses creaking and the curtains spotted with holes and cum. And who was I to believe in Santa Claus? What am I looking for? What love in a leaden heart? And then I was deeply embarrassed, which was funny being as I was a veteran of these encounters. Being, acting, playing the handsome young man apparently well off, the student who at last dips into the poisoned vials of sin, that squire from American shores traveling abroad. *Bien entendu*, I paid, with the easy smile of the wealthy rich, twice what I should have paid. They squealed with delight. Picking I don't really know why the heavyset one. Looks like sculpture. Wide wellworn creases lashed across her forehead. Promise of things to be, breast of my breast, wow I tell you, this wide wellworn woman, she just breathes to fuck.

William watching from the bed as she undresses. A woman without a top folding in beside me. Massive mammaries. Don't know what to do with themselves. Here, let me hold them for you. Smell them. Sniff sniff. Earthy odor, somewhat powerful. Like the dry matter in Central Park lying on the horse paths. Mother's dachshund rolling in it, his elephant ears flapping for vultured joy. And this rib cage. It's so big. No spider hair on her rubbery pussy, and legs like trees. The birds on their branches singing to me this night. Heaving, rasping, urk! O I shall farce you fat with the frivolity of fucking.

Sucking squishing seeking sin sex saliva . . .

Hey, watch it! Don't yank! It's not a garden hose. Just because you may not have one. Don't think you can have mine. Heh heh. That's a strange sort of kissing you have. Rubbing noses. Cambodian custom. Here let me show you mine. As I bury my hungry tongue in your thick fresh gum. Heh heh. The tight delight of bestial vice.

When are you going to take that off? That whatchamacallit? I hate to get to the point but now come here sweetiepoo (giggle giggle), now roll down on top of me. O whoo, you're heavy. Heavy is as heavy does. So don't fret your little Cambodian heart away on morsels of mortgages. Buy me.

Knock knock. Let me in. Into your warm lair, *chérie*. Your thick hand about my weenie. Lift it gently. Don't squeeze too hard now, mam, I'm a businessman. Make no mistake. A razor in your cave. A leather ring. Luring me to this foul den for my wealth. Then kill me. String my bones out in my throat balldry. Never quite relax. Sleep on my muscles. Best to stick this exploratory Lewis and Clark finger in here. There. Wag it about. Much leeway. Little else. You're safe. I'm sorry.

As we presume to resume. Your strong arms propping you as you fit your midsection like a vaulting parachute onto my plastic modelman erect and quivering with anticipation. That's a handsome head by the way. Wind and sunparched. Feeling these subterranean jibberings now. Wow! I always knew I'd fuck a real live Commie someday. It was inevitable. In the scheme of things. In doxspite's canons.

Sucking squishing, squish suck fuck . . .

O these words. Come fast when I'm drunk. In the night. By and by. How it hurts, ooowwww! sting of sweetness, tickling fingers on my groin, singing groin, finely tuned. And whistling with all that American milk muscle, exciting the physique. Sign of the mystique, drowning as I drown in your warm soft tender pleasant pleasing mildmannered hole. Making love to the enemy. Passing secrets. Shot in the neck. Till dead, goddamn mam! In a whorehouse that is Cambodian, on his back, grandfather subtended subsiding in her serpentine evatude. Adam's error. O sweet Jesus, what is it with me, that I want? With me. O!

In the rain. He had smelled it. Scented it. Ego to id. Moving with a panther's muscle. Away. His death. Hearing it explode inches from where he had just been. *Splut! Boom!* Hitting the earth with a splat, his face moiled. An edge of great final sadness tearing at his leg. And turning back to see where the other one—the one called William Stone—lay smeared in the soapy gumbo soil, pink rainblood oozing from his craters. "Isu . . . isu . . . isu," he was crying as he was dying, choking on the monosyllables which had no meaning but to him—"isu . . . isu." And then he died.

It was murder. A long time coming.

THE BATTLE HAD passed on. Distant pops of gunfire rustle in the high grass, and he lies there, on the earth, next to a tree, at the musicend of Death, and remembers it all. The fuse of the flower suffusive with suffocation. Move the camera closer please, closer closer, sablesweating cavalry mounts, flopped over and stewing with piping insect gases. Raw meat on the silk of seas. Stripped white bodies of the buffalo hunt. Charred corpses shagged, on hillsides lying. And as maggots and coyotes add madness to symphony, the blackbirds and buzzards, announcing their arrival with leaping shadows rendering the bluffs buffcold, come, they come. Skinned by stout squaws whose children have with jocularity shot the dead again and again. Broken bodies of the dead lie as if on cold unseeing snow. In quiet contemplate. Whinge and creedle. As fingerpainted Indians fight the horse soldiers on sleekswift ponies in scorching cold sun and melt with fascination behind poisoned mintgreen foliage.

In the East, the rainbow. Evening's mouth quick to approach, home from work and into the tub. Stretch my skin. Yawn. Move this athletic breeze to agitation, and cool my hindsight. And tonight, watch the lowlying orange-red moon hover dimly over the pleasemeye plain. Stranger.

Stranger Stranger Stranger

Beating like the thought of a tear at the side of my head. Grip my hands, pour down pots of pity on myself, cry cry your naked soul into the light of rainbow day, asking yourself.

What does it mean to die?
Or do I dare?
In dying to disturb
the universe?

O but I have a stern slicing headache which is ripping at the edge of my head. Standing up now holding my head with pain. Above the left eye, inserting its knifepoint, working down the perimeter of my cheek, into my twitching mouth muscles. It's the agony of an airplane, swiftly egressing from the clouds plunging to earth, my ears roaring with blazoning air pressure. A feeling for Death, wherein without warning things suddenly slip, slip away and as it is slipping—not knowing the "it"—I see in one frightening flash the military face. Bored and inexpressive eyes down through the centuries, hard unrelenting Spartan faces, crewcut hair and bodies that cannot possibly grow slack or fat. Nothing is left, not even so small a sum as the things of this life. It's tough! How sad this knowledge, this devil's egress, this lessening and lessening. A piano finger dallies in the depths of a Chopin piece, and with tensing fury comes a sound, how sad a sound, so sad! Clashing like science against the icicle of the stars. It's a hard life my father always said.

"*Yaaaaaeeeeeeee!*" ululates the oriental Indian and unwinds his shaft at ten twenty feet in the smokeclearing air, whistling winding into my gut, transfixing me, jerking me aliveyet and in searing pain backward back into the ground, not understanding, then understanding. What happens now, where is he, in what out there swooping in for my headshair dangling from his hunter's girth, treading orifices of ancient woods before the white man, with affection, arrived, yes what sights shall you see child, tell us of death's incense and its allure, o lie to us!

The Indian approaching, naked in his loincloth, sixfootsome, broadly shouldered, breast of my breast. Slowthinking asia-faced primitive, not understanding, not so much aware of mercy as sharp flashing points of victory drumming the dry air of his percussive drip drop life. O he will throw me violently to the ground and will clutch me tight as he clambers onto my supine form, sweating of whiteman's blood, with his big hand, his naked thighs astride asquat shouting bloodcurdling obscenities and hair-raising howls, will plunge his used blade into my dying ghost. Without pity he will cut me open, my balls and all, and smear himself in my warm blood, he'll rejoice and wash his muscles in me and mock me and eat me bit by bit. O handsome savage come! Together then. In communion be. All changed, changed utterly.

The boy William, his head no longer bowed in humiliation of death, but alive so alive, so filled with sex blood streaming freely over his frame in his dusty shirt in need of release and about to be freed, he picks that drooping head up right through the dollhouses of ardent death, right through earth and heaven and through the filmy mists of memory and questions and secrets and the prospect of tumbling down to death, through the protests of a mind which has already begun to separate from the body and has stopped in one last irksome chore. Stone William, who for all he has ever thought or has ever known and yet has never died, now ghosts the words—

"Kill . . . kill me."

And in the silence that follows, as hush as death, the bold winds speechless, the oriental Indian stood rigid in statuesque surprise, not speaking a word of the whiteman's language, yet feeling the force of his wrungout mind. *"Keemeee!"* he heard. *Keke Keke.* Until a roused primeval vengeance, angered, sets awork anew. And his face resorting to its chiaroscuro of hate, taking in one swift murderous stride the few separating steps to the dying youth, crying *"Yaaaaaeeeeee!"* home home drove the heavy tomahawk into William's haunted skull. *Crack!* It entered and sundered, shredding splitting, dissolving; the mind scurrying out of its short scut in time, in intime time. Oh yes! The naked savage straddling the dead form, the bending back of the elbow to reach the bloodied blade, the egress, and the hunter's scalping knife coming up swiftly, casting a shadow over the ashen face. Digging into me, dead flesh. Mocking the meat it eats, O green-eyed monster!

ON THE RISE above the river by the valley after the rain a sunset rainbow, and the sound of exhausted gunfire. Songs of the dead and the dying. It had better not be written, what happened. These things never are. Because no one who can. Really remembers. Sadly savage.

And if you tell me it is dawn and, brushing my forehead, tell me I must awake, I will believe you baby. The yawning yellowness. Staring into my skull. A generous dizziness and at the end of the movie, the faces of all the people I knew—Crazybush and Crummy and Cashdollar, Maloney and Rains, Crysanthefoi and Ridgeway, their blue and yellow scarfs aloft in the hot combat wind, it's all been a soldier's seasound, and in the end . . . in the end.

Oliver moves among the bodies. The earth is looking for friends and souvenirs. A tired slope of men wander aimlessly in the shouting distance. There must be hundreds of them. Little yellow men in green uniforms swimming without motion. Never be the same again, Oliver. Not quite. Ever.

He looks down at the spot where he remembers vaguely, in a concussion of sounds, that he almost died. Almost. But something *did* die here. An animal? Another?

Confused, he knows not what, Oliver stumbles on. Don't shiver, don't shake, above all don't squeal. Don't wonder no more, son. Your job is done. In the field with the buttercups and the daisies, though I never knew which flower was which, full of vague murmurings in my ear of things that creep and crawl along the earth. If only life had been more fun. Beauty was the darkhorse. It came in spots of small cups. Like the Holy Grail. Every thousand years.

But you won't forget then what I told you Mother? There was never any woman but you. You were there. When Death was as thin as air. My lips in your warm hair. And how we hid in the grass when the regiment of North Vietnamese overran us deep in the Ashau, and a mosquito got lost in my ear. I really grew up. And I'll never write about it. I don't want to.

We were on our way back when they hit us. Jungle eyes. It was like the sound of a pinetree cracking and crashing in a distant winter wood. The panic of a jungle when fire seals off the paths of escape and all the animals, cobra as mad as tiger, shriek in the unison of terror. My M16 jammed again and, surprised that I was still alive, I beat him to death, the little North Vietnamese man, with my plastic toy barrel, can you imagine that? This civilized boy who went to Sunday school on Madison Avenue at Seventieth Street where the pink-faced reverend always wore rustling clerical robes at the pulpit. Looking out with silver hair and hawkeyes at his well-dressed congregation. Foxhole eyes of sin and guilt peering back at him through layers of Christ and porous stained window light. I did so very much want to speak. I could at least have told them of the insides of my soul. Its compartments of wood and iron and steel and terra cotta.

But then I crawled away and hid in the bushes and I went to sleep for awhile, maybe a minute, maybe twenty, and when I came back, there were thousand-pound bombs and gunships and jets overhead and everybody was blowing everybody up and they were overrunning us and we were overrunning them and it made no sense to me but I was alive, feeling my penis and my sac of hope, still there! I look pretty ferocious now.

Why am I still here? Ask not the silly question, you're in the Army now. Soldiers must expect to die. There is no reason really for them to live. We swear too much and we drink too much and we kill without wondering why, it is no wonder no one wonders why. When we die. Our graves laid out like a cloth of gold and the grass gratefully green and Hecate's womb blooming white with jeesus crosses. And I see a boy of small poetry, pretty with long lashes and smooth skin playing at the piano with his mother in the late afternoon shadows of the fifties, in a large livingroom overlooking Manhattan gardens that God and Saint James built in a way made for me. O soft mystery of naked gloom! *L'or dans les montagnes, c'est comme une femme que je n'ai jamais connu.* It's like a woman I never knew, through the smoke and in a dark manner, the absence of essence. I shoulda been a mercenary in the Congo and got cilled (fuck shit piss cunt!!!) but I was different after all and my memory too deep.

Because poetry is where the poet is, and in him, his peripatetic passions, the children of the prophets live and move and have their being. He is like a beautiful red and green serpent and he dwells deaf upon a log in a tunnel of hollow coiled darkness, striking savagely at the echo . . .

. . . echo.

Now comes the hour. His boot draws near. O Mother. There was never any woman but you. You were there. When Death was as thin as air. O Mom, stick around. I'm no suicide. Don't leave me, as when you said I would never die. Stay. O we were rough tough this day, the twenty-five sticks of June: Bravo Company. We roamed in fruitless flocks and thought ourselves as tough as the west wind, the zephyr, until it went and banged itself out to sea forever. Because they say, in dreams, the lightning it quickly comes, from the East, as when cats drag their childcats into the falling ball of flame deep in the distress, rocking the Ark and thus disturbing the winking tilt of the unified verse—the Poet he comes now, in a mantle of fire that crucifies tepidity and wakes the dead from the sunken slumber of life! O come.

come . . .

How we stood in the air and fought, the sergeant he said so. To the last man! You sons you boys you children, God-protected and Mother-loved till now, and then surprisingly forgot. Our souls have flown, and now it is written the eagles with the claws from the Mexican mountains come. But I'd just like to say. Before it's too late. That it's been an honor. Next to none.

To have served in this man's Infantry.

Oliver, on a western ridge of the Ashau Valley, scalping the dead Oriental, throbbing in his arms, his face torn apart with pistol shots, bleeding into the earth.

First the scalp, slowly sheared, dear, with my hatred, a ripping tearing sickening sound. O and then the ear. Just one ear. To send home to Mom. For Christmas. So that she might know. How serious I am. Because it matters. It matters very much.

Yes. He now opens the hour of the flower, he opens the o of his obliging soul.

O Oliver!

INTERLUDE

10. FUTURE FANTASY #1

AS I LAY DYING in a Saigon hospital with a severe amount of shrapnel sheltered in my leg and thighbone, a beautiful young woman came, with much fanfare, to visit the wards. She was waving to the flocks of sick and dying, flourishing kisses from the corners of a corolla mouth, and swinging tanned blond limbs with wild, reckless grace for the flocking photographers.

She was motherwordly and broke right open the hollow song with which we sang ourselves to sleep each night. In the heart, or where the heart is supposed to be, it can become so monotonous, and like a swollen blackened eye, the space carries with it a feasible ache.

"Who's the broad?" I asked the creep in the adjacent bed in my tough guy language.

"Where ya bin? It's that big moviestar, asshole—Julie fuck what'shername . . . Julie Christmas!" he replied.

It so happened at the time I was trying as hard as I could to wrangle a trip back to my homeland in order to recover not only from my wounds but also to get the fuck outta there. I was therefore feigning insanity—a psychopath whose legwound had traveled to his head. In the ward they were suspicious of me. I was different, from New York, perhaps a "pansy" and looked on as sympathetic to the "gooks." The nurse had already discovered an ounce of local weed in my toilet kit and the redneck element made it a point to say that if "that harp-head was in *my* squad I'd fuckin' zonk his ass!" I had few friends except for "Goober" who never spoke, maybe because he'd lost both his legs. He was always reading, either the Bible, which he said he liked in small doses, or the novels of Samuel Beckett. Which are about people who live without limbs in jars. He would read Beckett for hours at a time, page after page, quite otiosely, and on occasion would suddenly roar with laughter, then lapse abruptly back into his silence, causing the soldiers in the ward to look over and rub their heads in wonder.

The only one who wasn't fooled however was Doctor Spight, who warned me of my imminent recovery, whereupon they would send me right back to "the bush," and there for sure, I knew I would finally buy the farm.

The closer the moviestar came to my area of the ward, the more obvious it was that she was, indeed, a fire unto itself. She wore a blue summer dress over bronzed skin and carried a long loping sack strapped to a wide shoulder that vanished into a sea of blond blond hair with black roots. Catty she was, with limbs that hung loose, and white pearly teeth in curving global smile on a perfect face that was radiant in any language, she carried with her the inescapable stirring of mostmen's hopes and erections. There is indeed such a thing as Great Beauty in this life, there are perhaps a hundred thousand of them, while the rest of us are left to wonder what it means to possess that fire. So inequitable and impromptu life is. Moviestars mix with soldiery, united in the whorish name of publicity, each knowing they will never see each other again. I tried to look at it like a mercenary, and that there is nothing really wrong in mixing glamour with war. Perhaps a soldier should earn what he wins. But it was too much! No, I didn't want to meet her anymore, so I pulled the sheets over my head and concealed my emaciated limbs.

I could hear her thonged sandals slipping softly past Goober's bed. Suddenly, they stopped.

"Who's this?" Her crystalline English accent wafting in the air just above my bed.

"Oh," Doctor Spight mumbled, "this is Stone. . . . one of our more troubled cases, I think we should . . ."

"Poor boy," Julie murmured as she gently prompted the sheet from my face, just as my mother would do when I was a child. "Hello," her gentle face seemed to say.

O yes, Miss Pity, pour your pity on me! I gazed up at her. Too much light! She drank me in, by the quart, taken by my grace of face, she understood all with those ice blue eyes. Here at last was *an angel,* a real angel! Standing in front of me. She had come!

"Stone's a war hero, mam, he's up for the Silver Star," Goober suddenly volunteered from the next bed, the doctor glancing with undisguised irritation at him, as I continued to look at her without expression, deciding that my trip back to America was far more important than any fleeting glory wedded to a moviestar.

"Well, that's nice. And how are you doing, Mister Stone?" she murmured, placing her womanly finger on my fevered face.

Boing! A flashbulb popped and blinded me.

I couldn't answer. Her flesh made me tingle, my penis suddenly poking itself up and pitching an embarrassing penthouse in my sheets. It'd been so so long!

Seeing it all too well, Doctor Spight made a jerking motion

to move her on. "Er, Miss Christmas, sometimes . . . it's safer not to touch, you know. . . ." With his eyes telling her: he's *nuts!*

She hesitated. The patient, a tiny head in a sea of white, was looking at her with red-hot mongoose eyes. Time had improperly suspended itself.

"Miss Christmas," someone reminded her of her name.

Her eyes lingered one moment more upon me. But the gulf could not be crossed this day. And on she moved, shaking her head in detached sympathy. A little lump in my throat at having to watch her go. But my picture would be in the paper. It might help my cause.

Doctor Spight lashed his hand to her back and was hustling her out the door when the vociferation occurred. All figures froze in midstride. The doctor, glinting with illhumor, thought he might've heard a pinetree cracking and crashing in a distant winterwood, though there were no pinetrees about the hospital. Then again, perhaps it had been a table, rudely raked along the uncarpeted floor? But when at last he noticed the oceanic solitude of the ward, he realized what they all realized looking at me.

I was truly sorry but it was too late.

Flashbulbs were popping, matches were being lit, and the local scribe, encasing the wings of his nose between his thumb and finger, would soon mythologize the event on toilet walls.

Only Miss Christmas, unencroached by the deafening intrusion, stood firm. Because she understood that men are not infallible, that men, when they crack, fartfill the atmosphere and rend the universe with tears. And returning toward me, bending down in the stunned silence, she tickled her breath into my ear. "What are you really saying, Mister Stone? What's wrong?

Tell me," she asked with such compassion, known for her liberal causes on behalf of canines and foxes.

And I looked up embarrassed into those sparkling moviestar eyes, the kindest eyes I had ever seen, and began uncontrollably to weep! to sob! Utterly humiliating!

"Oh, don't be ashamed!" she moaned aloud, "you're human, we're all human. I cry. I cry more than you will ever know." She fell silent. My sobbing decreased, ashamed to look her in the eye. "There . . . do you feel better now?"

"Yes," I lied.

"What's your name?"

"Oliver," I mumbled.

"Oh Oliver. What a lovely name!" Her impeccable accent rang in my ears like crystal, so interested a sound. "And where do you come from, Olly?" Said the British way.

"New York," I answered, not believing she could be remotely interested.

"What was it you did in New York, Olly?"

"Oh I went to college," I said, ". . . nothing much," as I ran out of things to say, still worried lest the evil doctor recognize any symptom of normalcy.

"Well," she smiled, "I have a feeling you'll soon be back home and your mother will be very happy indeed!"

What does that mean? Oh, it doesn't matter when you have a perfect face only inches from mine. My inferiority arising, along with my penis, the old truth teller telling its truth again.

She wet her lips with a brief flick of a lizard that looked like a tongue, and on my hot blushing cheek planted a warm O.

"I must go now," she apologized.

Suddenly I blurted it out, "O Julie! I . . . love . . . you."

Nobody spoke. It was a strange thing to say, without context, out of time. I was utterly embarrassed and would never understand why I said it. Or what it really meant. I love you! I do. I did.

If at first a little stunned, my moviestar managed a warm elder sister's smile, though not much older than me, really, then gently withdrew her hand, warmth pouring from her like sunshine. "And I love you too, Olly Olly. *Ciao!*"

I positively glowed with a madman's smile. Oh, I felt loved, like the seals and the porpoises. Because in this lonely heart I'll take what I can get. Her slender frame moving away in the sunbeams, long crystal hair floating in the tepid hospital air.

Turning from the doorway and waving to us all. Avoiding my eye. I *had* embarrassed her. She goes off now with the stars in her eyes. And in the mud I stay. Never to taste the divine nectar. Soldier boy.

Within two weeks, Doctor Spight prevailed, and PFC William O. Stone was sent back to the jungle.

IT WAS YEARS later when we met again. It was 1999 in an era erraticyet, beset with the chaos of overpopulation. After the Vietnam War, I had written, as Oliver Stone, a first novel of widespread appeal, and with the gains therefrom I had retreated back to the East, where I lost touch completely with my mother and my native land, and as William Stone had carved something of a legend in Asian skies. Smoking ruth of a man. Rubber plantations north of Saigon. A helicopter and an airplane. Private game sanctuary. Of course many rumors abounded about me, mostly sinister, heads beating about for facts. Questioning *quidnuncs.*

Then came a time, before the turn of the millennium, taking philosophic pause before the end, I contacted my aging mother and asked her to visit.

"Mother!" I now call out in delighted reserve.

"Oliverre!" She beams back, busy supervising the jeepload of friends who have accompanied her.

"Hi, everyone!" I greet them astride my jeep at my private jungle airport. Sporting my knee boots and pearl-pommeled revolver at my side. "Hello Otavio! Ronnie! Jean-Claude! Joe! Kiki! Comtesse! Philippe!" Kisses.

"*O la la! C'est magnifique, Oliverre! Oh c'est beau ici. Mais je crois que j'ai pris trop de robes, non? Il fait si chaud!*" Looking about for her flock to agree, which they do. "Of course you know Julie! Julie Christmas, my son, *mon fils*." Mother anxious to introduce her, knows everyone, of course, and repeats everything twice. Not one thing changed in Mother. Except the face now becomes a mask, more and more.

Julie Christmas smiles warmly coldly, in that British way. "Hello."

"How have you been?" I smile, watching. Wondering if she remembers. She doesn't seem to.

Turning to kiss Mother, Jacqueline Pauline Czezarine Goddet. Old face of a growling meateater. Wolfess. Smart and cunning. Which attracts and repulses me. She notices my limp.

"But I never knew about zis leg, *chéri,* my *chéri?*"

"The war it was. I never did get to write you much Mother . . . I'm sorry."

"Oh but Oliv . . . Can I still call you Oliverre, *chéri?*"

Of course you can! What else but Oliver?

"*Eh bien!* Oliverre, all zis, you're rich! You never tell me, you never make it clear!"

No Mom, nothing was ever clear. I even promised myself

by the time I was fifty, I would have read every important book in the English language. But that never happened either. Every man being rich in proportion to the number of things he can afford to leave alone. Didn't Thoreau say that? Young man of the intellexion, now round about the waist and a little fat in my satupon ass. Things do take a natural turn. O come what will! The peace that passeth understanding. Or in your terms, Mom, pink almonds in the spring!

As I lead my gay caravan of jeeps and giant white guests through miles and miles of voluptuous vegetation and winding red roads rutted with the deep earth. Elephants in shallow pools of water, trunks shoaling the liquid. Orangutans gibbering and jabbing each other in the trees. All mine. My hand spanning the horizon. In *propria persona*. My land. Acres of beauty, thousand-shipped, aching, subtropic, tropic. And these my people. The Vietnamese. A hairless savage race. That by slow prudence, I render mild.

Julie in the jeep behind. Sad to say but Julie is no longer quite Julie. Nor I William. Time has come between. Healing these wounds. Creating others.

Mother in our reconciliation, sucking in happy breaths. Her son! He had left home a poor soldier years and years ago. And now zis strange dark Vietnamese female watching everything, no need to speak but from slitted eyes, who iz she? My son's *chauffeur*? His *assistante*? What was zis one's name? Tan Nuit?

No, Mom, Thanh Nuy.

Mom nods, her white lying smile. Could she be, *quelle dommage!* my son's wife? *O la Mon Dieu! Hélas!* Why? I never understood that crazy boy.

Orient orange sun setting in the west. Down to the Strait of Singapore. Flaming flamingo clouds. An abeyance of time. A pox on time! Between me and it lie the Himalaya. Hence, we must climb the Himalaya.

Stopping the vehicle on a foliated ridge peering down into an uncut valley. Here we are, folks, don't say anything just yet. Close your eyes. Simply smell. The lavender and the jasmine. The pall of air made dim perfume by purple violets. Inhale. Don't cough. Now open thine eyes and ears slowly, so slowly. Unseal them. O no, don't faint. Take it in. Glorious sin. And over there rain forests to walk in. Canary yellow days. Ivy so thick like Yale years ago and vegetation so voluptuous it cloys the senses. The cathedral light on the forest floors where foot-falls snap all the beasts and flowers awake. Sultry air and viscous unhurried heat. The rank smell of the swamp. The noxious sludge on the bottom of our souls. A chain of abandonment and surrender. Like life.

Yes, take refuge in this life while you still can. My hand sweeping to the ridges rippling to the east, maturated in moss. Terraces of purple opium poppies, poppling out in playful pop-ulations. And farther east, Chinese wisteria wippling in the wind. I like flowers, the sacrament of perfume. My hand ex-piring on its expanse. The senses cloyed. All these figures, one limping, climbing back into the vehicle. One last peek. Torpor straddling the rising moon. The jeeps revving and hithering homeward through jungle mouth, through jungle eye.

My mansion is earthred stuccos and cool marbles and painted walls of green, etched with ebonies and mother of pearl. The plants gleam of suetdrops. Spruce trees and thickets inter-twine a graveled driveway opening onto a circumambulating colonnade, encompassing stratums of fat English turf, rhodo-dendrons, syringas, and a green stream like light notes of music under a quaint cobbled bridge. And in the gardens à l'arrière, with their eristic bumblebees stone-deaf humming and tumbling through the late afternoon air, behold a den of Jerusalem artichokes, tulips and dahlias, equidistant and agape, as they vie with damask roses to catch the master's eye. Ho hum. Nondescript it's so rich. Poverty breeds similarity and richness breeds disease.

Monsieur Stone, weary with emotion, making in monosyllables with the servants, "Nuy, take Mrs. Stone's bags to the red room, Miss Christmas the blue, the others. . . . Mai, fix up some fizzlers for us would you please—*thich tai hai, dun le lo, otue phuong!*" Clapping my hands to the gibberish, it doesn't matter quite what is said as long as it is said with authority, the servants scattering. He'll show you to your room, Mom. I'm glad you're here, so glad. At last. Hunk of a woman, now old with gentle bloat, disappearing behind the louvered doors, already telling the servants what to do. All French, Mom, naturally taking to the colonial command.

An elliptic moon now showing its bedtime face. Bausondfaced deer grazing on the deepgreen lawn. Mongooses running through the grass, cracking the night open with their shrill warcries. The empty sounds of silverware banging on plates on the leeward side of the porch, with the parrots and the aspidistras. Wines from France and pepper from Mongolia. Birds communicating love songs in the distance. And way way up there, a cold interstellar wind.

I sit at the head of the long table like Hemingway, entertaining Mother and her fickle friends. Julie to my left, Thanh Nuy to my right.

"So Julie, you really remembered me then?"

"Oh yes, from the first moment, Olly. I never thought your mother could be my old friend Jacqueline, but . . ."

Once weak and wounded, now wealthy and wise, I smile, not for one moment believing her.

So I see.

Serpentsmiling

Sit down. Eat.

Her blonding hair coiled loosely on her head. Which, in my dreams of Siberian convict farms, is skullshaved. Portions of her calves revealing themselves in her freshly scented gown. Still a wench. Crystalline voice. And a rosebush tinted with tea. A silence now sits with us at the table. Yet no one speaks.

Mother of course fills it up, "It's so *borring* in Paris now. Always the movies and the fashionshoes, everybody with zere gheela monsters and whippets, zer Highness, zer Lowness, zer balonus tromponus!" The courtiers laughing at her overstatement.

While Julie tells me in clipped English understatement that she had a "marvelous day!" Really did. "You have such a groovy place here, a cove actually—and what elegant beasts, your horses."

"Oh, thank you."

"I read your book, you know," she says. "And I did like it. It was smart because it had nothing to do with reality. I don't think you know anything about colors or the interiors of homes or the way women talk or think, but your insensitivities aside, your work does have balls, you know."

"That's kind of you." Opinions have soured the gentle curve of her mouth.

Does she notice when I notice?

I fill the pause. "You'll like my new one. My new book. It's called *The War,* and it has nothing whatever to do with tactics or strategy or weapons. It's about . . . well, best left unsaid till done, no?"

"My little nephew calls you a romanticizer of death."

Ha ha.

"He's quite serious, Olly. He says you're half in love with death, aren't you? . . . I am too. The other half perhaps?" A little coiled quip of self-deprecating laughter from her.

Thanh Nuy's eyes move past Julie across the table, nibbling on a kiwi. The Englisher doing her best to ignore her. Does she understand English? I wonder, she wonders.

"If Death is a woman, let it come in high heels," I laugh back. Our eyes linger. Her eyes telling me I'm sorry if I'm too critical or forward. But I'm like that, no punches pulled. Her common sense like their sensible shoes.

Don't be sorry, I say. Life has many levels. Such as ours.

"The next book you write," she goes on, "you must put me in it. When they loose the final bomb, chemical, whatever it is, most of my films will evaporate. But books, they bury those deep in the earth for future nomads."

"Did you really remember me from Saigon?" I ask again, vainly, still not sure where the lie leaves off anymore.

She is surprised by the question, but manages to say gracefully, "I think so . . . that trip was so *sad* for me. You boys all looked so . . . My God, I thought you'd probably be killed. You stuck out. I could tell how much you wanted to go home. Oh, it was so . . . so *sad*. I remember, I just couldn't stop crying back in the hotel."

Yes, and it could've been about anybody. Perhaps if she'd remembered that I farted? But because she was so beautiful once, I am ready to forgive anything, anything! Lost in the memory of her face and eyes, no longer there, and flattered by her attention under the influence of the soft Mediterranean wine, I hear myself now blurting out my past. "Well actually after you left Julie, they did send me back to the jungle. I was more miserable than I'd ever been in my life . . . God! in those black months it was only *you*—the secret thought of you that kept me going because I promised myself that some day I'd be rich and find you again. . . . And I'd *be* with you. I'd be good enough for you. God! How young and silly! But it kept me going for months, for years! Because I really did fall in love with you in that hospital. I told you so, remember!'' I laugh.

''I remember,'' she was blushing too, a little practiced for my taste.

''But then we got caught in a horrible ambush. It was my conception of Hell. I was separated from my squad, I'm not sure it was an accident, and I spent three days crouching in the swamps. Leeches as black as night burrowed into my—excuse me—asshole and my ears.'' She reacted with horror. ''Then I heard the ghosts of the French soldiers, fifteen years dead, whistling from the marshes. My cousin Claude. The sweat of pure fear washed me in my stink. And I thought this is it, this is really the end, Oliver. I shall never see her again. . . . But each time I was on the verge of dying, your yellow hair would encircle me, your limbs entwined with mine, your mouth kissing me deeply, telling me like an angel that you'd be there at the end. And then you were making ferocious love to me, wanting me, devouring me, rebirthing me. It was so real. It was so real.''

Her eyes were panting, reviving the abandoned dream of finding her lover.

The table too had stopped to listen. As Thanh, with impassive gestures, continued to suck on luscious fruit. A great appetite this Vietnamese.

''Well,'' I went on, ''somehow I got through it. On fantasy alone. When they found me, I was barely alive. They sent me back to the States a hero, a second Purple Heart, and I shook the hand of the President and a hundred different Senators, and they asked me to run for public office. But instead, I wrote that book, in a fever I guess. It only took six weeks. The rest . . . you know.''

A silence. Eyes moving about. Mother hoping.

And now? Julie asks without asking.

O Julie, how do I know! There have been so many. So many years of rein. Years of loneliness. What mind's meanness, what cachinnations of conspiracy have been launched in verses against me, years of crinkling averted icelation, and now these country manners asking me to transcend all this, much indeed, o halt, be kind, be sweet. Come!

Looking deep into her, my old double William rising, kissing her, my hands thrusting through her hair, into the steaming hot warmth of her flesh, under the croissant's crust, bringing her into me.

You've never had a woman like me before?

No.

Inside you're trembling, you're trembling from head to toe?

Yes.

But you're not really at ease in my presence?

No.

Your hands are ice?

Yes.

And your heart?

No.

Can I warm you?

No . . . not really . . . Nor I you.

In my silence, Julie Christmas reads her rejection like the oracle of Apollo. All air and sounds of tinkling paper bells and wind and you will never know. What is in another person's mind. Or that something ugly has come to live in you in these intervening years. Cells of cynicism as eroding as cancer. Not your fault. It's Life we blame. Illusions that crack and crumble with the attack of Time. Yet we are responsible for our faces, are we not?

Her eyes withdraw, frightened, terrified of the abyss that has just opened before her. A woman they say is only beautiful when she is loved. The saddest look. I wish. I wish I could reach across this gob of air and. Warm you. But pity destroys love.

She was gone from me. Forever in a woman's way. Hurt feelings are so predictable. Perhaps that is always the problem. The predictability of feelings. Surprise me always. Never take anything for granted.

The dark Vietnamese eyes to my right follow the silence without comment. Perhaps she understands, more or less. It doesn't matter. We trust. That is all. Her beauty blooms precisely in not seeking to define. With words. Only feelings. Which, by sweet Asian custom, are kept in reserve. Unstated. Thus life becomes more delicate. More appreciated. Words so often kill, do they not? All that chitter chatter, like Mom, where does it get you? At the end of time?

Dinner is over. The mucilaginous pods of the okra and helmeted guinea fowl dozing in our duodenums. Alongside tamarinds to tincture the temples. A massive mickle meal. And whirling oriental fans overhead that strum thoughts on the sleeping sucklings in our souls. No, none of the noisome odors from some rearward middens, as I revive in my philosophic breast idle thoughts of Xanadu and its caverns measureless to man. So happy. We must savor it for now. Bottle it. Good night Otavio, Comtesse, you all . . . Julie. As she goes, smiling and kissing and saying goodnight too too much, too hurt.

And now good night to you, Thanh Nuy. Her silent eyes like the black leopard Komo. Very dangerous in the midnight arts. My wife taking leave, her footfalls like snowflakes.

In the living room below, mother and son alone together at last. Each stoned, together blind. Well, Venus, what brings Psyche?

"But she never speaks, your Vietnamese?" comments Mother, always critical in her French disguise, wishing Julie to my bed this night. "How does she say her name? Tanka Ne-gee?"

"No, Thanh Nuy, Mom. Like *tant pis.*"

"Do you love her?"

"O how do I know these things Mother? I love her. As much as I've ever loved any woman."

But it seems the same at the end. Like a mirror, reflecting. Narcissist, perhaps. If so, then you taught me how, Mother. *But . . .*

"*C'est la vie, comme on dit.*" O the piping pomes of peace! Oliver laughing this late jungle night. Mother smiling coyly, happy for her son. You old witch, you always knew my thoughts, he thought. Couldn't keep anything from you. Remember when Father and I used to make bets that you wouldn't find the baseballs we lost in the thicket. He always said you'd find anything, you were a witch! And you'd go right in there and even if it took you an hour you'd come out with the bloody baseball. Mother smiling her potato eater face. The cockles of chalcedony. Remember when you won Pee Wee the parakeet at Coney Island in the raffle? Thaumaturge. That last night at "21." Winter glooming. We were both so depressed. You said I'd die in Vietnam. Pythoness.

Mother laughing nostalgia's little laugh. "Oh yes I remember so well. You were so crazy as a boy! You never listened!" As if you did?

Figurines talking on late into the tropic night. Wails of cicadas. The servants sleeping. Mosquitoes thrashing their bodies up against the illuminated windows. As out on the high seas, the ghosts of Drake and Hawkins heave to in the moist South-asian wind. Whatever happened to little Uncle Leo? And did Karlo ever come back from Yugoslavia? Is Colette still married? Olden times in the West before the lights went out. Poor Father. Never did recover did he? Drank and smoked so much, and more and more, the closer he came to death. But he was giving up the sex, you know.

Mother looking away. "You hurt him so much. You never wrote him, why? He always want you to come back, he always say I gave zat boy everyzing he want and all he give me back iz a kick in the face: oh he was so angry with me but he always love you, Oliver, he love you more zan anyone else he haz in ze world."

Oliver asking, "Then why couldn't he show it?"

"Because," Mother sighs deeply, "because zat's ze way Lou always was. He was a man who never could show his feelings. Oh he broke my heart!" And the tears tarted from the corners of her eyes.

"I guess you always knew that he . . . he didn't love you the way he should've Mom? I don't know really if he ever loved you at all?"

"Oh yez, he did!" she cries back. "He always love me Lou, he love me very much!"

Yes, Mom. She cries quietly, long tears like boats sailing from the ports of her eyes.

Father dying peacefully in his New York bed. Attended by drinking friends and boring relatives. Telling his brother Leo, "Leo, you'll live to be a hundred and twenty but you won't have any fun like I did."

Thinking back on those jocose days when he made it a

promise that when he went. He would take me with him. Little William Oliver, my boy. He never did. Dying without your son must be miserable. Cremated into ashes and dust. Never forgave the Nazis or Roosevelt, we all hold on to these old grudges. Each generation grows into its grudge. Obit column and picture in the *Times*. Economic intellectual. One of the best. He came in 1910 on the year of Halley's comet and, like Mark Twain whose humor he genuinely adored, went out with it seventy-five years later. Tears suddenly tumbling from my eyes. I never could get it straight with my father. And now it is too late. Ancient Stone curses passed down generation to generation.

Yes, Mother, have we or have we not seen the chimes at midnight together?

Sitting in the Sixties in your New York apartment, in the early morning hours, after the gay parties, both of us baked out of our brains, talking about how rich we'd both be some day. Gilded thoughts of the mounds of money you were going to marry. And never did. And for me, hamster farms and squash courts. I promised you I'd support you in gala gaiety one day. But Father never believed me; he never believed in all sincerity I would ever earn an honest nickel. Almost right too. Weird prophecies father curses son with; and then they go and come true. Can't tell you how close I came. To giving up. But, as it turned out, it was he and not I who lost everything. What a blow. It killed him finally. A conservative man, every risk he took backfired, and when he died, after all the argument and anger over money through all the years, only twenty thousand from several million was left, all pissed away, he said, by Mother, to whom he left a modest insurance policy. In many many ways, a selfish life. God is cruel, but life is crueler. O Fortune! *La richesse!* Plutocracy.

Now I am rich, forever rich, *delenda est Carthago*! Done! *Hinc illae lacrimae*. Oliver laughing. Mother laughing. In 1999. And now pausing. Looking at one another in this time of summing up. *Multum in parvo*. Mutual deracination of hearts. Grafted in grief. Growing back in granite. Oliver saying: "Mom, I love you."

Mother hugging me to her, "Oh Oliver, Oliver, I've always always loved you so much! You are ze only one I have!"

Yes I know. But why couldn't you show it more? Walking down the Boulevard de Courcelles in Paris, past le Parc Monceau. *Clickety clack* on your black alligator high heels, swinging your shiny black alligator bag. Perfumed by Chanel, you go to Van Cleef's in the Place Vendôme. And then perhaps to Dior at four. And then you must of course leave me behind for the summer with your parents in the countryside, distracted woman heading off to Saint-Tropez to have Fun! Fun! Fun! And I will wait, forever, like a faithful dog for the month week day and hour that you return, laughing with your friends, always laughing Mother, great sadness there. . . .

Through the lighted windows on the great green lawn, winding down to the tall eucalyptus trees by the river. It is cool out. Yes. Mother and Son. *Qui mal y pense*. In 1999. At long last.

PART THREE

HOME

11. THE BOILERS
OF THE MOON

HAVE YOU EVER seen the Mekong up in Laos at break of day in the rainy season? When the waters return to flood the valley, as if it were the Bible and time had never flown?

I have . . .

I have followed the river down to the sea, and the sea has stayed with me as fierce a prophet as any of the old Canaanites.

My story is of a man named Crummy, one Samuel Crummy whom I knew but a little time in my life, though he too has stayed long with me.

I met him in a bar near the Mekong River in Saigon. I had been working as a novice wiper on a ship that was waiting without purpose in the harbor that ran like an artery through the city. Often in those days the port was so overcrowded that ships bringing war materials from America would be backed up waiting to load or unload for up to six months, stacked all the way down the Mekong to the port of Vung Tau on the South China Sea. The pay, however, included war-zone bonuses, so the sailors were making small fortunes for doing nothing much except the minimum maintenance. But they grumbled all the more, the day being long and hot and the boredom high.

On such a night my fo'c'sle partner, Jimmy—Jimmy Eliot

I think his name was, from Mobile, Alabama—was badly drunk. A filthy strapping young man, not very bright, he was the more experienced wiper, and because the crew made fun of his dim-wit manner, he sometimes, when drunk, felt the need to hurt someone besides himself. This night was such a night.

The whores had boarded us from Saigon, and Jimmy had picked out for himself this candy-faced, petite girl who went by the name "Jenny"—Jen-Sing her real name was, of Chinese origin. Following the usual night of drinking in the bars along the port, I had returned late to the ship when I heard her cries, pursued by the thundering sound of someone crashing into a wall of my fo'c'sle. As I blearily stuck my head in to see, Jenny was screaming something like "you crazy in the head, I no fuck you, never fuck you!"—something which always makes me wonder why a woman, who should know better, will always say the stupidest and most dangerous things when angry. Jimmy slugged her for that. Hard. I could hear the dry pop of either her jaw or neck as she caved downward. I could even discern the sickening distortion of her face as she received the blow.

I have vague recollections of trying to get her out of there, of Jimmy giggling at me with a guilty look followed by images of myself grappling with Jimmy, whose eyes suddenly turned insane. Then something moving out of nowhere and a blinding blow to one side of my head, stunning my thought process even further. Then Jimmy was vomiting on the floor as I was clumsily pushing Jenny out of the fo'c'sle. Bizarrely, she was slapping me and scratching me as if I were Jimmy, and we were all so stupidly, intensely, and egotistically drunk that we had no realization of the blood that was being spilled and the anger that would never be satiated.

Once I'd gotten her to the sampan at the base of the ship's ladder, she cursed at me in a harsh, guttural Chinese, wholly ignorant of her recent proximity to death at the hands of Jimmy Eliot of Mobile, Alabama. There was something inexplicably ugly about Jenny, drawn to and attracted by violence in a strange alluvial relationship of her blood to her anger; sooner or later she would arrive at a violent end, this I felt as she gave me the finger, the engine of the sampan drowning out her curses and disappearing in the smell of oil.

I knew then it was impossible for me to room with Jimmy any longer. He was simply too dumb and dangerous a human being to trust; it wouldn't be long before I'd be in his line of fire, or else cringing the whole voyage just to please him. Returning later, after some anguished thinking, to the fo'c'sle, and grateful to see he had vanished elsewhere, I quickly packed the few small personal possessions I had and departed the ship, hopping a battered French *quatre cheveaux* taxi to the stately Majestic Hotel on the central waterfront. There, in a crumbling once-glorious French colonial room with an overhead fan looking out on a sidestreet of the Mekong, I passed the night in deep drunken slumber.

However, the next morning I told a young crewcut graduate of a Wyoming college, now an assistant consul in Saigon, that another, unnamed crew member had tried to knife me and that the captain of the vessel was cheating me out of my war-zone bonus as I wasn't legally in the Merchant Marine union. The State Department man was surprisingly empathetic and said he'd try to get me another ship, wondering no doubt how a person like me had gotten into a situation like this. He gave me some money from the Embassy's traveler emergency fund, and I moved into a smaller hotel across the river in the poorer "black" section of the Saigon waterfront where, dating back to the French North African troops of the 1950s, the bars and whores were notoriously cheap.

Each afternoon for several days I trekked back crosstown to the Embassy in the brutal heat to inquire of another job. The gonorrhea that I had contracted in either Laos, Cambodia, or Thailand, I knew not where, had mysteriously returned with a vengeance, tickling at the head of my penis with an insectlike fever. It was an imprecise disease at best, but it was painful to urinate and I was deeply worried and bored at the same time. Could it have been the finely spider-haired Mei Lin who'd given me this? Or the fat rubbery *mama-san* in Cambodia? With diminishing funds I bought another penicillin shot at a cheap clinic on Hong Thap Tu Street, and, neutralizing any positive effects from the antibiotic, went out and got irrationally stoned that afternoon on marijuana, whiskey, and beer, and vomited on the floor of a rickshaw of an irascible old cyclodriver who started yelling and pushing me. People were looking, a whistle blew down the street, but before the police arrived, I overpaid the crazy old man and vanished into a Vietnamese movie house where at least it was cool. Later I bought some dirty pictures and masturbated back in the hotel. Then I went out that night and got drunk again. Such was the nature of my days.

The man from Wyoming had an idea. Newly arrived in town was a merchant captain named Bogolm, Simon Bogolm I believe, who was looking for some local American to show him around Saigon. The consul thought it might lead to Bogolm taking me on as a wiper since he was heading straight back to the States, and that suited me just fine, though it seemed strange that the captain of such a vessel would be lacking for companionship in such a large port.

When I saw him I understood why. He was one of nature's

beasts, an extraordinarily ugly man, with cruel mouth and eyes cut short by a flat top, of mottled complexion and far too fat at some two hundred seventy pounds. The man was one of nature's beasts. He sweated, farted, ate and drank excessively, and he could hold no conversation beyond its surface; his only real interest seemed to be in captaining his ship, and that he wouldn't talk about because it was what he did, and thus it merited no discussion with the uninitiated. But, given my upbringing, I felt sorry for him and tried to be especially kind, with the possibility of course of a job. It took some effort.

At first I tried to sophisticate him to the city, but all allusions to culture, politics, and local custom met with bored and beady eyes. It was only when I described the sex life I had with some of the locals that his froglike eyes would jump out of his sockets in caricature of a lecherous slob. The thought of screwing two Vietnamese girls at once particularly appealed to him, and one afternoon I altered my destiny by pimping some ugly but lively girls I knew to this sad hulking heap; my remaining image of the captain after all these years is of this gigantic blubbery mass squeezed into a ridiculously narrow rickshaw, his thighs overlapping the sides, being pushed around by a tired, old stick-legged cyclodriver, who I speculated was destined to reverse roles with Bogolm in the next life. I pointed out the sights as we drove along the hot afternoon streets into a darkened alley rotting with the smell of fish and fresh fruit and garbage.

Several hundred yards down the winding maze, the two chickenpox-scarred girls I had in mind paused briefly as they watched the captain struggle like an octopus from his rickshaw. But the Vietnamese had learned long ago to delicately disguise their distaste, and, abiding by tradition, they welcomed him.

And he paid well, and, unbelievably, there was no problem, in fact a sort of sullen gratitude on his part. And as a result, I was given the job of second wiper on the USS *Red River*. Nothing, I have since found out with much difficulty, comes for free in this life.

That night I met Samuel Crummy. Bogolm had taken me to drink at one of the waterfront dives near his ship where several members of his crew liked to drink, although he deliberately avoided all contact with them and barely talked to me—he had tired of people long ago—but as he grew drunker and more morose, he walked out with barely a goodnight nod in my direction, and vanished from my life. I believe it was the last time I would ever see Bogolm. Like many such ghosts, he would become more fabled by his absence than he would ever be by his presence.

Eyeing a Vietnamese beauty engaged in conversation with two Navy types, I approached another section of the bar. On closer examination, she didn't live up to her promise and I fell into conversation with an ordinary-looking fellow, meek and thin and faded by time, a sort of sad hooded owl look in his eyes. Somewhere in the course of a long, semidrunken meandering conversation that would include several asides to other drinkers and trips to the bathroom, this man revealed himself as the actual first wiper of the USS *Red River* that I was joining. When I introduced myself as his new partner, he smiled with a slight upturn of the corners of his mouth, which was over with quickly lest too much joy spread elsewhere along his features. He lit another cigarette, shoulders slouched. I remember that moment now because it was one of the few times, if any, I saw him smiling, as he generally kept his head and eyes directed downward, watching the ground or the bottle or the glass as he spoke. His voice had no pressure or command but a certain humility, especially in its silences, that I found endearing.

Crummy seemed the sort of man who travels the world and is never seen or remembered by others. In later years of my life, when I would work alongside fabled, powerful people, I would come to recognize the charisma of presence and what it meant. But in Crummy there was no such presence, none at all, and hence for me, oddly, there *was* presence, albeit a strange aura of hopeless sadness. Not that he hadn't tried in his life. In fact one of the schemes he revealed to me that night was his tenuous connection through another sailor, his "buddy Kolby," to a tenuous entity he called "the Company," by which I learned he meant the CIA. He said he'd hooked up with "them" after he got into the Navy during the Korean War and he'd done "some work for them, secret stuff, y'know . . . black ops."

It was the first time I would hear that terminology, but in later years I would think back on Crummy, wondering what truth there'd been in these stories that sounded like untruths, but to which I listened with the nodding courtesy of the young. He spoke of "ops" he had pulled on trips to South America, dirty things, get-rich-quick schemes, arms deals, phony passports, murders even; he'd worked in Cairo in the Fifties for or against Nasser, I couldn't determine; another time he talked of a scheme to import mushroom hats from Vietnam to California and sell them as beachwear for triple their value. Almost everyone on the ship, I was to learn, had his own version of such a scheme, and I should have suspected such when, without hardly knowing me, Crummy was more than willing to cut me in on half the deal if I put up some money; of course, at the time I was flattered because at twenty I didn't have many worldly connections.

But the real point in all this was to create a dream so that the dreamer would never have to go back to sea again. I eventually figured out that the opposite was true—that all these sailors' schemes were doomed to fail because they secretly loved and hated the sea at the same time; that the sea, in its final brutal stage, was the single most elemental woman of their lives. Hence the myriad broken families, tragedies, and tales of woe that would pervade my ears through the next period of my life. It taught me sadness, the sea did. The sadness of the ordinary things like the emptiness we all carry inside.

I grew to love the sea, but it has taken me many years to find that out too.

It was clear by now that Samuel Crummy had an addiction to alcohol, which he drank in enormous silent quantities, methodically, briefly pausing. A professional drinker, I would say, of the wrist and elbow technique, a golfer in another life. But the reputation of drinker, once affixed at sea, is a terrible classification and cannot be shaken; its victim is to be rejected as an undesirable, even by other alcoholics. Of course most merchant seamen that I came to know drank heavily, but the key was in the perception and in that way, Sam Crummy was damned.

He was not in the least puffy or florid, as an alcoholic might be, but extremely withered of face with what seemed a small reserve of good health remaining. He could in fact have been as young as his late thirties back then, though to my eye at twenty, anyone in their thirties easily slipped into their forties and fifties. I ventured him married at one point, perhaps even missing from his Navy unit, escaping some early dawn when the rattlesnakes are still asleep in the backs of barbecue yards in places like Alabama or Texas. Thus he would remain among a class of people who, no matter how honest their intentions, find themselves fugitives on this planet, forever bereft of a home.

Crummy had apparently toiled for a while as an "ordinary seaman" on the decks, a category just below "able-bodied seaman." But later in his rambling conversation I gathered he had fallen through that crack and was assigned beneath deck as a "wiper," a comic word perhaps for a job which I was proud to have, though considered the lowliest category on ship; the deck crew being the outdoor symbol of a romantic seadom; the cooking crew revered very much the same way serpent gods might be viewed in Africa—with fear and need; leaving the grease-ensconced blackened fingernail brigade from the engine room as the "unmentionables" of their profession. It falls to that category to "wipe" the dirt and grease off anything on which it accumulates; it means "blowing the tubes" on the main boiler, scrubbing out toilets, cleaning and putting tools away, and doing anything asked during the 8:00 A.M. to 4:00 P.M. shift. The wiper's duty it seems is to grow dirtier and dirtier till he is so dirty he must be banished from our sight like the biblical leper; from his pockets dangle oily rags which revile him, and on his feet the machinists' clodhoppers are plumped like boulders. Hefty slices of black grime lie encrusted under his fingernails. He stinks of grease and oil and fingers cigarettes that are always stained. The wiper belongs no more to the spirit of the sea than to an auto repair shop on land. It was a job given generally to beginners, foreign labor, the mentally retarded, or any available riffraff without a union card that was wandering overseas—such as myself, the "smartass kid in Saigon."

It is thus strange to meet a man who is a career wiper, because it doesn't take much time or study or money to become an "oiler," the class above wiper, who is accorded the dignity of a craftsman. It is a bit like getting to know a man who shines shoes all his life, or works tables and plates, or a bellboy who's old. As the years have gone by, I have always taken that extra pause around these people, my eyes crossing, knowing painfully of a feeling between us, knowing of the gulf and also knowing, sadly, that I can never cross over to this other human being because long ago I gave it up to become part of a mobile, money-driven society. Though I wish, I wish sometimes I could reverse my biological clock and be young again; when there was so much more time to listen, just listen, to men talk in strange lands about their strange lives.

Crummy thus talked, and I learned once more of the power of fantasy in men's lives. He talked, drunkenly, not always rationally, of another ship during the Second World War in the Atlantic. It was freezing cold in the water and it seemed that this friend of his, a French Canadian ''cat'' with a name like Henri Langlois, had gone and fucking jumped into the ocean one night . . . yes, jumped off some cursed vessel in the middle of the North Atlantic. In winter too.

''Harry, he had problems with the booze. With the broads, too. . . . He was just crazy them last days, gone outta his mind 'cause the captain, see, was fuckin' with 'im,'' he said.

And then he was rattling on, without much sense, of how badly our present captain, Bogolm, was fuckin' with me too . . . ''Goddamn Greek, he'll fuck with you too, kid! His bastard brother-in-law's counting the dough in New York an' stiffing us and the union can't do jackshit 'bout it 'cause these bastards got it all figgered out, see?''

He'd sputter on for awhile, long loopy half-punctuated sentences that I could partially hear under the bar noise, though I did learn that Harry had gone out owing our man Crummy forty dollars which he'd lent him "on the beach" down in Australia. And each time he thought of his old friend Harry, he still thought of him as "forty-dollar Harry, that sonufabitch went and disappeared in the fucking North Atlantic with my forty bucks!" Some epitaph. And he broke out laughing, exposing an ugly set of cigarette-stained teeth.

But then his viciousness abruptly receded like a scared mangy dog who'd shown his fangs in one last show of self-respect before retreating to its natural pusillanimity—or was it real humility? No one on the ship, I found out, really knew much about Samuel Crummy, or cared to. He was one of those men who'd just pass you by a thousand times on a thousand streets in your life and you know you'll never talk to this type of stranger. You avoid such men. In the language of the sea, he was simply, if occasion arose, called "Smiley" or "Crappy" or "Crummy," or better yet, No Name At All. He was a You, one of those people who are always told what to do, a shadow of Yourself saying Yes to You. Go clean the floor. Now go away. Don't bother me. Above all. Don't Talk to Me.

"It's not the thing to do all yer life," he was saying, "young guy like you . . . can make it other ways. Go to the city, you know. You're edeekated, you gotta get edeekated, that's the only way now."

Then he added, "I always wanted to be an engineer . . . or a musician. Play jazz in a club someplace."

It was a strange thing to say and it lay there on my ear, at odd deference to his other cruder remarks. From the light in the side of my eye I sensed him looking at me. I didn't take his eye. I want to help you friend, I do, but if you, then everyone. And that is my fear. Having to share of Myself, dividing

Myself, the fear that would shadow my entire life. Because I can't trust *anyone*. Why should I? I gave him a polite little deathmask laugh in return, and proceeded with my boilermakers; it would later become vodka and then wine. All sailors waddle in self-deprecation. It is a form of romance, of felony, of bursting through the barriers of a constricted life imprisoned in tons of ugly steel and noisy engines grinding through years and years of oceans without women to civilize.

As he talked of his travels down through the Arab ports of Djibouti and places with strange names in Aden and Yemen, the Gulf, Madagascar, and the east coast of Africa, I studied, sparingly, a thick red boil on his nose. Boils are terrible-looking things; they shine and they ache at the same time. At its tip was a tiny puncture, clotted and sealed, through which the pus ultimately vents itself. Boils grow on the face like cancers, literally pushing outward seeking release. They ache slowly. They shine perspicuously. They glow with malignancy. A boil is a very public thing, stuck without nakedly on the face calling attention to itself from all passersby; and if not actually seen, then thought to be seen by the paranoid victim, whose life is suddenly made dark and portentous. His boil is a way of life. He has been selected. He suffers.

But that is me. Not Seaman Crummy. It has taken me many years to realize the difference in the narcissism of our sensitivities. The boil's presence, which conspicuously marred his face, probably did not even *occur* to Crummy. He was one of those dislocated people who could not be bothered by modalities. He lost his toothbrushes, he tore the seat of his pants, he was dirty, he suffered from sinus conditions, his buttons fell off and were lost, his posture was urban poor, slouched in a kicked cat's gait. Life to somebody like myself at that age could never be satisfactory unless I put myself to bed having completed something of significance that day; that was certainly the motivation driving me out of Saigon. Naturally then, many are the nights that I went to my pillow drenched in inadequacy and depression, a forlorn wretch ill-conceived and intended for no passable purpose, the "bum" of my father's mythology.

Crummy, on the other hand, could stumble into his fo'c'sle at five in the morning, befuddled with liquor and painlessly, without a word, a happy drunk in spite of it all, slip into sleep. He could not anaesthetize his life through means of regulation or qualification. He was the sort of man who must face the prospect of wasted time. Hours do not matter to one like him. A day is justified by a drink, by a single spot of joy. Activity is not an essential. And why should he be any different? Taxicabs don't stop for him on city streets. He'd never think of registering in anything other than a seaman's hostel. He is well aware of class distinctions. No one looks at him in a public place as he strolls by. He saunters through this life anonymously. Though not an egotist, he is entirely concerned with himself. He never ventures upon thoughts of beautiful women or the finery that wealth delivers to her flatterers. No, more likely he wakes from his somber nightmares with the nauseation of drink upon him, sweating the curse of this life in the bottom of an insentient and unforgiven soul, and invariably when it comes time to tie on his clodhoppers in obeisance to the engine room, it is then that the shoelace chooses to snap in two. In such small action, many are those who would seek out the influence of God. I tear my flesh, it pains me, I blame God, and eventually myself in the sight of God. Perhaps God is at work in every insignificant action.

But if so, Samuel Crummy was a man without God; he was forever missing the train, stumbling in his shoes. He loved travel, falsely thinking of it as the *summum bonum*. There is philosophy in the sea. He thought himself extraordinarily fortunate therefore in having seen a great deal of life, of having combined the sea with the land. A man not solely restricted to one *modus vivendi*, he has had a finger in a few pots. Nevertheless he knew that experience was not a solution. Rather he had come to accept the fundamental discontent of our human nature, and he had vaguely realized that the best thing he could do in its terrifying face was to move, to move much. He had to his satisfaction combined movement with permanence, function with environment—life and art in a single existence.

A HOT WIND was sweeping in from the sea, the kittiwakes shooting up out from the deep as we sailed down the Mekong Delta under a late afternoon sun, the rich rice paddies taking us deeper into the primitive colors of a green and yellow land. The *Red River* was a Victory ship, a "class 8" built just after the War in '45 or '47, the first of the post-Liberty ships, slightly larger but already antiquated by the massive Lykes Line oil tankers and container ships now passing us on the river. Any information given me by the crew was cursory, their glances brief though they seemed to learn everything they needed with that look. I still wonder, walking on streets of strange cities, how much we reveal in one glance to the thousands of people we exchange looks with? It is truly the only look we'll ever share with each other in all our time on earth. And some learn all from it, some nothing, but you must wonder, after years of such accumulated glances, what They thought of You.

That night we lay out on the deck in the heat, moving lazily downriver like a Congo ferry in a Conrad story. We could still make out Saigon around the bight, flat and shimmering, recalling soft Vietnamese nights and women I had known in that cowboy town. I fell quiet and pensive. Tracers were being fired by our helicopters into the surrounding rice fields. Thumps of artillery, supposedly obliterating Viet Cong units moving at night, occasionally boomed in the distance. We'd heard of other merchant ships that had been fired on by the VC—nothing serious yet but for a few dimpled smokestacks. Johnson, a bull-chested thick young black pantry steward with a cute hog's face from Georgia, was talking in a high energetic voice of his favorite trips out of New Orleans on the legendary "Romance Run" down South America way. Every trip but the one you were actually on always sounded better at sea.

The big guy listening, who heard everything, was "Krazy Kat," sitting there wearing a weirdly colored hat that I later learned derived from the Rastafarian sect; he was the most seaman of them all, classic pirate looks, albeit black, with some eye-popping tattoos of dragons, eyes like sharp hooks, six foot long and slim strong, he talked in words I only half understood.

There was also a heavyset white fellow with a severe crewcut I only knew as "Sparks," the radioman, who seemed to know all the current gossip on ship, and was describing the long-term cancer that was devouring his knee. Rather cheerfully he told us he'd have to have it amputated this time, and that it would be his last trip. We'd be back in the States in about three weeks and then he'd qualify for the highest grade of insurance, which the shipping company and the merchant union would pay for. Wondering how you get cancer in a knee, I asked why he didn't get the company to fly him back now? He snorted loudly, avoiding my eyes, looking only at the ones whose favors he was currying as he replied, "you don't know this company, kid."

Krazy Kat nodded sagely at this, but Jack Boggs, another "ablebodied seaman," with trashy Elvis Presley looks, now hard and lined, expressed his anxieties about getting back at all "in any three weeks, who you shittin' Sparky?" He predicted terrible weather in a deep smoker's voice, "the North Pacific's a motherfucker midwinter, the ship gonna ride high in the water, no fuckin' way! Get yourself a plane, Sparky!" He laughed cruelly, coughing on his cigarette.

When I asked why we were so above the waterline, Johnson pointed out there was no cargo to take out of Vietnam, except bodies; everything was moving into the country. It dawned on me then because we were traveling "empty" that we'd have less ballast against the weather, and that there was no real purpose to this voyage beyond getting the ship back to the States, trading crews, and reloading for Vietnam. There seemed something hollow and ominous about that, as if we might be on a "death ship." The men were "antsy," Krazy Kat was talking now, they'd been "sittin' too long at anchor" in Saigon, almost five months now, and they wanted to get back, take care of business, do some things with the big money they'd made on the 'Nam run.

What Boggs had said concerned Sparks and he now expressed fear for his leg because his knee was hurting worse than he first told us. He was deeply worried, it seemed, about the Greek in New York, by which he meant the ship owner, "the cheap bastard," the same fellow Crummy had earlier referred to, who somehow would manage "to fuck me out of my insurance." The malignant knee, wrapped in leather like some sadomasochistic exhibit in a museum, dominated our eyes.

The men listened back and forth to these various tales of woe and small hopes, sharing a night as old as the Illyrian war. I looked off at Saigon's lights now disappearing around the river's bend. Thinking this would be the last time I would ever see the little graceful mistress on the Mekong where I passed from my youth.

Near noon the following day we debauched from the Mekong into the South China Sea, where it was rough and windy, and our ship took very little time to have its first nervous breakdown. We came, unbelievably, to a complete stop. The main generator had failed and for some reason the emergency backup wasn't working, a bad sign as the engineers went to work while the ship rode at bumpy anchor off the coast of Vung Tau, a provincial capital on the coast once called Cap Saint-Jacques by the French when it was the "Cannes of the Far East."

As my looks out to sea rocked sickly from side to side, there hove right into my mind's eye, onto the surface of the water, a sea monster! At first the prosaic of my mind was telling me it was just a rubber tree. But no, this thing was *moving*— and moving with power. It was an incredibly long, thick, brightly colored sea serpent. I had never seen such a huge creature. I was stunned by it, in awe. Because it was what it was—a rare mythological creature of the deep, long rumored, little seen, save by the Few.

Chilled, no longer attent on my stomach, I screamed out to the men on the deck, "Hey, come here, look! . . . It's a sea snake!"

Johnson, the black kitchen steward of last night's talk, his transistor blaring ugly sounds into the wind, ambled over and stared at it, chewing on a ham sandwich, his blub eyes expanding. "Judas fucking priest! Ma Gawd, dat what I think it is? And I was gonna go swimmin' in dat water?"

The serpent hung there, no longer moving, deathly still, bobbing in the windy water, as if watching us, watching for signs of what? Other men were coming up now to look.

We studied it from the railing, our elbows and eyes cocked over the side, entranced, the boat weaving off the sandy tropical Vietnam coast, this giant omen staring back in a strange silent standoff. Some of us commented with deep fear and respect in our voices, but after a bit of waiting, some walked away bored. Johnson threw the remainder of his ham sandwich into the water, as if to see if, like some pigeon, it was still alive and would take the bait. The chunks of starch-white bread bobbed soggily on the waves.

The snake suddenly moved, with an amazingly fast unwinding of its powerful coils shooting it alongside the pieces of ham and bread. In a flurry of electric speed, the snake's head struck the bread, stunning it with its jaws. Without a moment's doubt or mercy, it rolled like a big sweating stallion jacklashing itself, its jaws clamped, its gelatinous eyeball suddenly visible to me, perhaps locking on me in memory or forewarning, and, with a spasmodic thrust of its tail slapping the surface farewell, dived down deep into its lair in the ocean. Then I saw it no more, the bread gone with it. All this in a moment of time, no more.

My God! All of us, mere humans, continued to stare at the roiling water, wondering where and what fell fate awaited each of us now. Johnson's eyes were like ghosts wearing white sheets. "Holy shit! You see that!" he repeated, "I was gonna swim in dat water? Man that's the last fuckin' time I ever go swimming!"

The men laughed nervously. They had already started making light of it—just another tall tale from the sea—no one really believed them on land because land is another element. Water is more fluid and allows the dream life to flow closer to the blood. But there would be many such tales this voyage, as there always are, some half true, some not so true. And who am I to talk of myths learned in schools of the Greeks seeing snakes as evil omens and making offerings before they set out to sea? No, not I. I dismiss the omen. I live in the present.

But somehow malice was born this day, malice was everywhere as our little puffball heads vanished into the size of the clouds spread vast across the wine-colored sea. And after several more hours, the generator was fixed and the ship began to move again and later, as twilight set, proceeding at a biased angle, the coast of Vietnam folded itself up on the horizon and disappeared forever.

We made our way up the coast of Taiwan, past several mysterious-looking private islands shrouded in fog and mist, the crew dreaming aloud of the fabulous wealth of the secret man or corporation who owned those sanctuaries; who this was, to this day I still wonder. I learned of the sea as I went, vomiting my way through the first several days until I was expurgating nothing but dry white spit; it was then I achieved my "sea legs." But the toughest part of my newly acquired life was without doubt "blowing the tubes" of the main boiler each afternoon. It took a strong shoulder and arm and Crummy was not particularly strong, or helpful, wiry perhaps but tending toward sickness or complaint most of the time; in a shrewd union-member way, Crummy was never a reliable partner as my wiper, and for this reason I now understood why he garnered no respect from the crew.

The main boiler is, in an exalted sense, the true mistress and keeper of the ship, for it was the boiler in the end that determined, like some mythological fairy goddess, if we were to live or die. It was this towering, fire-breathing, steel-cabled dragon that I approached with dread and humility each afternoon to blow its tubes. This was achieved by tugging with heavy workgloves on an ancient set of steel chains that would in turn pry open the individual boiler plates, each one emitting several hundred pounds of hissing steam per cubic inch, ventilating the pressure buildup in the boiler.

"Red" MacGuiness, the second engineer, a burly redhead with a mouth fixed in a scowl, would take up his position one or two stair levels above me, opening and closing the valves in conjunction with my blowing them out; we worked tandem like greased ice skaters who had to feel what the other was thinking. The scalding oil would drip down heavily from these valves onto me below, wearing a wide-brimmed Australian bush hat to avoid any burns on my shoulders and face. Nonetheless hot oil soon became second nature to my skin. There is something carbureted, almost dinosaurian, about the smell and feel of an essence such as oil; it is a smell far more specific to the engine room crew than sea and salt to the deck crew. It gets in your clothing, in the softest part of your skin, in your fingers and under your nails, it gets in your crotch and no matter how much you soap yourself down, it seems to inhabit your very cells as you sleep at night, as it finally invades your dreams. Soon I was as grimed as any wiper had ever been, boasting a new Oliver, these dark black hands holding my cock peeing, so strange a sight. As the lingering venereal sulfur still bubbled and twitched in me with its reminders of my recent dark libidinous past, I felt something wrong in myself, something poisoning the very seat of my fertility, but I knew not what to do or whom to trust.

I didn't see Crummy much; he came and went from our fo'c'sle at his own hours, distantly polite, helpful when asked, but not really interested in sharing anything with me after that first night at the bar; it was as if he had his own secret rhythm at sea, his own "con" on the world, and he didn't want anyone to know too much lest he be hurt once more. Secret lockers, secret drinking depots in the kitchen, perhaps a liaison, but never tell the other of a third; always compartmentalize your private hurt like a mistress you don't want anyone else to set eyes on.

For that matter, no one shared with me, except the most basic "howya doing kid?" By their standards I had no life yet. In all our time in the engine room, Red MacGuiness barely acknowledged me. He'd ask, you'd reply. He'd tell, you'd do, his eyes green and huge like a frog's, Cyclopean in his forehead, and, like most engine room personnel, highly irritable and worried about the next thing on his watch going wrong. I never saw these subterranean men smile, as did Krazy Kat and the deck people.

The captain had long since disappeared into his cabin somewhere in the areas above, where I was never allowed to go and where he was only seen by the exalted ones such as the chief mates who ran the ship for him, the radioman Sparks, and the kitchen crew who served him in his cabin and told us he had the gout in his swollen feet and couldn't move very well. They struck me all as men with solitary problems and dispositions, captive on a boat together, each with his different dream, each counting the days till it would be over, each ultimately missing what he'd hated, and each assembling once more to travel together. Perhaps like all armies, all navies, all men break back down into their molecular oneness, alternately integrating and breaking apart.

It was a magnificent clear cold sky a few days later as we rode through the Hokkaido Straits of northern Japan, the icy cliffs refracting the sun, white snow curling up like dogs in the laps of the mountains. The day before we'd seen whales hoving onto our port side, spuming joys of water and frisking so merrily in the sun. An hour later porpoises as fast as lightning had lit the waves, calling us to join them at play in the fields of this great paradise the sea could be when she allowed. And when they left us, it was as if they were our friends, somehow the last good luck we would have. But of course suspicions and legends abound at sea.

Suddenly from around one of the cliffs, two small Japanese fishing boats veered out, thrown wildly back and forth on the choppy waves. The little spidery men working the boats seemed fearless, totally preoccupied with their task of fishing in this impossible wind. We cheered them on as we crawled against the current, but they ignored us, totally concentrated on their work.

When night fell, I watched the Japanese mountains disappear as we entered the great northern Pacific. It was the last piece of land we'd see until we reached America. The nights on ship were quiet and private for me, and when I could steal the time, I would go up to the prow and stand there and watch the ocean breaking just ahead of this giant beast plowing the furrows with its groaning will, pumping the night with its kitchen oil and lights and massive throbbing engine. One such night Johnson, the steward, came with me, and as we were standing there sharing the hypnotizing pounding rhythm of the ocean, he started talking about sex and how "bad" he needed it and how guys "could do it" for him. He said he still liked girls but guys were "real," which somehow I didn't believe, that he liked girls at all, the way he talked about them; and then the conversation moved onto me and I was not saying no and Johnson liked me a lot and I was "like a virgin you know and it'd be somethin' special" but he'd give me, "you know, fifty bucks to get some quiet time together, party a bit, y'know." He was embarrassed suddenly and he giggled, a little nervous.

Yes, well I liked him, I tried to tell him but not this way, certainly not this way, because I found Johnson to be repulsive, not only in the ugliness of his complexion but for his silly piglike lust for all things material; I enjoyed his company, nonetheless, for the insight he had, as a kitchen man, into the common nature of all people; all his stories were meant to reduce the human being to its animal realm, which is the zone wherein Johnson was comfortable. He took my rejection well, perhaps assuming that it wouldn't be long till I came around to his point of view, and then he drifted off into the warmly lit interior, leaving me by myself on the deck thirty yards from the pilothouse, lost in the shadows; this late in the journey, the deck watch had been abandoned as the sea was considered far too cold and rough.

As I stood there now astern looking out on the wild raging frozen ocean, stranger and stranger thoughts came to my mind. Consumed with appetite and the piercing pain of the wind, I am become a legendary King feasting on the sport of the sea from whence my fishes come to my banquet table. Glorious in solitary splendor, I eat and not a soul to share with me. The flambeaus flick their bloodwings over the walls and the fire rolls with the roar of laughter and I glut myself in secrecy, and as the raw flesh descends into the secret conduits of my warm naked body, I cast quick darting glances about the immensity of my shadows and up into the stone staircases and catch nothing, absolutely gloriously *nothing*! And all is silence once more as the strangled animals on my table ready themselves for my gullet. I pick at their bodies, crack their bones, and my teeth tear into the moist red flesh. I eat, and it listens to me eat.

I shiver.

It became like some dread game a crazed Edgar Allan Poe might play with his own mind, but believe me when I say if you have the courage to stand out on the prow of a great breaking ship and stare down into the water crashing beneath you, under the coin of a moon that darts back and forth with its austere light onto the pounding waves and at other times falls jet black and the world is nothing but shadows, you will understand the treacherous feeling growing along your spine and into the branches of your brain. The feeling of ultimately betraying yourself. As the ship plows a new wake and you hear the thump of its belly hit the ocean, and a new white wall is overturned and its waves slash and gush at the sides you are standing on, you will find that inevitably, if you stand there long enough, bundled up in a sweater and jacket that are futile against a cold that whistles as harshly as any oncoming train, then a proposition will arise in your mind, dancing back and forth, teasing you, almost whispering to you like a siren, which now says sibilantly, ". . . go on, why not? . . . We're waiting. . . . Come on, it's not so bad. . . ." The creature speaks in defiance of all logic, all reason, all desire for life, all your past and your future and, perhaps the wicked final truth, in defiance of your cringing aversion to the freezing water that will kill you by way of disinterested accident.

"Jump! Jump!" your own devil voice tells you. Yes, if once and for all you could discover 'neath the thin sliver of a moon the virgin hymen with its fragile unknowing—or else the deeper knowledge lying beneath the waves, waiting like the suspenseful mouth of a silent man. And underneath, or inside, to find finally, the answers, the words—even if it's a babble, they are words and to your starved mind they can be salvation!

"Jump Jump . . ."

I was about to.

The ocean was waiting, Oliver, it was ready for you that night, the devouring lion of your Judah mind.

"Jump! Now . . ."

I ran inside that night, terrified as a child.

As if I had seen some horrifying truth of myself. And I didn't want to know. Ever. I would run as far away to the ends of whatever earth as humanly possible to avoid my Death. My self-inflicted Death.

And I never returned to the bow at night alone again. In fact, very rarely have I ever been out alone at night the remainder of my life, fearing, I suppose, that my deceitful demon double will appear again.

The weather tilted for the worse. Sparks reported a looming hurricane, cited "Emma," coming down from Kodiak Island to the northeast, heading over us toward Japan.

The men grew cranky and anxious. The ship was far too light in the water to absorb a powerful hurricane in the winter Pacific. The tension mounted subtly as men became sick, or pretended to. A pastry cook called "Sinbad," another Jamaican, contracted a pneumonia and rumors immediately swept the ship that we had been contaminated through the food supply he'd been touching. An oiler was coughing blood.

My partner Crummy, who had complained every day about one physical ailment or another, now took himself to sick bay with a pain in his groin, talking of appendicitis, which is a frequent and vague ailment sailors and soldiers will often cite; the upshot being that I was now left alone to handle all wiper duties. For this I would soon pay the price of my inexperience.

Around four o'clock one afternoon, blowing the boiler tubes, one of the chains stuck and wouldn't budge no matter how much force I applied; I called up quickly for help to MacGuiness above me on the boiler. He looked down, studying the situation, and took his sweet time bulltrotting down the ladder, his small dancer's feet encased in ugly metal-lined work-shoes. Straddling his red crewcut was an awkwardly sized Washington Redskins hat that perfectly matched his floral skin tone.

I have since wondered if he could've prevented what happened by alertly readjusting the valves he'd been working upstairs, but the cause of the accident would never be known due to his denial and my lack of knowledge. The very last thing I remember was a terrifying whistling sound coming from the depths of the boiler inches from my face, alarm bells going off in my head that there was something structurally wrong in the boiler, the whistling now urgent as a police siren, instincts yelling at me to run, to leave now even if it meant losing all my dignity in front of sloe-eyed Red MacGuiness.

It was over before I could barely react. I could taste metal searing my skin, ringing in my ears, heavy black smoke rolling over me, and I was howling something half conscious, strangled sounds, bits of flesh, purplish tissue. I was trying to speak but making choking sounds.

They told me later that twelve hundred pounds of pressure per cubic inch blew itself across the empty space where my head had just been. I had pulled away at the last moment.

My consciousness returned on the stink-oiled floor of the engine room, the worried eyes of a big Polack first engineer called Mulanovitch or "Mule" staring down at me; other faces were around him, but certainly not Red MacGuiness's face. They told me later, when he saw the black smoke pouring out, he just took off down the alley. He never even stopped or looked back—he'd left me for dead. I was now swollen red with thin steam marks on my face, my neck, my arms and hands. They were telling me I was lucky to be alive, but they were avoiding the issue of Red MacGuiness and his betrayal of a fellow sailor, a nervous fraternity of men not about to turn on one of their own.

"Good thing you got outta there kid, that was a motherfucking steambath. Shit!"

"New York Greek bastard's too fuckin' cheap to replace the goddamn boiler parts. Next inspection he's gonna get busted big time, big fuckin' fees! The greedy fuck! . . . ," expressing the view that instead of returning with a normal cargo load through the Near East and Africa, we were going back empty in the middle of the winter storms only because the Greek was making more money on the West Coast of the States, loading war materials back up as fast as he could "so's he could rip off Uncle Sam." It was also rumored that the Greek was pulling some insurance scam by carrying no cargo.

"Anyways you cut it," Boggs, the gravel-voiced, able-bodied seaman would conclude, "that prick bastard's making money every fuckin' minute, every lost fuckin' day we sweat it; they make money you betcha your ass. Anything goes wrong this trip, the Greek's got his ass covered at Lloyd's. Howd'ya think they own these fuckin' ships! They *don't*. Banks and insurance companies own 'em. Suckers like us work 'em, they own 'em."

Yes, to the "Greek in New York," it was Economics 101, no less no more; there was no feeling or relationship to the employees of some ship-owning entity perhaps paying taxes in Panama or Greece. The captain, Simon Bogolm, was nothing but an insurance guarantor; until, of course, "he fucks up, but long as he don't fuck up, long as he don't get too drunk or too fat, and there's no warrants, lawsuits, or fights, then he can stick it to us." This meant pretty much any degree of tyranny or mediocrity was tolerated. The Greek in fact might have told you with great fondness of how he too as a young man once worked the ships, and those ships back then would break the back of any man. And he had worked for grease wages; he worked banana boats and coal tramps. He might even have remembered, when he had the time, how it really was when he felt the fear. Otherwise no, it was too long ago, and he had since forgotten the wealth of sea forms. The song dies out in the ear and the body accustoms itself to the secular seat. Who cares! Greed always wins out because greed has no ministry. We do what we have to do. Why seek out an explanation—danger's hatch and brood.

Regardless, my issue, my connective thread, was not with the Greek in New York, it was with Red MacGuiness right here on the ship. By the code of the sea, he had violated his bond with me, and by that same law I would not be respected as a man until I confronted him with what he'd done. And in his cold red-green snake eyes, I felt my own fear. Having been raised a polite and considerate boy from Manhattan, I knew I would never confront Red MacGuiness and in that knowledge lay my own corruption, my own sense of worthlessness and shame.

In the fo'c'sle, before sleep, I ran my fingers along the edge of my razor-sharp Cambodian knife, marveling at its death, polished with images of Asiatic tyrants driving their chariots to war over the groaning bodies of expiring sixteenth-century minions. It had been sold to me in the back of a dusty store by an evil-looking, one-eyed Cambodian hag who swore to the naive eyes staring back at her that "yes, this antik, very old! Worth much more but I give you good price, you take America, against law, no pay tax," though a dot of suspicion arose when she readily dropped the second price in half. Regardless, this particular Cambodian knife became my friend, by dint of being the only thing I still had left after so many travels and so many thefts and losses on drunken nights in drunken hotels in drunken countries.

With Crummy still in sick bay, I slept that night in my fo'c'sle alone, licking my ugly face of its wounds of sorrow and shame. Unbeknown to me, the Fates had woven their own threads about me in ways I have not to this day understood. Life in all its complexity has truly eluded me of its meaning. Or so I think, until the next outrage mocks me again. On this night the sea woke to its full anger, and the gods, of whom I counted Pallas, Pallas Athena my protector from long-ago days at boarding school, in vengeance rose.

You cannot imagine what twenty thousand tons of steel suddenly tipping over in an angry, unforgiving sea in the middle of the night can feel and sound like; my first consciousness of it came and went within a moment that perhaps consisted of seven to eight seconds, perhaps less, but forever forged like manacles in my memory. The crash of a hundred or two hundred plates in the pantry is the loudest sound I remember. In that instant, I saw the ocean outside my porthole glass unbelievably, staring right back at me inches away, like the face of a giant waiting shark, as I slid from the top bunk, flying feet first at the tiny porthole. The innards of the ship were creaking with an awesome finality and we all were going over, yes! the whole lot of us, enemy, friend, history, schedules, anger, all swallowed in one Moby-Dick gulp of the ocean whale, ingesting us, Jonah-like, all forgiven, all forgot, all gone! My time had come so young, so unfairly it all seemed as I instantaneously prepared for the shrieking cold water to swallow my body, mind, and *me*, to die, aye, by drowning, thus was the mystery we all ask of our God now being answered. It was to be. For me. *Death by drowning*. I surrendered, what else could I do, lashing my eyes shut in fear, careening off the wall, clobbering my neck and knees and shoulder and feeling no pain as I was consumed by the great yawning arising mouth of Death. In Vietnam, the rehearsals were only rehearsals for Now. Now is . . . too late!

How a ship of twenty thousand tons righted itself at the last possible moment in a forty-four (of a possible forty-five) degree tilt in a rolling ocean, I, no engineer of such details, shall never know. But pause was given, capriciously I will always feel, as if playing with us, soft hard reminder. Moments of such death are always based on proximity—a car roaring past us at sixty miles per hour, we turn, we *feel* it a moment too late, how close we were to dying. One more step and . . . such is the feeling always, boat or car or bullet it matters not, you are there in the momentary maw of Death and no matter how irreligious you are, how profane and desecrated your mind, you feel the awesome sacredness of your own egosatanical, specially defining moment in its awesome watching face. And you know that moment will come again, yes it will come, in your final hours and you will only really know you are dead when you cross over. Till then you will always be a half-step away from the end, drawing back in the nick of time from the abyss, perhaps even given to revisiting it again and again in your life.

The *Red River*, for whatever reason, did not go down that winter's night. I heard shouting, yelling in the distance but it took a while before I could even feel the weight of my feet in my metal-lined shoes, putting myself back together like a shaken Humpty-Dumpty, nursing the terror away. The crew—even the oldest among us—was shaken. The ship continued to yaw in the sickening swells and unabating anger of the storm from Kodiak Island, but lessened somewhat as the night died down. At dawn, we warily cleaned the halls floating in shards of broken crockery and glass, the toilets congested with filth, much of the food spoiled; several men were injured to the knees and head, none seriously except in retrospect on the insurance forms.

Rumors spread quickly that a Norwegian tanker was in deep trouble two hundred miles northwest of us, and that signals had been sent for us to go back and rescue the men; our unseen captain radioed back that we were unable to return. Arguments and gossip spread from there, some saying the Norwegian ship had actually gone down, others that another ship accomplished the rescue operation; another group claimed this was untrue and that the captain had a failure of nerve and would be brought in front of an Inspection Board and never allowed to go to sea again; and yet others supported Bogolm, claiming our ship would've been torn apart had she moved any closer to the center of the storm. The confusion was unresolvable at this stage with the radioman, Sparks, sick from the effects of his cancer medication and now isolated like the captain in his cabin, unable to authenticate any rumor.

I never found out what happened to that ship. If it even existed or was a figment of a collective imagination run amok. Like many of the combat stories heard in Vietnam, the fabric of the story-telling would become part of the tale, believable only given the access of the teller to the powers that write the histories. I've since come to believe all history is like that, the lower-class men having the least influence and access, and even those men who survive the epic battles are very rarely capable of describing them correctly, having knowledge perhaps of only a section of the land or sea they fought on; thus the history of the world comes down to us in teleological myths often justifying the vision of life necessary to the present age.

Of more immediate concern to the men was what the captain was thinking. Would we pull north to the Aleutians to seek shelter as quickly as possible? Or would we continue on our present and no doubt doomed route? The issue was compounded by the spreading pneumonia afflicting Sinbad, the pastry cook, and the dire state of the appendix of the wiper Crummy; Krazy Kat was saying that Crummy's entire right side was so tender it couldn't be touched, that his rectum was inflamed and he had a fever approaching a hundred and four. The danger was that he would develop peritonitis and the appendix would burst. He was indeed in great pain, moaning and on the edge of delirium. When I heard how insane he'd become, I knew I had no desire or reason to visit him; after all he'd done nothing for me. And I, a still hesitant youth, had little capacity for compassion of this nature, frightened as I was of most everything, especially illness.

The correct decision, it seemed to most of us, was to go north to the Aleutians and evacuate Crummy by helicopter, but the captain, according to Krazy Kat, was likely to make the wrong decision for economic reasons. Because the insurance company contracts do not like to reconfigure the economics of a costly voyage around the health of only one man, Crummy would simply have to tough it out till the States, which loomed perhaps as far as two weeks away.

In this atmosphere of chaos and dread, Johnson approached me in a quiet corridor and offered a substantial increase on his fifty-dollar offer; turned down his hundred but could, in his bulbous eyes, see the encroachment of fear, at which point the need for sex inflates to unheard-of levels in one such as Johnson. I had never been so dispassionate an object of meet adoration in my life, and turned him down with sensitivity to his brute feelings, though I believe Johnson felt it was only a matter of time and asking.

The madness among us attained its natural vacuum within a day when the USS *Red River* itself responded to all the wild vacillations of rumor and lie by once again shutting down. At noon, she came to a complete and stubborn stop in the middle of the North Pacific. The old boiler, the troubled shadow of which we had, on several occasions, ample warning, shuddered and concluded its participation in our voyage.

An urgent yet silent panic spread through the engine room as the ship shivered back and forth in a turbulent daytime sea that had somewhat calmed from the previous night. Mulanovitch, the large, stinky-underarmed first engineer, discovered the problem in the main steam pipe and muttered something about one of two gaskets being damaged and that it would have to be removed quickly.

Four of us from the daytime shift, including Red Mac-Guiness, quickly set to work cutting away the plaster encasing the area around the main steam pipe. In a space the size of a running board protected by thin steel piping, and using heavy, two-man wrenches, it took us more than an hour before we were able to loosen all seven bolts rusted with disuse. By then it was boiling hot in the engine room and the bowels of the ship were rocking back and forth with the four of us squashed together like writhing snakes in a milk carton, the redhead MacGuiness's sweat glands souring the air. I excused myself to go and heave my insides out into a toilet, but the second time I couldn't check myself in time and my vomit spewed out onto the floor, splashing MacGuiness across his shoes and trousers. He swore something at me, and moved in a flash, his wrench coming up to his shoulder as if ready to snap my brains into my face. Naturally fast of reflex, I recoiled in the same instant. We froze, looking at each other. The others all looked a bit surprised by MacGuiness's overreaction, but Mulanovitch gruffly told us to "knock off the grabass, assholes! Get to work!"

With wary eyes, we both went back to the work at hand, as we tediously, with great sweating concentration, finally removed the faulty gasket and inserted a new one, Mulanovitch egging us on with pressure from "upstairs." Using a hollow metal pipe to lever the handwrench, we screwed the bolts back into their threads and tightened the fissure.

Mulanovitch now went off with another engineer to open the main steam pipe. We relaxed, like only those who have worked mightily at some backbreaking task can do, and, sighing and putting our tools away, we gratifyingly heard the first roar of the pressure coming up the pipe.

And then, without any warning, the noise of the steam suddenly deflated into a whining hiss, gradually creaking back into silence. We all stared. The pipe was dead. The steam was nowhere to be had. We had failed utterly. The ship continued to heave back and forth, passive in the ocean.

Mulanovitch, furiously cursing imprecations at us, the world, and his Polish grandmother, set us to retightening the bolts. Straining with his own great strength, he brushed his lard-stinking underarms into my face, nearly knocking me off the running board, crying, "Heave! Heave!" as we strangled the faulty gasket into its tightest possible embrace with the main steam pipe.

We passed the steam through once again, hoping but knowing it would fail. Which it did, hissing briefly into our hearts before falling silent again, mocking us for our effort, taunting the four of us as failures, as more and more of the men from the upper regions now came to the doors of the engine room, peering down at us, wondering: What the fuck!

We set to work loosening the bolts in order to inspect the gasket, all of us now caked in black sweat and grime. More frequently now, each of us went above for air, but there the ocean provided only brief menacing respite with its dark gray waves rising ever higher as the twilight hour neared, and the captain, it was rumored, going wild with worry, and with him no doubt, the big Greek in New York and the insurers in London and all the men the world over who make it their curious business to watch the money all day all night twenty-four hours winter spring summer and rain thunder sleet and snow.

I vomited once more in the engine shop inside a pail until nothing was left but belches and hiccups. I caught my breath and, overcoming the ardent desire to lie down and sleep and never wake again, I forced myself with sheer will to curse loudly and walk back to my post. There was always in this boy I knew the ardent desire to show up and fulfill the image in this life he had projected for himself. And if that meant following the canons of the sea and the twice-told tales of Jack London and *Two Years Before the Mast* and *Captains Courageous*, all rolled into one defining imagery that would rule young Oliver's life, as the war gods had ruled his land adventures, then all would be sacrificed. Two years . . . three years, soon it was going on four, five years out here in the Orient, feeding these, my fantasies. This day—this night—would conceive to be the greatest such tale of my sealife, but the truth was it was played out in pain and guts.

Mulanovitch demanded where I'd been. ''Puking man, fuck it!'' I lashed back in anger, finding my place in the circle of sweating men heaving and ho-ing until we had loosened the bolts once more and removed the bad gasket, looking around like dumb apes, peering in all the nooks and crannies of a boiler and a main steam pipe for evidence of things gone wrong.

By this time, there was a large crowd of deckhands and mates coming and going or peering down from the entry doors at the great pit of What Went Wrong, and with our lights burning and valves grinding and all the yelling, we looked like a small city in the middle of Saudi Arabia working the oil fields at night pumping gold gas and greed.

It was Mulanovitch, I think, who figured out that in our

rush to tighten the bolts, we had raised sections of the gasket disproportionately to other sections, thus crushing the gasket itself into a distorted shape that apparently rendered it ineffective. We should have raised each bolt in equal simultaneous steps instead of finishing one bolt and then moving to another; or at least that is how, with limited technical knowledge, I understood it.

"Get me another gasket!" Mulanovitch barked, and I ran. Back in the machine shop, I stared horrified at the empty gasket box. There were other gaskets in other racks but none the size we needed. Given the inspections and the needs of safety, this was inconceivable, as if the gasket had been deliberately stolen by an agent provocateur of Fate. Mulanovitch blamed me for the bad news and stormed off in frantic search for what he assumed I had mislaid in my amateur attempts as a wiper. MacGuiness glared at me and called me something ugly I couldn't hear, his voice trailing off as he too went searching.

Yet I felt I would somehow save the day, as was my mother's custom and instinct for finding baseballs lost in the brush. And I did, redeeming myself, finding an old rusty gasket hidden away in a footlocker that perfectly matched the size we needed; desperately, now heroic in my mind, we set to work for another two grueling hours. The weakest of the four men finally dropped out, but MacGuiness stayed, so I stayed, too.

"You wanna go?" Mulanovitch asked, tightening his six-foot-three biceps on a wrench; he probably didn't know my name or cared to, but there was a certain pride in the way he asked, as if he at last recognized I too had expended everything in this effort, and in that there was a kindness in the strong sweating Polish engineer unknown to Red MacGuiness, who had long ago given up such feelings.

I shook my head at Mulanovitch. We continued slowly,

cautiously, to bring up each section of the gasket so that it would not bend itself out of working shape. Slowly seven times, seven bolts. It was now after six o'clock and we had been rolling in the sea since noon. Rumors came down that the captain had actually been *seen* outside his cabin in the wheelhouse, considerably bloated from his gout, yelling at the chief mate before shuffling back to his cabin and slamming his door.

As we plowed into our seventh hour, there came to me a clarity which I have rarely experienced, the sort of diamond-cutting skill which always seems for me to divide the true from the false, the real from the unreal. It seemed to say, with its beastlike breath, that I could now know the truth if I wanted. And in looking back, I wonder why, if it was there for the having, didn't I take it? The thoughts involved the raising of the circumference of our lives, in equal parts and at the same time; the parallel precision this required; the concept of expending great effort without there being success or reward; and the nature of existence eating up and destroying the hopes of men like these, in the dirt of their sweat, wrestling the unknown nature of the sea, trying to fix their little hole in the world without much more knowledge than the need to make it one more inch at a time, praying like worms for nothing but rain, nothing in it for them but the doing. But these thoughts vanished in the sweat and tedium of our enterprise.

We finished near eight in a sea that, though less turbulent than the awful one two nights before, was rocking us mercilessly in its grip, paying us back for our empty cargo holds, paying back the bastard Greek, who wasn't here, for his greed. The effect of such battering of the senses left us benumbed with the coal miner's bleary stare. I remember not caring anymore, the tension drained from my exhausted body as I retreated to the main floor to watch as Mulanovitch opened the valves, letting the steam start through, sounding like a suppurating bubble, coming higher, higher, with obvious and evident success. Mulanovitch, his expression almost insane with excitement, whose life in mechanics had rarely risen to these heights, was ready to thrust his arms in the air for the one small remembered victory of a long life of drudgery. We were all excited. We had won, this we knew; even MacGuiness would have to smile and finally surrender to the barest murmur of a collective smile.

The boilers of the moon came roaring up!

And then *hissed*. Hissed with the dragon's mockery of our best-laid plans to move on, because moving on is what all of us expect and demand; because we do not allow the moment of death to stop us; it is rude interruption, not tolerated, and then when grasped, is a hysterical fear that grips the heart and the mind, and surrender follows spontaneously. The captain himself, it was said, reemerged into the wheelhouse giving his first command in days, perhaps years.

"Okay, let's make it up!"

The whole ship rocked at once with the same forked and hissing tongue of failure. One giant reptile consuming us. We died in that moment, all hope of human life and decency shattered. If we were not able somehow, by some miracle, to extricate ourselves from this killer ocean, we would drown here. This we all knew. As Boggs succinctly put it, "Now we're *really fucked!*"

My eyes and mind were hollowed, a door had slammed shut in my head, leaving me moon-eyed for idiosyncrasy, standing there in a fog of my own devise, hardly noticing the fresh clean face of a new engineer, risen from sleep, passing me on his way to work. Stunning in his calmness, he was our third engineer, on the eight to midnight shift, a Japanese-American sporting clean glasses and overalls. As he began methodically reexamining the boiler pipes. I drifted around the engine room, lost for the next few minutes; there was no place to go except sleep, but sleep would be impossible in this ocean. I would have to, of course, put in for an overtime payment for these hours, but probably the paperwork would never see the light of day because *we* would never see the light of day. It was all irrelevant, including my efforts, and I soaked myself in pity and numbness, and, above all, took solace in the known feeling of having lived up to being a member of the losing football team, which is what, I have come to believe, most of us as a race belong to.

It took Mike, the third engineer, who belonged obviously to another race, less than fifteen minutes to find out what was wrong. And what was wrong was that we had been working the entire day on the wrong gasket! And that if Mulanovitch had played closer attention at the point of origin, he would have fixed *the other gasket,* the second one in the main pipe. How ridiculous! How very ridiculous, how like life, I thought. It is where you start that you must also end. Inbetween is the maze, and like Theseus we wander, some with and some without the thread to lead them back to the beginning. Very quickly, within an hour I believe, our Japanese had replaced the defective gasket with the original gasket we had removed some twelve hours before and the boiler was running beautifully, if suspiciously, with steam once again rising through the ship's innards, aerating its old lungs, sending us hurtling forward, cantankerous waves now joyously smashing once again at our feet.

I dragged myself up to my fo'c'sle, where alone, smothered in grease and failure, tired of broken hopes and a life that always seems to triumph over its occupants, I yawned once and slipped deeply soundlessly into the black bridal gown of sleep. . . .

ROUGH HANDS WERE shaking me.

"Get up! Get up!"

Dizzy and wondering how long this man had been shaking me, I came up out of the sea and saw it was still night? Was it this same night, or was it a night later?

"A man's overboard!" is what he had been saying to me, or was saying for the first time.

Something exhausted in my voice muttered back, "What! Who?"

"Crummy," he said. "He jumped!" That's all he said. Not why. Just *he jumped* is all that is necessary in the parlance of the sea. Motive is attenuated, discounted because it's ultimately "bullshit" or "philosophy," however you choose to define your corpus of thought and opinion.

I remember rising and tying my shoelaces, realizing I had fallen asleep with my shoes on, wiper style, but I don't for the life of me recall the face of the man who woke me and left quickly as I staggered to follow. He was another stranger in the shadows in a life full of strangers who always seem to give us the most shocking news and then disappear to tell others.

Vaguely following the clarion call to assemble in search of Samuel Crummy, I went up on deck into the cold four o'clock night, feeling the silence of the dry sleeping bodies rustling up against walls, the shuffle of shoes, the stares, others muttering, irritated at being roused, "It's fuckin' Crummy! He went and fucking jumped man, the fucking guy, fuck!"

Crummy! Twenty minds echoing the thought. Weird as fangs stuck in an arse. Pangs of icy wind trapping our faces. Why Crummy? Bodies breaking into the cold night air. Werewolf fears and the shafts of a searchlight zooming out into the seadark shivering the web. Now I see Krazy Kat, and he's got a green baseball hat on his head and it says "Polo Grounds, 1954," and I think I will freeze without my windbreaker. Dark forms moving on the rim of the ship, and someone says, "I give him twelve minutes in this fuckin' ocean. If he's lucky!"

And then Johnson's voice muttering to no one in particular, "He gotta have hit the fuckin' screw on the way down. He was dead 'fore he hit the water," but given all the speculation, he died, that he died this we know.

At sea, men don't set much faith in the collective. Each one does what he is told to do, no more, no less, and though the confinement is intense, the sense of getting to know one's fellows is in no wise encouraged. This was the way it was. Until the ugly boil started to sprout on the endless nose and Samuel Crummy had passed into legend as Emma had broached Samuel and Samuel begat Ezekiel and Ezekiel's real name was Oliver, and we may be thankful to Father Fiction that memory is but our servant. In books like this—my story—you die, Samuel Crummy, in order to nourish our bland factlives with wild infusions of fantasy. As we powder our wrinkled bodies and congratulate ourselves for knowing the width of despair.

And yet we never know what it is to die.

Imagine the chaos of this death. The insurance forms, cables, paperwork. New York, London. The world will know an obscure man died this night. Money will be passed. Papers forged or stamped. It matters not. A smart Greek ship owner on Wall Street does an immense job with immense labor. He is perpetually reassured by forms like secretaries and business lunches and telephones, a woman who is his wife, and small people who are his children. He can never simply lie down and die, that is impossible, the form will sustain him, he can go to an office, he can even be sick to the very root of his stomach and suffer its intense appendicitis and he will continue to exist. Because he will hide behind and be protected by the security of his forms.

But out at sea, in the nothingness, such illusion is foolhardy. There is so little of this life-preserving mesomorphic form. A captain yes, a bark on the water, a salaried job, but nonetheless, against the rage of the elements, the war of the sea, the slow passage of weary steps, the fading margins of each sunset, by day by night, by definition, definition is dissipated and discipline loosens its grip. Man evolves into littleness, perhaps eventually autistic nothingness. He lives by the sea now, the sea's organic discipline, and when on land, he is forever dislocated.

In the corners talking of death by drowning, the men all sensed it, they knew and they were vexed, like the dim sea, enshrouding crowding, the truth was everywhere, whirlwind swiveled. The rumors spreading: Crummy had apparently been to see the captain before the suicide. He had asked for things not granted. And the fiction grew through the early morning hours. They even *heard* his cries earlier, weird and woebegone, screamed through the timbers of the clipper, blowing in the fierce nightwind, ''O fuck holy jeesus get me to a hospital, willya! You gotta take it out, you gotta take this out!'' Gripping his abdomen, because no longer could he urinate, with his eyes so large and limpid, and in his agony arising, rumor abides, he crawled elbow over elbow to the captain's cabin. Throwing open the secret door, he at last saw the puppet pulling the kingdom of Id, the ugly Simon Bogolm of the USS *Red River*, lifting his hideous flapjacking two hundred fifty pounds of blubber gut from its drunken slumber in a small, too small, cracking bamboo chair, so frightened now out of his mind bugeyed with fright of this small limp pathetic form lying like tuberculosis in his doorway, yanking his revolver from his desk drawer and in panic chopping at the poor man's head. So the rumor goes. And Samuel with blood in his eyes, and clutching his cross lurching blindly about the cabin, hurling cries of ineffable pain and pity as Simon, driving the demons from his own drunken terrified mind, shoots wildly, *bang bang bang*, out out sweet ghost! But the ghost doesn't die, so the rumors go, and with agonizing raw persistence, clutching his belly and his cross, the hot sting of the bullet in his flesh, he crawls onto the raging cold deck and then with a single cry in the night, hurls himself into the raging fury of the midnight ocean.

He thus
Disturb the sense
with sleep

I shiver. Or was he pushed? Some say. We wonder but no one will ever know. And no one will ever explore. Because no one cared about Sam Crummy. It's the way the game is played, Oliver. Learn fast.

Krazy Kat moving slowly, as in a movie frame, toward the metal door leading back into the heated corridor. A liquid ray of light shoots out, producing a long narrow green hat, a snub catnose and a crooked smile. It *is* Krazy Kat. And I am here on this ship with the memory of a man named Krazy Kat. He is retreating; he opens the lumbering door and looks back furtively. The door closing. Krazy Kat is extinguished like a fly. The frame fades into blackness. Cut.

For one hour, then two, the ship patrolled back and forth like a giant Cinerama horror bird looking for her egg, which, if you don't know, is in the belly of the sea scrpent. All iridescent yellow and slimy seagreen. Who, as she licked the aspic from her livid jaws, watched from her coign the ship. Krazy Kat, perform proceed. His rehearsed retreat. The conspiracy of the sea. One man more. One mariner.

I shivered again, as if the conceit were centered in the deciduous earth of my belly. Some dizziness that snatches desire and renders proof self-evident. In a dream once that sundered sleep, and I was in a bare bare desert they call it Golgotha and fell upon a growth of cactus strung diagonally with human skulls. Like a thin tassel lying bent and broken on a Christmas tree, I found the butchered body of a green and yellow sea serpent smeared in silk red blood.

"I see him! There! Man starboard!" Hysteria borne from the foredeck. Eyes fled the frost and thawed, the call relayed.

"Where!?"

"There!"

"Where?"

The eyes strained to see, before the dawn, an undigested corpse in a dyspeptic sea. The stare of the skull within. A body, wrinkled and hideous in the seed of death, borne aloft on a bobbing sea, resurrected!

Slashing puissant swift through the sea, the serpent, observant god, sank its head and swam smoothly back into the silence, satisfied.

"False alarm! False alarm!" A deeper, huskier voice assured us from the shadows as the cold recoups our shame and it is finished now, and now I know. That all the world is as a movie, and we its playactors have conceded. To technologies of feeling. And if only in long involuted prose sentences do we revolt, then it is in the sentences that wind themselves out pages without stop and filled with words of incommunicable wealth and little less reason, that we can say, you see, in talking of the dead who died at sea, like Boggs did, in his deep tobacco voice with the once-handsome face, who had fucked all the women in all the ports and who was our resident philosopher cynic, summing it all up later over a warm black cup of coffee in the mess, "Well you can tell his old lady, she can sell the shithouse now."

So said, Samuel. But he had no "old lady." None at all.

There was a pall that traveled with the crew thereafter. Emma, sweet hurricane, subsided into the memory of history, categorized as nightmare, near miss, death experience, but essentially catalogued by the human mind and thus rendered impotent and forshorn of its immense and terrifying power over us.

It wasn't long before Johnson, given to earthly things alone, returned to sequester me in one of the toilets I was numbly cleaning with mop and pail. His offer now stood at a mind-boggling $250! Take it or leave it but it was definitely without doubt the most he'd ever paid for "pussy."

Although I said "no" this third time, there is no doubt that, under the sway of the moon of Sam Crummy and all the foretold incidents that had occurred to me and further partitioned me off from the world of the known to the netherworld of surreal shades, that I began that night to complicate him in my mind, forming a vision of Johnson as a young black god. The smell of strong sex coming off him. His bulging muscled belly feather tickling me and in his pants a mysterious swelling mass taking shape, finely carved and piercing through my belly wall, up and up, deeper with each thrust from the jerking belt belly, o smash me! crush my intestines where they stand and force it up, hold it tight, twist my vines, smell me, eat me, dip me in the boilers of the moon, but *don't* let it out, keep it in, keep it in, force it up, fuck me good!

In such a moon of madness, I went after MacGuiness. For truly he was the one who had rendered me impotent in sight of myself. He, not Johnson, had spit me into the oil of the engine floor and rubbed his oil-soaked clodhoppers across my sperm; it was he who had abandoned his engineer's post and fled for his life, leaving me to die and not once acknowledged it to crew or me, needless to say, said "sorrree!' And until he did, I was just another cipher soul like Crummy, whom I had now replaced as first wiper and would grow old as such. Vietnam and its meaning to me were already shorn. And in the knowing indifferent looks of the crew, in my nothingness, the voyage would end these ten days and then? I would never see MacGuiness again, he would vanish into the world, another anonymous user sinner desecrator rapist violator with the core of his humiliation rubbing my seat of sperm cowardice till the end of my recorded petty time. Aye, but what's courage anyway? It comes and goes, does it not, it blows like the wind, and sometimes it's here and sometimes it ain't.

In command of my newborn fleet, I vow, Red MacGuiness, I shall return to slay you someday. Ahoy, maties, man the furls! Let's shred this jeesus wind with Bible sword! Because, in a little train station, in the rain, I know she's there. And she's been awaiting my arrival now some number of years, sweet dark woman of the sonnet, Who art thou? Who ist thee?

He came bulltrotting on duty, scowling as usual, his Washington Redskins pig hat on his head and of course his heavy oil-soaked metal shoes. A man out of my worst nightmare, thick and powerful, with no good in his heart, he actually did look, on closer scrutiny, like my conception of Edward Hyde, his face squat, mean, toadlike, with bulging greenish eyes pinned between red lashes and sandy, nearly hairless eyebrows. I feared him preternaturally.

But it was now or never, Oliver, now or never. He had his back to me as I edged closer, a wrench gripped in my hand, thinking like Hamlet suspended over the praying Claudius, Don't fuck this up, clobber the slimy bastard right fucking now!

But I couldn't, because violence is not second nature to me. And he turned and he looked me square in the eye and scowled as if he knew the very thought that shone through my forehead. Trembling inside, I sneered back at him, a practiced false sneer and said something so stupid its memory eludes me but sounding something like, "By the way buddy, thanks for leaving me under the boiler that fucking day."

Stupid things are what get said in moments such as these, and then I thought he said "so," or something like that. But the scowling, red-freckled, pig-eyed Irish bastard didn't. He didn't say anything in reality, pretending not to hear anything above the whirr of the engines. He kept perfectly still, the sweat glistening off his red sideburns, challenging me. The ship was swaying, his feet were planted well apart, a taut scary rock of man, shifting back and forth with the swell, his beefy hands akimbo, sleeping on his feet, he hardly moved a muscle, hardly twitched, hardly breathed. I knew the fear in me. A practiced gladiator he was, strong and used to these barroom brawls and brutal beatings that sadly I would now have to undergo.

I couldn't hit him first. Old fear signals of the ape cave. Above the roar of the machinery, I screamed finally, "You fucking fuck with me again MacGuiness, you fucking coward sonofabitch, I'll kill you! So help me fuckin' God I'll fuckin' kill you!" For all the rafters to hear! The engine room's attention now focused, cheap ringside seats.

Grimacing, I took my wrench like a sword, and making my point for all to see, smashed it on the handrail inches from his hands.

There followed a moment of pure silence. We were staring right into each other's hearts. His pride and ego were so towering in their red rage, he could not tolerate being told to his dogface that he was a coward; he would risk a little to defend.

So he hit me. Hard and low and surprising, first in the gut with a swiftchopping beefy blow and then a glancing sound over my right ear where it was soft, his hook coming out of nowhere. I heard myself grunt, realizing through a suddenly blurred consciousness that I had not done what I had set out to do, that I had been listening to some still rational instinct over something darker, baser that this beast knew. Then there was an explosion of that familiar surrendering blackness and a sound coming from me that I could only hear from a distance as his heavy clodhoppers caught me painfully in my thigh, missing my groin, and I was tumbling down, another numbing chop to my right shoulder and neck which reeled through my brain like a flashbulb. God, was he dirty! Fighting from where? Now he had me by the throat scraping his jagged fingernails painfully against the skin of my throat, and I saw the wrench in his hand, and the wrench would come around faster than I could handle and my brains would splatter all over this greasy stinking engine room floor.

I struggled hard to my left as I was pushing back the other way, but he was short and close to the ground like a bowling ball, hard to dislodge. I got a hold of his wrench arm and put as much pressure as I could on it, but there was no question he was built stronger than I. Then he bit me on the arm with a mark that stayed green and black like a scorpion's sting for weeks.

It was this moment I believe that I went sailing out of my rational mind, jumping blindly into a black sacrificial hole of adrenaline, screaming in a voice I had never heard before, hitting him hard and leveraging him off me at the same time. He was quite surprised to see I had transcended myself, and he suddenly lost his grip, as Fate, or luck, or some deviously whimsical Homeric god, had irrationally intervened in his or her way, and MacGuiness no longer seemed so all powerful and overwhelming. Now he was *mine*, this I knew as I was smashing him against the railing, and then the floor, and then I was hitting bluntly and flatly into his face without feeling, knuckles that would gloriously ache for weeks with the pleasure of revenge, and I was screaming insane words and now my hands were around his throat and he was collapsing with fear, I could see it in his eyes, what had happened? What moment had sparked this transference I had no idea, some Edward Hyde of my own had emerged and I was going to kill him as I was going to kill my crewcut cousin in France so long ago, and I saw the wrench in his hand and he did hit me with it on the side of the head but I felt nothing, absolutely nothing, blind with my own pain I wanted to strangle this evil fucking redheaded second engineer all the way to dusky death, his ugly bulbous purple-red orbs jutting from his squat face, once and for all to rid the world of all the evil there is. So I squeezed harder and harder and I knew he'd be dead very soon, but it was, I think, Mulanovitch the Pole who pulled me off him and then big Nelson and Koombs and two or three others rushing down as Mémé had in that distant bee-ridden land, and then Boggs with his cigarette voice who had done me the honor of coming all the way from the Olympian decks above, yelling, "Get off him! Get off! You're killing the guy!" All of them yelling at once in a red vortex of madness, and somebody was yanking Red up by his scalp and slapping him to see if he was alive yet. It was all confusion and I felt like puking now from the heat and the madness and the oil, but the triumph was vivid in me, gloating glorious summer sun, I was, I am, I will be!

And the last thing I saw of Red MacGuiness was the blood streaming from his nose and ears mixing with the red shorthairs of his scalp, his shocked leviathan eyes rolling up and down like he'd lost control and shit himself, which he had, fumbling for gravity, yelling something repetitive and stupid like he was still in charge when everyone knew he wasn't and everyone knew I'd just beat the shit out of him and done the only thing I could do, and by so doing become a sailor now!

And a man.

Fumbling out of there, shaking like a leaf of pride, I made my way onto the deck of this lawless tub where the gray wind was scraping the decks with an icy fork. My young hair was blowing wildly back and forth, and the waves were cresting green and white on either side of the ship, beautiful slimegreen breakers fraught with the smell of salt and sea, and the ocean looked like a giant semicircular screen through which the point object of this ship was gliding.

The first seagull croaked from somewhere hidden low in the breakers. Did I hear something? My senses perked like bells. Then the bird suddenly rose up from behind the waves, flapping its large graying wingspan, croaking out a second greeting. What's up Doc? Eh heh eh heh. Flap flap flap! Looking for some garbage, I yam. Got any?

I wanted to rush down and tell the others. But I resisted. Feasting on my secret knowledge, I stood proud and exhilarated on the deck, the wind washing my face. I had slain the dragon in me. But would it stay away? Leave that for another day. For now it's over, Oliver, God bless, it's really over. . . .

Enwept, I looked out to sea, whole again, and tasted the passive power of the ocean. And heard once more the song of the sea, the eternal silence now of Samuel Crummy back there somewhere in the deep, his old man's soul flapping in the undercurrents of the ocean, his tattered shirt hooked to an old footlocker.

It is a cry in the night that will never leave me.

1 2 . O R E G O N !

THERE! THERE IT IS!

The cliffs of pine. The forests without fear. O Oregon, so big, so wide! Hello, how are you?

Is it really over? My youth. When the bellying sail is furled, the hatches are closed, the last sailor is down the ratline, and the clipper, the great white blooming clipper, which treaded the Hudson when from the rocky gloom perched falcons stood tight vigil, is home, home from the sea.

I hope so, for we are tired, we seamen from the sea. Grazing in this vast greenery. O Sinbad, we are sad birds, without homes, no end to our travels, no arch to our experience, no tongue with which to tell. Of that which we see. Or know. And we do know. That in this moist seawind, there is the breath that blows the soul.

O but you are a liar Oliver, aren't you? Moist monologue. These red gashes on my face. Boiler wounds. A hero to myself. But I am no hero. The dull, the dreary, and the dry. Believe you me, you great flock of greeting gulls. Blanch at our tails. Shame for this ship. Came with curse. From that way. I could shiver. Thinking back. But shan't.

Why are these tears tiptoeing across my face? Weeping like

a wind, from where does it blow, this wind, washing sights seen by eyes so small a sum as two? Scepters shattered, myths mocked, wills broken; testaments made practical, and beasts as savage as a dream, o eyes the barren shell, punctured like a pornocracy, women despoiled and crippled, hidebound life made lewd and lust noised abroad. I had told myself that before, and before that. I thought Hope had roads and time schedules, o yes, and I thought other things foolish as well.

The minuscule pilot boat swimming out from the timber port of Coos Bay to meet the USS *Red River*. Surging in the choppy sea. The pilot coming aboard—the first land species we have seen in years. We stare. His lean unspeaking face, he looks among us. He too knows I am guilty as the next. And would never believe the yarn I could spin. O he's just another sailor, long on the leatherstocking. And a scar from a sabre's slash cleaving his face open. Take me then to your lair. Bring the wine with the women and I'll furnish the wit with the whiskey. And turn us all to swine. Because we're back from Vietnam. Aye. The land across the sea. O yes it was hard. What happened was this.

And then I begin. *In media res.* Of how I crawled into the jungle badly wounded one June day. And spent three days hallucinating as friendly leeches sucked my fluids dry. Nearly expired, but didn't, and dragged myself into a Comanche village. Near nude. And told them *je suis français.* The doctor came. He talked of a big battle in the valley to the west where the Americans were caught and massacred. Yet he gave me his old clothes and helped me to get to Quang Ngai and thence to Saigon by backcountry bus. Living silently off the edges, I bummed around, caught the clap in Laos or Phnom Penh, I'm not sure where, but I did fuck a girl in Bangkok. Named Mei Lin. Pretty as sin. Who I will always . . . always. I longed to stay with her but the ship was leaving the next day. I spent the last night with her, smoking cigarettes watching the light break, caressed and cuddled together, she'd long turned off the meter, Mei Lin; one of the saddest things about growing up is that you come to realize you're not as handsome as you think you are; this I felt in the throes of fucking. Maybe I should have stayed behind, in the East, and married her. Slopehead.

I got her name written on my arm. Yeah. Mei Lin. And an arrow through a red heart saying "Bangkok," yeah. And the date. Funny thing is. See I could write a book now. An adventure story maybe. But, sad to say, I can't. It works that way. Too bad.

O but this is a bonny day. And that is faraway. And my parents lie in this land. Many many moons across country, back along the Oregon Trail, many buffalo between here and there, yes, but they're there. Father, in his wealth, lying in the sawdust of some Third Avenue saloon, saying he doesn't feel well, my only boy is dead, and they'd better put him in a cab because he wants to go home and go to bed and read the *Reader's Digest*. And my mother, o so, they woo my mother and waste my house. Here I am. Home. Your boy "Oliverre." Whoremonger. Sailormaster. Thug. Thief. And Killer. Reunion in jungles deep to man. That is, unless they both died while I was away whaling at sea. And were embarrassed to tell me. For how could I ever go to their funerals in good taste. They'd sniggle at me behind heirloom veils. Because I got the clap. Because I precipitated their public demise and peed on the first fright.

I guess I never told you that my father was a handsome man, with a wide wonderful sense of humor and spoke French. Or that in his spare moments, he wrote some beautiful poems about the girls he loved long before he met my mother, whom he never loved. Or did I tell you my father never hit me once in his life? But that he could never kiss. And did I ever tell you? That I took my father forgranted.

". . . Hello, operator . . . I'd like to speak with New York, please. Yes that's right. Templeton eight, thirty-nine eighty-one. Thank you." Click clack. Rubbing my finger on the pane. Nervous. Will someone be there? The telephone suddenly shrieking in an apartment three thousand miles away. My heart leaping higher on each echo. The approaching landfall of feet, gliding over the carpet. The lift of the receiver. The hesitation. Yes? And then.

"Darling! O my little darling!"

Mother!

The operator. "Sir, I have your party for you."

Thank you.

"I know you are alive! *Bien sûr* I know you are alive. I know nothin' can happen to you because you're my leetle boy. Oh zey told us you were dead, o zey told us you were dead, but I know you are not dead, it is impossible! I say—I must see ze body! O my darling, o my little little darling."

Slurps in the phone. And we talked and sometimes couldn't talk there was so much inside. What it's like to be a ghost? And what did the obituaries say about me, o I don't really care. Mother, I have to tell you something. Yes? Mother, I.

"Yes? . . . O come home zoon, darling, my darling, come home zoon!" Yes. As soon as possible, but I have to travel a bit first. . . .

"Vere?"

O, the West Coast, I don't know, maybe Mexico, I'm just not ready to come home. She wants me to explain but it would take too long and I don't want to get irritable with Mom, not

now, so . . . as soon as possible, yes, goodbye, good . . . replacing the receiver and standing in the gray aluminum booth
by the deserted cold lumberdock this January in Oregon—I
didn't tell her did I, about these things, or how I killed or how,
like Magellan, I returned. I shall surprise her—when it rains,
rains heavily, and I see her again . . .

. . . gliding over the thick carpet, echoing in my ear, and
lifting the receiver, the hesitation. Yes? And then a pleasant
mild-mannered voice saying, "Oh, I'm terribly sorry but Mrs.
Stone hasn't lived here in six months. Mrs. Stone moved back
to Europe, yes, I don't know where. You're the first gentleman
caller I've had in over four months asking for Mrs. Stone, I'm
afraid she . . ."

Click. Maybe I'll go to Mexico now. Keep going south with
youth. The eagles in the Mexican mountains and the dogs barking in the late afternoon behind stucco walls. Maybe. Like the
Vietnamese used to say when I was over there fighting when I
was young. Maybe twenty soldiers, maybe fifty soldiers, maybe
two miles maybe three. Maybe many more.

The USS *Red River* edging in. Watching from the deserted
dock, a gawky teenage boy and two numb-looking girls, in
white socks chewing bubble gum. Some other America after all
this time. Other people too, nondescript, waving hands, muted
smiles. Vietnam yes. That is where from which this witch
comes. Is that your car, that eight-cylindered Chrysler? What a
silly question. Hail the homeward hero. Populations of people.
Parade me through American streets, embarrassed and shy with
secret history, and then. Put me down. I'm glad. I don't know
a soul.

The short squat man coming on looks like a rep from the
shipping company. "A goddam' Greek fo'sure," says Boggs.
The sour-faced man is angry. Looks like he's going to fire every-

body. And those state troopers, with their smokey bear hats and big boots and 45s derricked to their sides, look like they're here for the captain. A little matter of incompetency along the way. Many questions to answer and many miles to go on the matter of Mister Crummy, I suppose. And those other men over there, all gray and worried, look like people who work for insurance companies, hungry to pull out their briefcases stocked with papers and get to work counting the counting.

O don't quibble over Crummy now. Don't tear him in two, he's gone. He didn't like scenes in public places. Neither do I. Oops! There go the ropes. Launched like pythons over the side. Wiggling down to the dock. The fresh smell of cut timber flowering my cold nostrils, out of which winds a thin streak of frigid snot. Wipe it away. There. Quenched and quaffed. Somehow. In television declivities. God, does America seem . . . quaffed this sullen day. Dry as a cinder. Hit by nuclear attack. I shall weep in Xanadu. In the shadows of these pines. And sawed-off parts of amputated trees. Piled skyhigh on this atomic little dock. So amiss in colors. So amiss in humanity's hullaballoo. Like the cry of a yipping coyote on a Mexican mesa. Looking into the moon with its bereft eyesockets. Wriggling with worms of seacold. Herr Stone. A tenor among basses. And all this time at sea without a woman. Forty days and nights, and no self-wringing of the insane penis. I conquered. What? This young woman waving onshore in tight slacks and wool jacket, pimply and poor. Granted. That I have gone wild and crazy with lust. Riven driven, denied deprived, making a firm point to myself, firmly. Suffering silence. Accruing asceticism. An impractical lamb who can walk through history and still be what he is: neither eating nor eaten—I should have fucked Johnson— that is until the day the cruel young Goddess of wisdom with the blond hair swinging like a wild wind down her back and wolfgreen eyes came sauntering into my prison cell, and shooting me full of leaks, says, "Oliver."

"What?" I ask the Goddess, worshipping at her altarcunt.

"You should have fucked Johnson."

The gangway lowered. Must go. Party's over. Johnson's not even looking at me, eyes clacking forward to the next San Francisco bar. Go home now. Walking slowly, unsurely, down this metal staircase. Must hold on. Just a little longer. Might make Mexico yet. There goes Krazy Kat. Wait up! Where goest thou so quickly without fair word or farewell?

Now, crumple and kiss. This American soil. Like a hot steaming bath. Stepping in, now rising up into my legs, grasping me, reaching my brain. For richer for poorer, for better for worse, forever fornicate. Forever and forever, feel free to fuck. Stretch and yawn and feel this soil. I do. O I do! A numb ringing to my ears. The harsh scrape of gravel on my shoes. This is not how you walk. My legs twaddling here and there. Give me some support, someone.

There goes MacGuiness. Goodbye, asshole. Yet I will miss you. Part of all I have met. And now—don't go!—Mulanovitch, Boggs, and Krazy Kat, vanishing to hotel rooms in St. Paul, trailer parks in Utah, threadbare marriages in Mississippi, all waiting till they get bored or broke or the next divorce or battery, so that they can return when they run out of dreams, preferring the schemes of the sea because there'll always be another ship going east or going west or going to Arabia, it matters not where, the dreams died long ago. Schopenhauer once said, every parting brings a foretaste of death. Perhaps. Perhaps that is why no one really says goodbye. They just split quickly. Into lesser parts headed like crazy molecules in all directions of America. I doubt if I'll ever see the Pacific again. Say goodbye at least to that. This ocean. You know it's really like walking. Keep walking and you'll be in Japan. So far away. For there will come a day, I say. A highway stretched taut in the sky, over the sea, and ships will be obsolete, and no more mariners under the sea sun in Phoenician lands, and a bit more of that misty margin gone. I wonder yet: what sharks are poised between here and there, their pimpled snouts furrowing the waves? This disproportion in mine eyes. In this feeling, in this day. I shall never forget. What?

Breathing deeply. Arriving at the American status quo. Must pee. Badly. The cold gnawing at my ears. Must walk. Over there among the pine trees. Or maples. Or firs. Whatever they are, never much good at naming things. Let's just slip in here and hide. Lest the smokey bears see and growl. Sliding my zipper down, looking over my shoulder, squeezing my frightened penis into the freezing cold. Thank you. And securing my shaking sea legs still unbalanced in this strange land like some stag-eyed Columbus, pee behind some tree.

Ahhhh! . . . it feels *so good.*

13. FUTURE FANTASY #2

ONCE OFF THE ship in Oregon, my future hanging in the balance before me, I ventured into the world of Greek shipping, where Fate and the gods favored my boldness, as did a natural ferocity. By my thirty-third birthday, I had outwitted the wiliest of my cutthroat competitors and owned perhaps the eleventh largest fleet in the world. Liberian, Panamanian, South African or Brazilian, my flag could be seen flapping on the seven seas.

The time had come to marry, and I married a lady named Isobel whom I met not in the South Seas or Afghanistan or a foxhole, but in as simple a spot as Southampton, New York, on a cool September night, which spoke then of visions of a future home with clean toilet bowls and the coffee brewing in a bright American kitchen, and images of sending flaxen-tailed girls off to spotless rural schools knowing they will never die because there are so many signs on these clean cold country roads saying DRIVE SLOWLY, SCHOOLS ARE OPEN, ADVENTURE IS CLOSED, and DEATH IS DEAD.

She was rich and I was rich, and the golden slipper was only gold. Mounds of it. In both families. People swarming like luscious locusts over the lawn. Insunsilent Indian Summer, silly and no longer snotty, the fountains swept with decadent moss, and lavish poisons mantling the surface of the wines. On my spine, a beautiful soft velvet black jacket, rustling in the breeze and whispering in elegant contraceptives to this tall green-eyed redhead who seemed to be drinking twice as many stingers as I, and explaining it away by saying she was half-Indian, of hostile heritage, and shot caribou and I asked her were they geese? The crickets rattling madly in the bush, warning me of a wedding with a woman who wore big boots to walk through the marsh and bang the white bird from the sky.

"You don't like people very much, do you?" she stated.

"Hunh?"

"Because you don't pay any attention to them when they talk to you."

"I don't?" I wondered, not quite paying attention.

"Actually you remind me of a cigar-store Indian," she added, examining me with a smile like an insect under glass.

"Right," I added to the broth, and you can depend on it dear, and digest it in small quantities, then die with me in dignity forgotten in foreign lands. Only when you arrive to replace me, be awfully sure the plastic robot is sapient, cold, pedantic, and if possible a coward. Because I will never be loved, as I am cunning and calculated to mystify, no, not until you pop the reinforced glass of my bulletproof showcase.

"What you need, Oliver, is a mate."

I think she said that too, though by now I had stopped listening to the tall half-Indian, but mercilessly American, red-head, and it merely wounded like maudlin truths far in the dying drunken night at Southampton. So potentially fierce, so probably possible, so remote at a remove. And yet in spite of its ennui, fiercely wanting her freckled rounded ass, and to teach her that to love is to share, and above all bung her tongue!

I was falling in love with Truth. And that was bad, because

this night she was Truth. Though if she had been the sun itself I think I would have embraced it as well and pressed the boiling liquid down the yellow brick road into my walled world of dadaist desire and muted enchantment. And eventually into that aperture protecting my soul. Told her too. I want you. Tiptoeing through the statues and fountains on the lawn in my black silk socks. Sense other than common telling me somebody in the bushes was pointing a blunderbuss at my spine but I couldn't because once you laugh. It's hard to stop.

And then you ran under the heavy-duty sprinkler and your hair emptied onto your dress and, stumbling, you fell into a flowerbed, luring the hefty caribou and said, "Ow! my back hurts!" Removing the tiny gnarled branch from under your strong spine, and slyly winking at the elf, prepared like a moth of ice to plunge into the fire and pierce you purple, I lay my weary weight on your titties and faintly detecting, for a finale, a rifle blast traveling up my ass like a young second lieutenant I liked who got dusted in the Vietnam War. Watching his Iowa eyes closing slowly and forever. Peekaboo, Pocahontas, don't you realize? This is simply not done. To have sex with more than one. Of the six senses. And in the bushes too? Especially in Southampton, where one, if one must, must have sex alone. Palm of the hand, bird in the bush. Though I gather waging war is acceptable, especially in distant lands killing foreign skins in the name of money, but fuckers beware, o Isobel! Identifying it merely as a tumble in the prenuptial hay and by the way, I am available, reminding me once more. That sex tells me I'm alive, something which I too easily forget, o jeesus that I *am* a human being. And not just a rich man. Who thinks sex is simply salt splashed on a pheasant's wing, just a taste, you know, under glass. Though I am never bored. In fact I enjoy it more than once each day. Ho hum. Why do I tell you these things? If it doesn't really matter and we're going to do it anyway? I wonder why? I do these things. Fall for your hay. Then walk down the aisle into your church with all your friends and family wishing us well because it isn't them. I wonder why it is. I do these things.

ONCE MARRIED, THE years went swiftly by with Isobel and, as often the wont of the rich, I don't really remember much except that Tara was born, my baby, the most beautiful thing I have ever known or achieved. It seemed from the first we were destined for each other. Tall like her mother, with flaming brilliant black raven hair, even when little she would tap me on the knee and, winking an eye, would exclaim in her cadenced little-baby talk, "We must always live dangerously, Papa." The very mention of her name brightens these pages which now I write with aging fingers and, speaking simply of her, my pen could fill a volume.

One starry summer night we took the raft out on the Atlantic, off Southampton, and we lay there, the two of us, the water lapping at our sides, giggling at the z-shaped stars and talking about most everything as the hours climbed past, and then she asked, "Papa, tell me a story of the sea. Tell me about the Pacific. About when you were young and Mommy said you did so many dangerous things." Silly girl, I still am young. And I tried to tell her what the Pacific was like—demonic and brooding and so very vast, but she giggled and pressed her small arm over my forehead, clumsily running her hand through my hair and said, "Oh Papa, you're so funny when you're serious." Not knowing how serious I was, or how very important you were to me and how simple life had suddenly become and that as far as I was concerned, you were at the center of it. It is a fool who rejoiceth not in the day of his prosperity. What a fool I was not to know this when young.

She so much liked that passage from Ecclesiastes which went, "Rejoice in thy youth . . . and walk in the ways of thy heart and in the sight of thine eyes, knowing that in all these things, God will bring thee into judgment,"—all of which you achieved, my daughter, unashamed to walk with beggars or kings—"and remember now thy Creator in the days of thy youth, while the evil days come not, nor the years draw nigh, when thou shalt say, I have no pleasure in them."

While the evil days come not, nor the years draw nigh. And that night off Southampton, the sky suddenly crackled with thunder and poured down torrents of rain, rattling up against the makeshift tent we threw over our heads, as we sought land, yet feared the worst, and you held me close in your fear and murmured, "Why if God is God, does he make rain and thunder and snakes?" And I whispered, "So that they might be, my sweet, and live and die like us and nothing more. These are but the outskirts of his ways, and how small a whisper do we hear of them." She shuddered because she couldn't quite understand and the thunder roared and she clasped me closer, fear zigzagging down her innocent face, and she did not yet understand that faith is little more than imagination, and that Beauty is as close to anything eternal we'll ever have. Yet she believed in me, my daughter, and thus through me, in the Lord. I taught her how to pray that night, and like a little monkey she imitated me. The Lord's Prayer first, which is the most wonderful of all, then David's Twenty-third Psalm, which I loved, and after that, a gentle little prayer I never forgot, which I taught myself in a moment of trying to relieve my suffering, and which began "O Lord, *surprise me.*"

These words somehow meant a great deal to me, and Tara too liked this prayer best of all. And that night she prayed as she had never prayed before. As our raft rocked back and forth in the blinding rain and Death seemed so close.

"Papa!" she shivered, "do you remember what you said— 'ask and ye shall receive, pray and I tell you, whatever you ask in prayer, believe that you will receive it, and you will' . . .

"Can I pray now, Papa?"

"Yes, I remember," I lied. "Of course you can, and whatever you ask, you shall get." If I was wrong, did it really matter anymore? Only if I was right.

Thus she prayed that night. And it kept her mind from the raging fear all around. I worked the engine as best I could, finally with great luck maneuvering the raft back to the beach after two hours of terrifying storm. And when her toes touched the sand, running up the beach to safety, she said nothing but courageously preserved the silence. Because she had learned the first lesson taught by the sea. Starting with the humility of fear. We must learn to expect the silence of adversity now, my daughter, but not to seek it. Not to talk of it. Not to suffer. But only to feel. Because to feel is to suffer.

When the Third War of the twentieth century began in the 1990s, the American Government, thinking I was secretly supplying the Soviets, mercilessly hounded me into taking great risks with my shipping in order to attest my allegiance to a plutocracy I was fast growing to dislike. In one brutal year my business was almost totally ruined, ship after ship blown up or torpedoed and invaluable friends as well as memories destroyed. I began to ride the ships myself to change their luck. Long trips to the Orient and to the Northern Independent Republics of the Soviet Union that would separate me from Tara and Isobel for six and seven cold months and sometimes more, during which time I could never rest in peace, thinking of them as hostages in an unfriendly land. I finally made provision for them to come away to Switzerland, but Isobel balked saying it was too dangerous as Switzerland could be invaded at any moment. Always worried by things unseen, she revealed my plan to her rich and scheming father who had never accepted me as a fellow *nouveau riche,* and he in turn told the Government, and it was then I began seeing American spies wherever I set foot; the strain, combined with wartime conditions, was intolerable, and I cursed the day I had first met with my wealth. I thought then anything at all would be better than the position I found myself in!

So I thought until a night in June of 1995 when we were sailing from Rio de Janeiro to Tripoli with a cargo of arms and supplies and a secret cache of plutonium. We were off the coast of the old Spanish Morocco and it was near midnight when, obsessed with a premonition, I rose from sleep and took a turn on deck. Just then, in a flaming ball of hell, my ship the *Tara,* the flagship of my fleet, exploded and within seconds sank in a molten debris to the bottom of the sea. Every man was killed but me. O don't ask me why or how miracles are made, they're made in madness. I'm no prophet with a premonition. I fear of knowing.

I spent twenty-two days at sea on a raft. I ate sawfish and sea fowl and I drank rainwater and survived to face the sabbath sun that first vexed my brain. Day from day, hour by hour, trying to remember and yet impelled toward thoughts of icy lakes where I had swum in Vermont and Switzerland. Thinking now by night only because I feared sleep and the fears of the dark. The fear of time, chronophobia, and the kidneys; there's never been an account written yet that I know of brute survival, and now I know why.

Ideas break themselves off in revulsion to each other and there is no longer such invention as sequence, but only scratching squeezing sighs and you find yourself so bored with living, giggling when your mind goes blank, as it does for long periods of time during the daylight, and even the music in your breast is stolen from you by the insipid sun which suddenly seems to ripple with waves of gold opening to disclose a Christ crucified, as large as a tarantula spread-eagled in the heavens, it fades, the buzz besetting your ears and a dream dredged from the dynamite of the mind, of a face scarred with fire, emerging beneath a pink parasol from the primeval jungle, you fall to the knees of the water-washed raft and pray to creation, ''O Lord, *surprise me, surprise me!*''

Do you too have a numbness at the center of your brain? Do you too batten on the howling waste waiting to engulf the rest of you? At sea you do. Have you ever talked to the sea? Has it never sighed back again? Have you never prayed to the sun? In a speech that marches to the winds? No, few ever have. So please don't speak to me of guilt and right and wrong when it's as simple as memory, and Memory is right and Forgetfulness is wrong, as you slip imperceptibly, insensibly, away from memory into a chasm of action reaction, and you wake up one day and realize that jeesus, I have done murder. Unto thyself. It is truly as the Bible says, ''Unto him who hath shall more be given and from him that hath not, even that which he hath shall be taken away.''

When the cutter found me after twenty-two days, they told me I had gnawed into my wrist and was sucking my blood, and had passed out and was more dead than alive. And they wondered how it was. That I was still alive. I tried to tell them that I was really dead. But they wouldn't believe me.

They took me back to Rio on a tropic night in July of '95,

licking and crackling with a violent red sky and blue thunder scratching the horizon. I wasn't the same anymore, and in my throat there was a motley pink foam and my body was crisped black by the sun. I wanted to be a father again, and Tara was in Paris playing the piano for a Polishman she claimed to love, and I was young again and headed for China. Only I lay there, in the rescue ship, terrified of what I had become, the lilies dancing along my veins, the cry of fear upon me, breathing desertion yet rationally prophesying that if I should flee I would never again be able to look upon myself or my daughter. Everything I had, I had to cast like bread upon the waters, O glorious unsacred freedom!

So I ran. For my life, my heart! I ran!

I ran through the streets of Rio and near dawn, on the outskirts, fell upon a woman's footprints in the sand by the sea, and watching them, slept like light foam by the waves. When she woke me and said I had been crying in my sleep, dreaming of my youth and my grandmother's ghost accompanying me through the streets of Paris, and then dreamt I was weeping (how strange to weep in a dream), I noticed her eyes and her bare feet and knew it was in her footprint that I had slept. She came to me there on the beach, bare-breasted, and gave them over to me to kiss. For nothing, and for the few years we lived together, I never passed a month without once weeping in my sleep, and each time like the moon, she was there. Her name was, ironically, Isobella as well, and with her I had two children whose names I cannot reveal. She never once expressed a desire to speak English, and together we were as poor as birds, yet I nursed my health back, and set to work to make another, better way of life.

I must hurry along now, the end approaches. And it all went so fast with her. First my memory returned, slowly at first, but by the Third World War's end, it was an integrity again, and I knew I still had another race in the north. Strange that I didn't return right then to Tara and Isobel. But worked harder than I had ever worked before. I learned Portuguese and became half owner with a Russian ex-officer in a large nut and rubber farm north of the Amazon River and east of the Branca. From sunrise to sunset, I toiled in the fields of my plantation like any native worker, painfully learning the just truths that the land holds. Backbreak, harvestal heartache, pestiferous disease, as indwelt as the fish in their seas, the passing infirmity, what is its suffering when measured next to the light God holds out for us to *see* but goes unseen? Ask Ahab.

When I wasn't working the land, I was prospecting in the mountains to the northwest. For three successive years I mounted expeditions with my partner until one inexpressible day in October 1997, deep in a quarry in the mountains near Los Chiquandos, something suddenly glistened in the dark and I thought I was at sea again and had seen the same star. I shivered and that night came down with a strange fever where I thought myself drifting on a raft off Algeria again. We stayed up in the mountains into the next year, mining the large quantities of gold we found with God-helped ease. I sensed this life in Brazil was over now and that the gold was a denouement to a bizarre dream begun on the raft, and if I stayed I feared the fever would kill me in the end.

But it was another year before I could go back, addiction being sister to my veins, and in that time my partner suddenly took sick and died, in the mountains mocked and at the end, the illusiveness of it all. He died writhing with maggots in his hair and ears, and I closed the mines and pulled up and left. I explained to my children that I had another family. But to Isobella the tears would come after, never shown, never expressed, but felt so deeply I knew that next to Tara and my mother, she was the only woman I would ever deeply love and be loved in equal if not greater measure. But even love cannot hold the march of the warrior ants. I don't know, in hindsight, if I was ever fair to my brown-skinned family, but who has the luxury always to be fair?

From Brazil I returned to New York on a rainy night in March 1999, and walked through streets growing wet, looking at the other million passengers expecting to recognize a face or two, or perhaps be recognized. But here was a race of strangers, as New York always is, its revolving cycles of worker bees destined to be replaced or die. I drove down that night to the Island, to Southampton, to see Isobel, who happened to be alone, and visibly whitened when she saw my wet, gray ghost come walking through the French windows overlooking the lawn. I said, yes it's me, what could you expect, having married me in the first place on that nutty night not far from here? Some twenty years ago. Where's Tara? And learned she was in Switzerland, married not to the Polishman after all, but to an Englishman of some shame and wealth, dodging taxes in havens abroad, belonging to an unworking class of men whilst my daughter wrote recipes for food books and played pianos and wove her tapestries in meet adoration to her household gods. And that she thought I had been a dream which had passed through her youth. But then I studied her picture and knew that she would understand why I died, because she was a level-headed little girl and once she used to live dangerously, or does she still? I never told Isobel about what happened in Brazil. I changed my identity there, and to this day it remains a dying secret.

After that, I lived mostly in Europe semi-anonymously, while Isobel preferred the life she had in America, promoting painters and traveling to Europe in the summers. In my energetic moments, which came fewer and far between, I worked at what was left of the shipping company which was mostly Isobel's now. I sold off the Brazilian estates and goldmines for far less than they were worth and, giving a fair share to Isobella and my children, with the proceeds bought, under an assumed name, a rubber farm in Malaysia, which marked the first time I'd been East since my early youth. There it was I took another wife, a dark yellow one, and had another, my last child, but that is another story and not for telling, because in the end it was a similar life and its true significance belongs to the East.

Tara had remarried after the disastrous drinking of her English husband who, on occasion she told me, had beaten her, her first such experience of the wretchedness of this life. Her new love was an Austrian with a "von" in his name, and though I claim not to be a snob, what father is it who doesn't express innocent pride at the concept of royalty in the genes? The Count, contrary to all my aged expectations, was a generous young man, an international banker, handsome and spirited of manner, who took time to share his joy with his aging father-in-law, to whom he owed nothing, sometimes skiing, with Tara and me, the highest mountains in the Alps, at the tops of which we would grow very giddy on schnapps, especially when the descent was icy and required a great deal of courage. Warm blood was always a temporary remedy, and heroes like the Count, I have come to know, have cold golden liquids running through their veins.

At the millennium, a terrible thing happened when Isobel, dramatic to her core and always subject to apocalyptic moods, killed herself with sleeping pills in California. I flew to her funeral alone because Tara didn't want to come, and to my surprise discovered that my half-Indian wife had long been living

with a gambler named Frank, and he was there too at the grave-
yard, a big handsome confident man, just what Isobel, in her
secret self, really wanted and never had with me. I later heard
he locked her up for weeks at a time in motel rooms on the
West Coast and in Nevada, and would sometimes thrash her,
and she'd love him more, dying in the end from an addicted
heart, because she knew he would never love her. In a way I
was happy for Isobel; with me she had never been real, and
after the marriage, and especially Tara's birth, she had left me
in spirit. Now at last she'd fallen in love, and that too was
painful to me, but in spite of her tormented life she had died
for something; however silly, it was for reasons of the heart,
which is pure in its ferocity. I think perhaps the key to life is
character and the key to character is the ability to reject; until
your ball of character rolls upward and upward and becomes so
strong and pure that at last you have the strength to reject
everything. Including life.

Her sister, unfortunately, was at the funeral, and recognized
me in spite of the sunglasses I was wearing. She cried, "You
asshole, you adulterer, you murdered her! You killed her, it
was *you* pulled the trigger! You kill what you touch, mister!"
She shrieked, as the priest of the church, to which Isobel never
went, tried to calm her and the crowd gasped and turned all
their eyes upon me, and Frank leaned over and whispered to a
burly associate. I crept away, quickly, and that night flew
straight back to Europe, never to return to America again.

From Munich, where I now kept my offices, I could easily
travel to Tara's ancestral home outside Salzburg. She was expecting now with the Count, and I would drive down Thursday
afternoons with my driver and come back early Monday. The
weekends were long and beautiful there, and when my first
grandchild, Jasmine, was born in the spring, I must've looked

an old fool dawdling about the estate, jumping at the thinnest excuse for staying the week, telling her ghost stories that made her shiver, sending her running crying to her mama who chastised me for frightening her.

But as she grew older, like her mother before her, she wanted more and more, and begged me for the stories of Orpheus' head floating in the sea, of Zeus who swallowed the heart of Zagreus, reborn of Semele, of man risen from his Titan ashes, of Mama Dyambo along the Red River banks of the Senegal, in 1732 a boat, painted glorious white, that up the Red River swam, they pointed their Aethiopian fingers and danced screaming: Mama Dyambo, Mama Dyambo—mamadyambo! in evil blessed, in goodness swallowed, and then in the widowed haunches of late afternoon when I would lie prostrate on my belly on a cold floor with my granddaughter, the soul thirsty for truth and weary of religion, I would talk to her, when she was old enough, of how God, if He is there, must be approached over the course of a lifetime. That we grow into him, that we learn year by year and there is no other way than through the evolutions performed by time and fear. Isobel used to say weak people needed God. Was I weak when I was first deflowered by the concupiscence of my curiosity? Is there no room for the ugly unquenchable thirst of the soul? I first discovered fear not on the raft off North Africa, but as a child, when my mother promised me I would never die. The inner certitude of faith—O child, have you seen the infinity of this existence? Have you suffered through vast complexity and the cluttered coevality of thought, and how is it your poor grandfather needs recourse to something like faith and love and all the shadowed attributes of religion now that he is old? Who am I? I know not.

With these growing attentions to my granddaughter, my old

life withered away, my businesses failed, Isobella took sick and died in Brazil, and my children with her moved on to ordinary lives. And finally the Count, Tara, Jasmine and I took a trip to the French Riviera, and, like a mad youth, I went dancing and carrying on to all hours of the morning with the voluptuous moviestar of the moment; she called me "Papa" and whispered in my ear drunkenly, "I want you to come and see me in Paris," which caused me to shed an inner tear in my wine cup because no longer could I go, on that journey. It was my son-in-law, the fourteenth Count of the House of Humbershalt, who took me aside, and with an aristocrat's refinement said, "We're all so fond of you Grandpa . . . but you understand we're young, we must live our own lives . . . and Tara, with the child you know, sometimes she grows nervous with all this talk of death and horror stories and God, and . . . she wants to be a mother, you understand I think, Grandpa? . . . "

He went on, my heart against my own wishes breaking that my own daughter could not tell me herself anymore; what had changed between us? What goes on changing between people through time, why do they abandon each other, or at the least, not tolerate each other anymore? God, life is so deceitful! Little do we know when young how endlessly *real* it becomes, how mothers and fathers age and wrinkle in front of each other and die. All falls away. Why not the night and lifespan of the butterfly, the moth, the winged chariots of the insect gods? I remembered my youth in France, back in the ancient Fifties. O families were families in those days! Sprawling luncheons at Soissons and far-ranging relatives of three and four generations married in churches and long lines of tiny tots walking behind the long bridal gowns down the aisles. *Les Grandes Tantes,* whose names you could never remember, introduced you from another century. Musty kisses and secret chocolates and hand-laced handkerchiefs heaving in sun-denied bosoms. But at least to know your children would never quit your side! And with the ascending years and the evolutions performed by time, to teach them to know, to read the great books with clarity and faith, and to know God. Or is that too just a lie of my own mind seeking better pasture?

After the talk in France, I didn't go to the Estate much anymore. And Tara said, "Why don't you come more often Papa, like you used to? Jasmine misses you so much."

"No, my little springdrop," I replied, "I have much business to do now, especially in the East." And to the East I went that winter alone, without my Asian wife and child who had long since migrated elsewhere, watching the dawns come up over Malaysia and the memories started pouring in again. Hello how are you my little hordes, and I was young and fresh with limbs of iron again. In seas of sun and other sunless seas. Have you ever seen the Mekong up in Laos at break of day in the rainy season? When the waters return to flood the valley, as if it were the Bible and time had never flown?

I have. . . .

14. FINAL THINGS

A SMALL MEXICAN hotel room. Overlooking a pretty little alley somewhere in Guadalajara. The dogs bark and the sun forever shines. My money is gone. The desire to travel further exhausted, yet I am comfortable. The hours and days go by. I never go out. I write. . . .

It was a slow and lingering death in the madhouses of the East, but the rhythms kept calling. I bypassed the rainbow and was writing of things which no one soul could possibly be interested in, and of which I, reading, am ashamed and could put far away from me. I was too exhaustive, too mystic, too irrelevant. I took to making illegible notes that began to make less and less sense in the margins of obscure books. I had strangely wonderful ideas about the repatriation of souls through the cryscumination of time. I made up my own words to fit my system of metempsychosis- *-intansification* I called it; I understood time as a crystallization of previous time, and many things you will find with my drawings of history and space and time in my last notebook. It's a mysterious muscled missymbolic realm where every step is dangerous, and as you read you will find it difficult to breathe. I sense that the charity of many will grow cold, the scorpion will sting the egg and in the ear of closets, the ravenfowl will devour the occult. It is our sole fate that passion must be vanquished, and whether by intellect or fate, it'll explain itself away and all I'll have left are words . . . silly jingles like the "penguined sea of odysseys," yes it was a slow death in the madhouses but the rhythms kept calling and neither sex nor God nor art could balm the agonizing dissolution of my mind. But I waited. Why? Playing chess with jeesus yet, blue-eyed boy, he was the only one left now; because I had poked my head beyond good and evil, where, I tell you, lies an uncharted realm. Past God?

You see if one were a saint and did see God, he would not tell; only the fool would rush in where the addled angel fears to tread. Yes, when I too was a child, I thought I saw God, but it wasn't really, it was His likeness. To know God by any created likeness is not to know the essence of God, and since I neither wanted to be a saint or a fool, I find it convenient simply to say I forgot what He looks like when He comes to me, as He still does in the childish image of my youth. O it's not so difficult as you think to see God and live, in fact I came to pity Him for in reality He has no control whatever over mankind. None.

Only Nature, and we are not part of Nature.

By the way, have you ever seen God?

I have.

At dawn, often, in my dreams. The fingers of the dawn they weep. Sweeping up over the purple horizon. I am awake. Staring flatfaced into the pond, who is that handsome figure there? Touch him, Oliver. . . .

It is . . . my God . . . it *is* God!

The man with the black beard. "Thump . . . thump." I hear his footsteps yet. "I am Who I am!" Lanklean curls. Ovoiding little children by means of ellipsoidal madonnas that strangle infant children with a nipple stuffed down their flaming gullets. No more! No more! Profane profane! My profile in the Seine. Like trying to beat myself at chess, o hurry, hurry, a mind is an infinitive thing, forever swiveling about to catch me doing it, doing the . . . I saw him!

He looked like a wrathful beast. He looked like a king from a playing card. Emerging from the mists of metempsychosis. Yes. Leaping up, like winter spring ardor, to fire sodden coals of failed creativity, the patience and passion that live in the horrifying alembic of seven thousand years, perpetual palingenesis, God, for, list list, I tell you God is not such a mighty horrifying or hard thing to see! (Or was it accidental Satan?) I trembled reverently, my imagination unpracticed, my utter absence of creativity or tenor o so evident, pray I tell you pray— *Boom! Boom!*—too late! (If only the windows had not been sealed from within from without!)

I wished him gone.

Boom Thump!

I knew him not, I know not God! The sting of death they say is sin—baby sin, fortuitously mine from my first dream, from my first rhyme, o then pray, pray to pray and then in spite to forgive myself, Oliver Oliver. I was conceived by my Father, born of my Mother, suffered under both, was crucified dead and buried. The eighteenth year I rose again from the dead, and ascended unto heaven and sitteth on the right hand of God the Father Fiction, from whence I shall come to judge both my Mother and my Father, amen, o wicked wicked child boy! Vague shallow philosophies of a wayward footloose fool who erraticyet rose to the heights of moral honor, o for olympic companionship! o for some confidence with which to fill the unfillable thing they call . . . "Oliver Oliver," He called.

I heard you not! stop, say no more! or I shall die when You tell me I have seen you. For this I know, "Oliver Oliver . . ."

. . . that ye shall inherit the earth! Thump, thump! and then He was gone . . . or was he, Satan? But alas, the birth of faith followed, faith and face, for have I not functioned on, samefaced everyday forever, believing, having to believe in as simple a thing as divine good, divine aid, all the divinities my fear urges me to snatch at, at any time, at any space.

I came thundering downward, how shall I function on, miracle of miracles, I felt suddenly sprung from the Holy Ghost loins of the Virgin Mary, made flesh in a ball of fire that had come to cleanse the Earth, and turn blood to water! For thus . . . but enough's enough, that was all long ago, watery and weak, when I was young and it was all so beautiful to think of puff adders who mate in insunsilent shadows and winter figures with long hair at the bottom of the sea, and Satanic silences perched in the air. The drip drop of tedium's sweat, like the movies, a forgetive imago, in black and white and chevied with chiaroscuro, and in the zoo it takes two days to say Yes, o Yes, how well I remember when from the French garden where He was walking He was calling as He was walking, "Oliver Oliver," and the spring vorvivid wind that was blowing over the flower beds and into the apricot trees. And from the upper story I leaned out and listened. Listened to His words which blew over the flower beds. And whooshed into the apricot trees. Whooooo. . . .

Yes, I envisage a great book in my mind. It would be a book of poetry, a book without sequence, a book unencumbered by the additive form, it would grow from itself, it would conceive a freedom no longer conceivable, a freedom of the womb, a salvation in deepening depth, a book that would, as it goes forward, also go backward, a book that as it swallows would be swallowed, a book that grows and a book that diminishes, until it is nothing but a single piece of paper—of the most perfect poetry this world has ever seen. A writer should no longer be a human being. He should by virtue of his diminishing effort be free, as free as the bowels that grumble beneath the earth's crust. He should live both in Heaven and Hell every moment of the day. He is beyond us.

So that, as the years pass, climbing upward as always, he would exchange the currency of the written word for the ether of the musical sound. Idealistically then I set for myself the final goal of "composer." Therein only lies the monstrosity of genius. Neither additive nor subtractive, divisible, multipliable, sequential, reasonable.

And in many centuries from now, when the futurians will archeologize the ageold crusts of the earth, they will discover a bronzed likeness of a human being from the twentieth century, and they will marvel at this figurepiece, and they will hang it in their lighted museums for all the population to see. They will flock about it, and they will celebrate it, and they will never again commit it to earth.

And it will be me.

My egotism was such that everything I saw for the first time I incorporated into my mind and owned because of the pure fact that I had wondered and marveled when I first saw it. The wonderment regarding other things bred the love of self. I even prognosticated an imperfect new liquid sun of decomposite language, lo a new age, an era begun!

. . . that is until I knew enough to know better, until I was swallowed in the immense indifference of loneliness and sadness and buried in the blind anger of hate, such hate, hates of doctrines sought and shriven—the battle between the Platonic concepts of Fixed Oneness and the Aristotelian concept of Becoming. And fierce dreams of my father in the great howling wastes of Hell, his earthly peccancies magnified a thousand times to repent for what one repentance on earth would have sufficed.

He shall surely return and search out Jerusalem with candles, poking his grayed locks through the crust of the earth, eyes above sea level like some great blowfish wheezing, "See where you have put me, in Hell Hell! In Hell do us part, by wisdom and by wealth, by richer by poorer, by fact by fantasy, by memory by desire, by hate by love, I'm here where you have sent me, creature of the deep relegated to dooms deep to man. Jungle creature of the green eyes, awake!" Thus I pitied my father's belated soul, his exigent wounds that bleed over the rainbow of a thousand years until, faced with his example, I became horrified by my very own hate.

We who travel in angry subways, who never knew of Zarathustra and Mithras, the mysteries at Eleusis or the oracle at Delphi, what is it that we have never seen that others before us have?—the wild Bacchae yells of the Greek night, Demeter and Dionysos, cathedral vaults burning with peasant prayers, the horror, the true horror implicit in religion. O Youth! its aged ways foregone foregoing, when young, in the Aethiopian gloom, in the shaded lice of memory, sing! cantabile and canorous, sing out! that once I stood on Atlantic shore and bathed my sandals at murky dusk beneath the sea-washed throne. That on frigid frontiers my armies roamed. That once I kissed the hand of Alice in Wonderland and bade my time in the jigging praises of Afjanistan. Of this and this more too: of Arabia could I sing, winds sought and shriven in the sapphire waters off Moorish Spain, or in muddy Flanders Field we died a million deaths of gas, and of the wheat that tumbled in the wind with the crows across the Russian steppes beneath the onrushing hooves of my Mongol band, all that when the Christ was long distant and light so far ahead, Buddha sat in celestial grove and Becket lay expiring on church steps bedaubed in reechy blood, behold the orphic world! *ecce signum!*

In the North there is the Nothing and toward the South the Void, and on it God hangs the invisible mantle they call the World. And in this abyss we laugh as we look across in boredom, because boredom is a sunset seen too long, boredom is exposition, boredom is basic, boredom is hell and hope is an abyss, drip . . . drop, the percussive drop of water, slipping on sound, it is wet in my shell, in my shallow shell it is wet yes, yet . . . to feel is to feel with an indiscriminate receptivity raddled with yearning, plaited with the long hollowness of time, wherein days melt into years and lightyears liquidate years, and through the lungs ghosts sing, yielding the fodder into air, air all about air, fixed and silent, long silences inhabit these longitudes, the dripdrop of air in my hear, in the air perched. Yes is the basic word in the language, it derives from the Hebrew and means amen but what amen may mean, that I know not, in my long suicide silences, where I stare, stare at air, amazed by such things as noise and leaky faucets . . . drip . . . drop. There is never thunder, just lightning—listen . . . drip . . . drop . . . o I am old old, indescribably old as if a puckered skin were stretched taut over my soul, a soul that can no longer be considered in the category of Socrates or an angel, old with thinking, too much thinking, old with the guilt of not being guilty, self-consciously old, old with the guilt of incoherence. All pertains in an ease of interrelationship, all winds itself out in one web and thus sacrifices its soul to its sanity. I am a student of simultaneity and I have discovered that complexity in degree is the highest level man can reach; it's ironic then that fierce complexity is the nurse of madness. O what distinguishes it, faith and despair being conjoined, being of the appetite, they urge one another on deeper and deeper into immutable sin, until when in the very pit, despair surfeited, and faith called upon to perform its most mighty labor, cries no more! and by reason of long separation from grace that is divine, disappears!

O the world is sorrow, nothing more, and in its void bosom I shall play the practice of my heart. Heart: art: rt : t. Done, die, death. So cuickly cuickly done. In the flicker of a tongue.

We each have our own ladder to climb; some, the innocent, cease their labors at an early stage. Others push on, sweating puffing, steaming with the damp. As we go, more stop and look below and contentedly sigh; they do not bother to look above and see the next step. They never really really know that others are still climbing; they can see nowhere but below. The rest, devoted and involved in something far more final than an innocent illusion, push on, a slower step succeeding a slower step, realizing with a forbiddingly rigid sense of reality that once the coil is shuffled they might be painfully, mortally wrong. Rebellious yet brave, faced with the prospect of plumbing the deep, they do not shrink back in fear or complacency. No, we go up and up, we try. We try hard and silently, in a dark manner. And yet the higher we climb, the more we seem to descend, as if unto a well, casting off skin after skin, reaching to the fingertips. But though we seem to descend, tedium yet reminds us there is one more step leading upward. And then again downward. Keep going into it, my fellow traveler, and you will never stop—going up and going down, higher and higher and deeper and deeper until you'll achieve the only thing you'll ever achieve—the perfect finality of utter madness! Leading you with halter about your neck to a despairing doom. Made up of normal people with healthy red faces and bills to pay who, as they do with insane people, will come and knock on your shell as if you were a turtle, and they will take you away, consider you not one of them, unfit for them, gone awry, and then, in the final and blackest degradation, they will take *care* of you, gentle care. . . .

Yet if Christ Himself walked through these Mexican doors, what then? He would seat himself, would proceed by docile methods to investigate me, would care for me, wipe my tears away, even love me, and above all would understand me and make it obvious, and then, bidding me goodbye, would walk out the door. And yet I don't honestly believe that I would try to stop Him, much less follow Him, or in any way prolong the fact of His existence in my life. I'm that way. I travel alone and I am so blind that I am not able nor willing to differentiate between people, for they are all the same to me, creatures to be met, interrogated, and left behind. I am a lodestone without polarity, the mathematician who has reasoned out the odds and decided against. There is a forever hopeless resignation in my attitude of arriving alone, of leaving alone. And God I swear there are times, there are times it's as if I were literally *starving*. A want of something in my life. The things which make the world go round, notional as they may be. It seems: all the meanings of life have been honed down to an inescapable in-eluctable implacable inexpugnable imprecise factor—inanition—One. And there are those times when in actuality all my quin-tessence could crumple to the floor for want of ornament, for style, for method. There is only unspecified substance and, I fear, that is not much of a specific . . . a driving drizzle in the soul. Empty streets. Anaesthesia. Thinking as I pounce from street corner to street corner, thinking, there's always one more thought nonetheless. Nonetheless, isn't there? Train of thought on the next corner. On the last corner. Inflexions of irony. Forgive me. I pass. I go. I passed it by. What was it? You search, you fail, you wish perfection in the mind, you are close, closer, yesterday but one, tomorrow but one, so close you are almost there (tomorrow!) but it collapses and where are you? Thinking, grimly thinking. On and on, through the threnody of streets, the rectification of rain.

To see a lightscape through the I. Is to see a note of lightning. To acupuncture facade. Is to see the genesis and the genius. For awhile, anyway. And then, *what?*

Our mind's prescience is its own nemesis; we realize, in anticipation, every possible course through which life can proceed, and therefore, through the pitiless employment of the senses, we arrive at a state of skeptical disassociation, at times romantic in essence, from everything envisaged in the mind. It has always gratified our civilized sense of work with the mind— man, in his mind, can be swimming in several different streams, of several different crosscurrents. In the same way then, working from a mind within a mind—disassociation—appeals to our instincts to an even greater degree. But the cost of this pleasure is that presently the supermind, fearing the trappings of risk and failure, retires to lie doggo in this new capsule—a now hydroponic mind satisfied with the *déjà vu*, the *aperçu*, the sketch, the detail, the survey, the fleeting impression, like a gull skimming the surface seeking after the gleam characteristic of fish—antipathetic to the deeper disappointments of detail. The acquisition of character is the acquiescence in stupidity. The mind now becomes frightened of true despair because the true moment of despair is a time of heightened uncertainty, and certainty is the only joyous feeling we can possess; despair itself is a horrible moment, it is a moment pregnant with the action of life, there is no pleasure in it, there is only pleasure in the knowledge of despair, and it is this to which our supermind has grown accustomed. Thus, no longer can it feel true frustration or real despair. It is as the parable says, "they bury their one talent in the security of remorse," in the security of knowledge. And this is iniquitous. For thinking itself immune, the disassociate falls prey to his own mind; thought is a hungry animal, and as the animal's unslaked hunger is heightened by the thought of food, so too is thought hungered by the thought of its own want; yet if that mind is intelligent enough to be disassociated, sensitive enough, it will naturally refrain from devouring that which lies about it in the material world; and in like manner it will be sufficiently omniscient so as to avoid being devoured by another mind. And so, in fine, with great remorse, it will curl in and eat its own self. Thus it is our sole fate that passion must be vanquished. Despair is a creature of superabundant imagination and little creativity. It is a growling dog forcing a frightened victim off a cliff. It doesn't even have to use its own teeth.

Let us go then you and I when the evening is spread against the sky, let us go together, for we shall go by the terms of the illusion because one way or the other, iron fist or velvet glove, *bongré malgré*, be we innocent or nocent or neither, we finish immersed in this life, competing at last, in outrageous perfidy, against one another. The villain is life. She sets us upon one another's throats. And we perforce comply. What wild dog is first tamed to the master's whip? What wild dog is never mocked? That wild dog, in the inexorable scheme of things, must die. Electric philosopher with the courage to seek the undiscovered country, and with great courage kissing the rest of us *au revoir*, says "no more!"

This is suicide, this the judo in my soul. An anthropology of blows. Out on the ocean where it is green and desolate and cold, and the big waves come up out of the emotion. Seagreen blue water. Thrashing down upon my skull as I dip my face inward and float my starved eyes on the wide window of water. Now lulling these eyesockets to wide-eyed sleep, strange sample

of the sea, transfusing the spark of ingenuity, there is no ingenuity in the deep, is there? nothing but what Hemingway saw
when he felt his hair splatter on an ioway floor. I too toasted
the stars and yet, a shotgun aimed at my mindfactorfunction, I
wonder: what of the men who go out to sea and spear the big
fish . . .

   . . . and fail to return?

What sharks are poised between here and there, what fish
lie lonely under the waves, their piranha teeth rising up from
soils of sea? I trust the water to wash me kindly, tumble me
through its foamish spine stretched by the Pacific moon—a
druid's egg, its shadow of the soul shimmering with hysteria.

A figure recalled. Jumping into the cold ocean. Lighted
laughter of insanity lit. Sundered by the wealth of fire. My
eyelids are fluttering shut in the Mexican sun. The wealth of
silence. The wealth of fire moving toward me as in a dream,
as when I sat at the piano in my youth, I would really be sitting
on the ceiling, my neck forever arching backward, attempting
to read this lentiginous music. The butcher's hands, shivering
in my sleep dysfunctioned, holding crumpled paper parcels running with pastense animal blood, and male bodies that smell
thick on light thrilling feet . . . a penance perhaps, is dizziness.
Sin by sin, is there no end to sin, no end to absurdity?

I think perhaps the greatest silence in the world is that of
the deep, beneath the water, where with the candles, prismatic
slow-revolving frames of renitent motion turn on their axles,
thauming with silver fish and green mirrors that splinter and
gleam. In the deep, what sounds? Longdrawn piercing phosphor
looks, elicited from skulls buried in ancient submarines, blow
wind blow, dark and stern, passing swiftly through the night.
From here to where: does this wind blow? Like the beat of a
hoof on a cobble. Like that of a noon on a face.

I cannot remember anymore, nor ponder the question. Who can at one sitting delve the depths in parentheses, who? Not Hamlet, a treacherous thing the sea, its smile, feathery crescendos that fade into baleful foolish fire, roaring "Jump Jump Jump!" I feel like an illusion-believing fool in a famished age. I feel we are like falling stars, expiring on our own wind, dying as we live, down disappearing, for soon our like shall be seen no more! I pass. I go. Forgive me. I am drowning baptized in the sea. "Help!"

My cry in the night brings my mother to the room, softly treading, is she my mother? Matrically wooing me, the ghosts of the lungs, the promise of things to be, whoossshhh, in what dampened bony cavern where women grow like seaweed from the earth, owling "iboo, iboo," her hand like an edge on my isolated shoulder—"Oliver, Oliver"—so sweet as I rest in her breath in her breast my head on her bosom and weep. Weep. Weep.

The fingers of the dawn they weep. Will I die, Mother will I die, is it so difficult to die, or so important? I look at the lilies in the field and I consider them. They love so little, yet they are legion, for they are many. Hi lily, hi lo, they toil not nor speak—nor sin nor saint—but are and are. Hi lili hi lo. And at the musicend of death, when the child's night dream must come to close, I believe they'll be there too, I guess, a sort of art. Daffy as the dew, cuckoo, cuckoo. It blushes at the profundity of my despair, and asks, why do you sow the music seed if you do not love life?

Why, Mom? What is it whispering in my ear now? The wind, your breath? Joy to me. Are you moving on, Mom, in order to vanish? I hope not. Yet. He needs you now. Your son. Forefather of his fathers. Death is with me every moment now, Death is like a sound in my ears, it sits in the terpsing movements of silent molecules, it is part of that day I reserve for myself, it is the silence that governs most of the day and all of the night, exasperating me into the hot dementia of wanting it, faith it waits, it sleeps in the air, it sleeps in the ear, it is silence, it is holy.

. . . my face in the mirror, unimpoverished and whole, my nipple teeth biting into the silvery coat of the scaly moon, hagborn—the gaping promontory under the El Greco sky, the wind skimming the ice caps and spitting full in my face. Do not fear, for you do not love and "He who does not love remains in death" and you are dead—dead! A stroke. A pain. A palpitation. The prescience. Turned into hard cold action. Hard hard Oliver, be hard for this, the hard cold plunge of steel into my soul—fiction's device and dowry. A last of thought. A pretty pit to thee.

. . . the Cambodian knife, drawn with kings, poised in the mirror at my throat. Myself looking at myself, about to die. Those who salute you. Many such men before me, noble and valiant, have been here at this moment.

I drew myself a man, his legs as knives as independent as souls, the incarnation of stoic pride. He heaved a breath, a mind now focused on one thing alone, envisioning such again and again, his spirit to speed, until it was pantomime, florality no longer frenzied by sight of blood gushing from a red ruptured wound, and trod, trod across the room looking out on the cluttered alleyway of the cheap hotel with no hope in the windows. A sleazy police chief wanders in the alley, speaking words at a beautiful prostitute. Who must of course. Pay.

I hate these gloomy shadows! On with the fluorescent lights. Luminescence and logic. *Pop!* Smash and shiver. Is that my soul? Crying out for mercy. For some salvation. For some sentimentality.

No, dogs, big close-cropped ones, they never seem to lose their nerve, do they?

Red shaving scars as ugly as death on the underside of my jaw . . . bloodred, balancing: ballet. I always loved that color. Red. Comic Oliver. In the deepest part of me. Deaf and dumb. Of philosophy frightened. Of ethic scornful. In adjectives, tame and notsotame, allayed. Have I too not been a student? Vague imagery of Innisfree.

It was Father who once said, "You know the story of the blind man and the elephant, don't you?" Being young I didn't. So he told me. Each blind man is told by the rajah whatever to feel this "thing" and tell what it is he thinks it is. So one touches the leg and thinks it a giant tree, another touches the tail and thinks it a vine in the jungle, another touches the trunk and recoils fearing a giant reptile, and the one who touches the tusk speaks of a great smooth treasure, and so on and so on.

In the very same way, life is predicated on this illusory belief that one mood is of greater importance than another; it fails to comprehend that all moods are equally impostors. Writing itself, God's ultimate trick on this paradoxical world, is nothing but a mood, dancing in the mind, bounded by pen and paper, expiring with the frailty of the author.

"God made not death . . . but the wicked with works and words have called it to them." Words that mean nothing any longer. And emotions that seem as lies as they come and go, feeling of Michelangelo, actions moviemade, our solicitude rehearsed and our fears premeditated. My life like literature is a falling away from the cosmic sympathy of Homer to the exhausted springs of earth fragmented. On occasion big explosions pockmark the skies. Aristotle. Aquinas. Shakespeare. Tolstoi. Terminating in Joyce's tower of confused tongues.

The sin of suicide is the sin of end things, is the sin of

death. Is an exhilarating violence, no more no less. The desire for violence like twilight arose from the violence done me. In turn I harmed not another soul. So now I must. Myself—my summer sun made discontent, I thus turn to paper death and sin by sin descend onto a maelstrom of false and fleeting dreams and words that madly twirl in the moist iridectomy of the demon moon which mirrors itself at the bottom of the ocean-opened floor.

To die is like turning a corner. It is already over and relaxation releases my limbs. Death is the ability to reject Life, it implies character, and at the same time, much against my previous predilections, it argues a Life after Death, a quaspire, a century's serio-loyalty. I say to myself, appetite grows again and I, like Edward Hyde, shall be reborn stronger and longer; as Zeus swallowed his own flesh in order to preserve it, so too do I swallow my own self in order to live.

The Cambodian knife. Pondered with the edge of a forefinger. The flower's whip. No more, merry memory, no more!

A loss of balance in the ears and Oliver tumbling down with one last long amylnitrate look at the earth, down a corridor of garlanded tassels and rubylipped cupids, sucking their thumbs, above, like a cloud, the orgasm beneath me, the blade embedded and caught, against its will, in my soul—soul white and transparent, crying out like bread in pain. Until it went and did it—it popped! And with an outstretched hand I gracefully expired. Death, be so lovely.

Sleep—a sodality oozing from my carotid artery. The moon, seasonable and pale and pink, lay on its back, subalterned to the silver sovereignty of silence, its anguish overt. From the aperture in the city lot, the cat's luminous green eyes pierce the passersby. And in my lightning-quick muscles, the tenseless shapes of sleeping forms in adjacent rooms. Rustling warmth.

A song that sighs with effort; sighs too deep for words and prayers from the deepest pit of the brain, o God!

A razor knife now dipping, its teeth filing across the angry salt. Squawk! Opening the oyster. Eyeball muscles.

My eyes flying open. Stumbling toward the toilet bowl, treading. Suchascope is man. I unzip my silver fly. Out with the hydraulic penis. For the umpteen billionth time, so boring, so *déjà vu*.

Squirting. A long sigh of silver urine into the bowl. Creeping up into my deep-seated distaste, and draining its juice. A boil of me, poisoned out of my technology, what comfort, hypnotized by the shooting chess circles of toilet water. Turning, reconciling my penis behind the arras, and moving away.

When suddenly it hit me. I was helpless. It came as a trickle. A tittle of annoyance. One drop of urine. Then another. And one more. Three. They slithered out in drops from my canal, fanning outward, witching the skin, impoisoning the nerveset, o God why do you squash me with this last indignity! suffer and addict me to passion! Mercy, have fucking mercy!

My fists clenched, I wanted to curse my very name, but what would be the point? How pathetic it seems, how boyish, reminiscent of a time when feces were evacuated in diapers, a neurotic void, weightless, timeless, perhapsless. How helpless man is, humbled and lost in the complexity of things, compelled after centuries to piss in his underwear, into the secretest part of himself. And when they find me lifeless, they too will find the permanent stain.

The pitch of instant madness! The Stygian darkness of my madness. The fear of death and cancer in my testicle. The void was couched in my mind, as nerve-ending as the inarticulate voicelessness of a sidewalk throng, the shuffle of pavement feet; no one knows, no one notices but me, there is no madness but my madness. A hole to my stomach, a void to my area, a want of life's energy. An inescapable and damned difference. Fate! Like the word "Never!" A historical term that fades like marmalade in the stupid face of fact. Fact: cancer: disease: death. Death is fact. Fate is just posturing about death. An all-too-easy fear has come, has seen, and with good-natured relaxation, has conquered. And once again, as if I had never experienced an emotion that was valid, as if in fact I had never lived a life natural to a human being, I deeply despair of being able to confront, from the narrow spot I inhabit, the cluttered complexity of the world.

I dropped across the ugly pink bedscape and the surge to sleep came zooming up, like a piano playing in the white Alps, from the tips of my toes, sleeping like a thief on its own muscles. Youth is an acid smear rubbing its liver in my pants, like rubber gloves. A notorious lick of gonorcanals at the head of my penis, tart, sweetly sleeping. For loyalty's secret sake. The doze was: is inchoate. As sharp a wish as. Deep in error. Two thoughts, preached by authors who are romantics and see iron where cheese only abides. You are easy with yourself Oliver, you always have been. In passing contrast to those such as Dostoyevski who live in spite of themselves, whose every act is an act of pursuit. You fool, you coward, acts of witchcraft perpetrated and coterminous with cowardlice. Truths, I tell myself, reveal themselves only in emotions. Yes, and sleep is no emotion. It is a painkiller, it is a sickness, it is a licorice attack drowning in the heart of the sea. Are you legitimate Oliver, I question myself? As legit as a flower, are you true and real, or are you a fake feigning suicide? Tails lurking. Balls pendant in seesaw sententiousness . . . for you know, don't you, that you will sleep and sleep ever so soundlessly until the sun comes up. Don't you Don't you Don't you?

Thus anguished, I fell asleep, overthrown by a powerful myopia of the mind, an overwhelming want of energy. It was the way of sleep, it was the way I slept conscious and gloriously free of sex.

And fell instead into a narcoleptic slumber characterized by fitful leaps of silver-minnowed images, flashing with brilliance through a gray nightcloud across the moon—momentary flashes of dream united in a single composition that detonates far in the distance. Bedcovers that roll themselves down. Large nomadic footprints in the waste. They loom imperceptible, setting over the summer, moving with a suprasaulsion that liquidates its own shortpast.

The sun, unremittent sin, porously pierces through my cheap school drapes. I overhear running feet and names dinningly called from the courtyard of my youth. I turn over and groan and wish for the rain to fall thick and cold, and lock the world out of my chastity drum.

A similar twitch, a cupid artery now begins to chirrup through my body. I see through the blur into the Cambodian chariot kings engraved on my suicide knife. Mutes. They sit. They seem. I collapse once more into the shadows. And smell an old acquaintance. I love the agony. I hate the madness. Red is for rapine.

It came upon me slowly, it was the kernel of genius. Because it was instantaneous and in the myths they say: never take candy from a stranger. Of course not. Yet I always do. It was brilliant, a fleshridden notion, and I grasped it because it was the only way out—sol ocean, solution! I *had* to do it.

I had to destroy the manuscript I had written!

There I was moving toward it. My novel is sick! My novel is sick! I wrote it across my mind, and whispered a prayer to the Good Lord to give me fortitude for this hard task. I had it now in my hands, and I tore it up page by page until a shredded pile no longer cogent or coherent, no longer accretive or sequential, lay on the altar before me. I washed it clean. The avalanche of whitewaste burying the basket alongside. *Finis*. The novel is dead, and I was right in killing it because Jesus at his most complex had merely wandered into the vineyards of parable whereas we, mere and mortal men, have sinfully and self-indulgently wandered into the novel, which is nothing but an artifice that disguises the simple religion of existence. Praise the Lord! Rejoice, for it is no more so, I repeat, no more!

And what's more, I had purchased, through this painful high suffering act, the necessary firmness that would allow me at last (I knew it was at last) to kill myself! I had forged, in this the real realm, no longer the romantic alleys of the rhythmical mind, no longer the fictions of suicide, but that which the suicide understood the morning in Idaho he fingered the shotgun, the hot holy humus of hell! Like a God flooding the pursy world in order to make way for the supraworld, the utopia of death, perverted as it was, now beckoned. Death was not merely going to be an experience, it was to be an event! Was there not horror here? Was I not already passing through the undiscovered country? All my faults, errors, frustrations, dissatisfactions, both of my life and writing, were behind me, and a feeling of exhilarating and doleful freedom ushered itself into my mind.

I had cut my eyeteeth on a failure that was, at this liberated moment, not only self-contained but also highly dramatic. What more indeed could I expect from life? What more had the great tragic figures suffered? What was there I didn't know, tell me? My entire life I had lived in the shadow of publicity—I was what you saw on the screen, I was what you read about in the book, and hence because I was both known and unknown, I was a most miserable failure. People like me—and there are others—invariably succumb to the enlightenment proffered by suicide. Is it Thursday or Sunday? The day of the crime. How good, how very gratifying to destroy a life's work in a minute. I had mistakenly thought in the deepest recesses of my optimistic mother-loving mind that I would have been a success as a writer, the very best, every writer a part of me, only a part, and me, I am the Earth Mother, turned on and floating free through the crazed cosmic cellulology of my teenybopper being. Lifetimes in my Oliver lightyears. Come all of you, come to heart, roost, roast, I am He, He. I am the greatest because I am the most puzzled about myself. By way of negatives then, it is me. And for all my exacerbating exertions at holding back this well of aggrandizement, for all the self-inflicted tortures rooted in the hog of my earthquake being, for all the merciless whippings administered shyly, I won, yes I did, I won. I held the fungus in, I squashed the cancer with palpitations from my heart, I cornered the spider with my thumbnail. I held myself in icelation so long I froze. My child, my poor poor child.

THE DREAM WENT retrograde. It seemed suddenly so unimportant now to kill myself. My grief was deeper, much deeper, and the misery I had engineered and sustained in order to produce the urgent hysteria of this manuscript, this access of despair seemed now such an irrelevancy beside the startling reality involved in the destruction of the manuscript. I felt as if I had misplaced my mind and made an error. Like Hamlet I had finally taken a decisive action and stabbed the figure behind the arras, only to discover that I had murdered the wrong man. My antagonist, watching me, had now been given the advantage of momentum. O fuck! It was fading beyond me now. And for all my Herculean adventures of the mind, who cares. Who cares? Greed. Greed. How obtuse and silly a boy I once was, talking tempestuously of suicide. I had been a fool, a self-indulgent fool, and now, fantastic to tell, I was suddenly a man! By virtue of suicide. By virtue of authentic emotion, I was happy to have destroyed a work so false to true nature, so cruel to God. Should I write another book? A better book. The idea of doing so leaned heavily upon me, until I saw my thousand-page book unsealed. It was sixty pages long, a slim volume of tender insignificant poetry, and in it was my unrecognizably butchered story. And there, off to the side, was Father saying, "They took out that verb, they took out that verb."

"What verb?" I asked him in annoyance!

"Penitent, penitent," he said. Perish the industrious thought, and now move toward the bathroom. And kill thyself, and be done with it!

In the dream, the boy takes the knife in hand, obeisant to suchathing as Fate. Many temples belong to Fate. He slices into his arm's artery. The blood bedewed squirts out high, leaping into his pained face like a spermdream. One sharp deep transverse rape of the pulse artery. *Swoosh.* Done. Die. Death. What is my pulse? How much: pulse. The minutes pass, scientifically beginning to faint. The lights opening their thighs and, spilled of milk, render out their orgasms. Bloodclots inhabit the brain. The time is swiftly up. Time! On your mark: gentlemen . . . The boy fading into death. An indistinct, beastlike, electronic groan heard fading away on the radar scream. Go!

I am. My name is William Oliver Stone. I walk on my fingers, and I speak with my nose. I sit on my peter and I think with my toes.

Now twisting and turning, teeming and seeming, the endless

insects of words came crawling over me, my eyes, my ears, my nostrils; cover me, and when from the side of my mind's eye (my back was turned), I could look out beyond, there was nothing but more words and more words, endless papers of unbaptized words marching over the hills, combing the hilly woodlands like an army of cannibals, words I had written myself and words I had never seen, never before guessed at. Never knew existed!

Roiling. Roiling. A *mons veneris* of vocabulary. Gush pond! foam, roll forth and over, rise and roll, rise and roll.

I somersaulted back into the lightened arena. The door was shut behind me. The lights were out. I lit the match. The personality of darkness is death. Death has no character. Liar. Liar. Everywhere. Everywhere.

Again the scream of radar!

The match burned itself down to my fingertips. I put the match to the rumpled fringe of the manuscript, and it began to flame slowly, like a cat slinking under a car. It grew. It flew higher. It is a high wind, bowelbound and visionary! The long romantic loops of my hand, scratching on the pen which is my intellectual equal and knows everything I know and am about to know, disappeared, etched by the insanity of flame into the writing fire. The fire is in my eye—a beam to my head. The blue fringe crawling outward, cutting a wide semicircled swathe across the page. *La Lune*. It said: The Age of Oliver. Suchaname, strange name for such a book. Burning in my grasp— my novel! Blooded spirit. The novel life—an economy geared to war, an instrumentality geared to loneliness—sits on the mind like a gargoyle, petulant and fed with boiling seething creatiousness, like a succubus, like a sea, like a Cinerama leech!

I put the second sheet to the flame. It started slowly but soon reached into irrecontrol. I added a third sheet, and a fourth and a fifth. It was too late to stop now. You see I had failed. I had gone astray. I had slept with the Fiction Goddess and hadn't known how. She condescended to show me. Sweet boy. Sweet thing. Some sample of thing. Gone nuts! I choked on my sperm and swallowed my toe. I marveled in the winds and forgot to forgive myself. I told myself I had failed even before I had inserted the ganglion, the organ of knowledge, shaped like a snakeshead, full of filth. Because I am an intellectual. By being false. And my core, and its fundamental supply of phlegmatic rot, is intellectual. And for these many years I have failed to think, to think deeply. And the hot heart of hell, I know, is no place for mother thinkers and soft souls.

The flames flew higher, throwing over the bathroom an awesome religious light that danced on my flushed face. In a frenzy I drove the entire manuscript into the fire.

I set alight the matchbook and watched as the paper waste began, like a pig rooting in the slough, to rumble and snort, frightened, so very frightened of its own fate, its awareness that I was real, a real person, burning the she out of her life, stealing the light out of my love, stealing o stealing, killing o killing, o goodbye!

In the dark it made a horrifying movie. The flames were spitting and crackling as over an ordinary fire; only that the fire was indoors, not without, and that in the broad highcountry mirror, my shadowed face flickered behind a garlanded wall of flame. My eyes were lit with the luster of iridescent wrath, as of pearls spiking the skull of a dead seaman, mired and moldy, lying in a slough of tranquil frustration at the depth of sea.

From the fire, black butterflies sailed up into the air and there, in the air, died, asphyxiated.

I watched stunned. The Age of Oliver. I backed away cringing from the heat until I fetched up against the opposing wall, where, above me, my shadow grew to immense proportions in the mirror darkness until its size flew up onto the ceiling and overwhelmed me. There was an immense blaze now eating with no degree of decorum and no hamper to its greed at the entrails of my body. The charred ashes, puritan thoughts of fire, my shadow pinned, entrusted like a scared cat to the white wall behind my head—a projected Oliver Stone, made in hell.

My throat raised above the fire. Fire. My throat is in the fire. The throat of fire floating backward, the knife red with pastense blood. It was roasting and revolving. Thwarters of reality continued to emerge from my being, the last juice of life, the last secret to madness, the core, the rot, the eccentric beinglessness to the being, the fanatic faith of the faithful, the delays of office, the decays of lust, gush pond! foam, roll, rise and roll! Teeming, twisting, turning through the night, the long last limblike night, words had devoured me, words writ on a celestial ball, forever oiled, that would never stop revolving. The knife was ready, the knife was hot and clean.

I stepped full in the face of the flame and embraced the steel. This knife in the tangle of my jugular and carotids, this knife invested with authority, this knife cutting through the neck of the flames, through the semicircles of the moon, the vanity of suchdeath. In the fire I see my blood spurting out from the cusps. It was fantasy blood, rilling down my chest into the purple flames. The windpipe was severed, and the *karos* was coming on. I didn't know yet, I was caught up in the vanity of the act, like a shockwave that prespeeds the noise— my cat floating fancy-free. Waiting for the pain to strike, when?

My ruptured face made a pretty picture in the mirror of flame, in the pitch-black bathroom. I had heard a gasp, but I was sure it wasn't me. I was feeling so drowsy, it had been, in truth, a scream from the radar, a call from within the wall. The gills, vested with authority, sanction, and dictation, first spit, then clogged, then choked. And then they were gutted, and my head sank into the wealth of fire . . .

. . . and then it was dawn. My throat was cut and I was peering dumbly at myself as through a net of water. It shifted its monster grasp, moving silently like a rattling chair overheard in another room. A hacking distant cough. Muffled. Ahhh . . . hem!

In the dream, I dreamt I was masturbating. On a bed somewhere in a room I had known in the past. A green-wallpapered room? I was only eleven or nine, but I was masturbating with my older penis.

The backs of a white woman's knees moving. Two dimpled hollows, a faint vein. A woman. Am I dead? A linchpin of bone protruding from the ankle. The feet. Swiftly.

Through the door, she comes. Dark and undismayed, across, athwart, in dreams these girls, they come for me.

Who is this face? What is your gift? Approach, spider. Coming, she rolls upward like an eyeball with a witch's smile.

My puzzled puppethead perplexed. Do I see? Vast emotion? Was I speaking French—a flowery corrupt blather, full of words I had never known, never guessed I knew? Yes, she wants me, at quirts lashing advancing. A walking smile. Her naked nipples. The ottoman hairs of her belly. Fear rose from her loins. Who are you? I cried. Through my head, the swoon of sin. Humiliation's flush spearing my body. Leaving me naked. Without my shirt and necktie.

Please, who are you?

My penis sprouting to an enormous length. Like a decadent French flower. In the garden calling, "Oliverre, Oliverre."

I was on my belly looking down from a great height at the

earth. Where, way below, my penishead culminated in a dark brown hole in the garden. No friction, nothing but the giddy sensation of height and strange swooping power.

Shrinking back to earth, I was fucking the hole in the garden, fucking it and fucking it! A great pulsing weight clamped on the head of my penis. Pulling. Throbbing like a piece of seaweed seized by a cranny in a rock. Washed by waves of water. Again and again . . . oooo whooooo!

I was drowning in the bottom of the sea. The skulls of Crummy and a thousand other sailors staring back at me. The puffy white dollsheads of their putrefactive faces, damp and gelatinous their sea wombs. And I was fucking. My pale white cheeks pumping a womb, the Mount of Love, damp and tight-crevassed, gripping me, suctioning me. Unlike them, I was alive. And it was my mother's face staring down at me, as she was doing this to me and me to her, both of us entwined like snakes of desire. My penis in her hairy hole. O how thrilling! How exciting! Against all rules! All flags!

Somewhere in my throat I was protesting. "Mommy! Mommy!" and it was the little boy in the green room waking from his nightmare, goblins already swarming up his legs, as Mommy raced up the stairs, her footsteps and Chanel perfume anticipating her, little knowing that goblins can also hear her, hurry! hurry! now is the crucial time, would I ever see her again! I closed my eyes in terror, "Mommy!" the silhouetted figure bursting into the room, grabbing me up in her arms, and me wailing, "I don't want to die, please Mommy, don't let me die! don't let me die!" sobbing uncontrollably with passion and rage, this soothing sweet-smelling woman above me cradling me in her arms with gentle kisses!

"*Mon petit chéri*, Oliverre, you will never never die, never, I promesse," until, serpents to the contrary, the child's night dream drew to a close and I would never die because Mommy said so.

And now her promise comes true. Her sweet kisses devouring me with exciting perverse poisoned pleasure. O it was good, so good, to unite in these human forms. Horror mixed with lust, fear with sensuality, blood surged into my neck and squeezed me with such implacable force that I felt I had not much further to live. Like a swimmer near water death, I came gasping for the surface. I urged a vague howl into the base of my throat. Collapsing on the tongue. My ancestors in the fire. My dog eyes moaning to growl. Whimpering. Dying.

Too late. My poem's body floating upward, liquidheaded, wriggling its sperm tail, through the muck, motioned muck, rising risen. O!

I burst the film of water and snored the sunlight as I came in my mother's dark eternal hole. I drank the stars, the million billion trillion stars, and I was gushing all over with warm beautiful white rushing sperm endowed with enormous strength and trembling, at last, at last, let free, let free! the dogs behind their stucco walls in Mexico are barking barking and out of the mountains, the eagles fly fly fly!

I AWOKE SHARP in a sweat, startled to be alive. The dream staining my pants with the force of cellular vision. I was in a dry hot Mexican hotel, and there was a dog barking from behind a wall somewhere close by, and the streets were silent and bored as only they can be in Spanish countries in the middle of the afternoon. A large bird was circling in the mountains beyond the edge of town.

Most of my book's pages lay in blackened ash heaps around

the room and in the bathroom. I had done it. I *had* done that after all.

The Cambodian knife lay on the bed with me. Unused. Its chariot kings staring at me. They knew.

Quietly, slowly, I crawled myself into the small shower. It groaned with ancient pipes and spit out a wash of water that cleansed a face and body sticky with suffering. My energy was exhausted and my brain suddenly felt very tired, without any need for conflict.

Dried and freshly clothed, I gathered the unburnt pages of the book, tucking them together in some surviving order. Perhaps a half of the manuscript was left. I sensed I had further appointment with these pages. But not here. In this time or place. Because Mexico was already a part of all that I had met.

I checked out of the hotel the following morning and returned to America. To what was left of my home in New York City. To a Father and, sometimes, a Mother.

There too I would find my parents were a part, and only a part, of all I had met. And that alone, through the coming years, I would seek the magic wisdom to forge a new life from the ashes of the old.

I await the dawn light.

EPILOGUE

THIRTY YEARS HAVE passed.

I wonder, having turned fifty, what strange, almost shamanic language invested this youth. In his desire to transcend himself and his earthly limitations, there is a recurring theme that yet haunts me. To this very day I still ask myself, can I go on? It is a question, I believe, that will only be resolved with my death.

But on the road to that day, I am grateful to have been able once again to encounter and remember this young man who struggled valiantly in his way to find himself, whether he was Oliver or William or all the ghosts he saw for himself. He seems to me a youth who lived many lives, perhaps not all in the age to which he belonged.

If I speak of him somewhat dispassionately, it's because he broke my heart, or rather he broke his own heart so repeatedly and sometimes unnecessarily. I still do that too, but knowing more, I do it less. And less. And with time, his passion and anger and savage love recede from me; his half-face, as on an Etruscan vase, erased by the layers of time.

But this I know. This boy Oliver wanted—no, *needed*—desperately to be heard and loved. But he wasn't, and as a result he inflicted tremendous suffering on himself—and thus on others too.

I apologize as best I can now to all those still living whom he—and I—hurt. And I forgive those who hurt him, and me.

From the perspective of advancing age, I am especially sad he did not have a sister or a brother or at least a friend close enough to pour his heart out to. For that young heart was full.

I hope, with this book, to be that friend he so needed.

—OLIVER STONE
Los Angeles, California
(1997)

ABOUT THE AUTHOR

Oliver Stone has written, co-written, and directed such movies as *Platoon, Born on the Fourth of July, JFK, Salvador, Nixon, Natural Born Killers, The Doors, Wall Street, Heaven and Earth,* and *Talk Radio.* His screenwriting credits include the above and additionally *Midnight Express* and *Scarface.*

Born in New York City in 1946, of a French mother and American father, he dropped out of Yale University in 1965 to teach in Vietnam and returned in 1967–68 as a soldier in the front line. He worked in the Merchant Marine and several other jobs before and after completing his studies at New York University Film School in 1971.

He is the father of three children, and lives in Los Angeles, California. This is his first novel.